The Fletcher
Book One in the Arrow of Artemis series

K. Aten

Yellow Rose Books
by Regal Crest

ISBN 978-1-61929-356-4

First Edition 2018

9 8 7 6 5 4 3 2 1

Cover design by AcornGraphics

Published by:

Regal Crest Enterprises

Find us on the World Wide Web at
http://www.regalcrest.biz

Published in the United States of America

Acknowledgments

I would like to thank Regal Crest Enterprises for giving me this chance to live out my dream as a published author. Cathy for the opportunity she provided me, Patty's wisdom, and Micheala for her patience. They are the women who worked with me most on this project and deserve my utmost respect. I'd also like to thank Helen M. for all her words of encouragement in the world of fiction, and for sharing her experience with me as she began her own journey nearly two decades ago. Last, I give thanks to those people who turned me down when I first began my publishing adventure. They were the ones who made me reach harder and higher to achieve my aspirations, and taught me that perseverance does pay off in the end.

Dedication

I started writing because after a lifetime of silence I finally had something to say. It wasn't easy and there are a few important people in my life who deserve the honor of my first dedication. First and foremost I'd like to thank my partner, Kari, for her patience and emotional support. Next I give thanks to my mother for instilling in me the passion to read and the acceptance to be myself when the time was right. And on the production end of things, I'm grateful that I have such an amazing beta reader. Ted's soul is gentle like spring rain but his mind is as sharp as the words of a professional wit. Thank you all for loving, listening, and laughing with me. Last, I give special thanks to my gram. She was the strongest woman I'd ever known, and she gave me faith that nothing was out of reach with enough work and will. This first book will be the beginning of a great journey that I hope lasts the rest of my life.

The Arrow of Artemis: Cast

Thrace

Kyri Fletcher – Daughter of Galen
Galen Fletcher – Renowned fletcher and archer of the region, widowed
Mira Fletcher – Deceased mother of Kyri
Soara - Kyri's mare
Dan - Kyri's mule
Lord Esteven – Ruler of Kyri & Galen's steading
King Colmenus – King of their region in Thrace
Lagus – First archer contestant in Kozani
Torrel – Bow maker and fletcher in Kozani

Telequire tribe

Lydella - Previous contentious Telequire Queen, killed by Orianna in a challenge for leadership
Orianna – Telequire Queen and Artemis' Chosen
Risiki – Orianna's sister who is married to a centaur
Shana - Amazon messenger and later Telequire Ambassador
Gerta – Head councilor for Telequire
Deka – Second Scout leader
Dina – Third Scout Leader (Moon shift)
Thera – Head healer
Coryn – First Scout Leader, immediate leader of all scouts, beneath Margoli
Sheila – Member of the First Scouts and Coryn's friend
Petrice – Member of First Scouts and Coryn's friend
Deima – Member of Third Scouts and Coryn's friend
Kylani – Training Master
Basha – Regent to the Queen
Steffi - Economic Advisor (Queen's Left Hand), in charge of trade and Amazon budget.
Margoli – Military Advisor (Queen's Right Hand), overall leader of all scouts and army
Gata Anatoli – Leopard cub rescued by Kyri after she killed the cat's mother

Tanta tribe

Myra – Tanta Queen
Culchee – First Scout
Tisha – Young trainee archer sent to stave lessons
Deata - Training Master
Baeza – Tanta First Scout Leader
Brandel - Makes brandy (strong Tanta spirits)

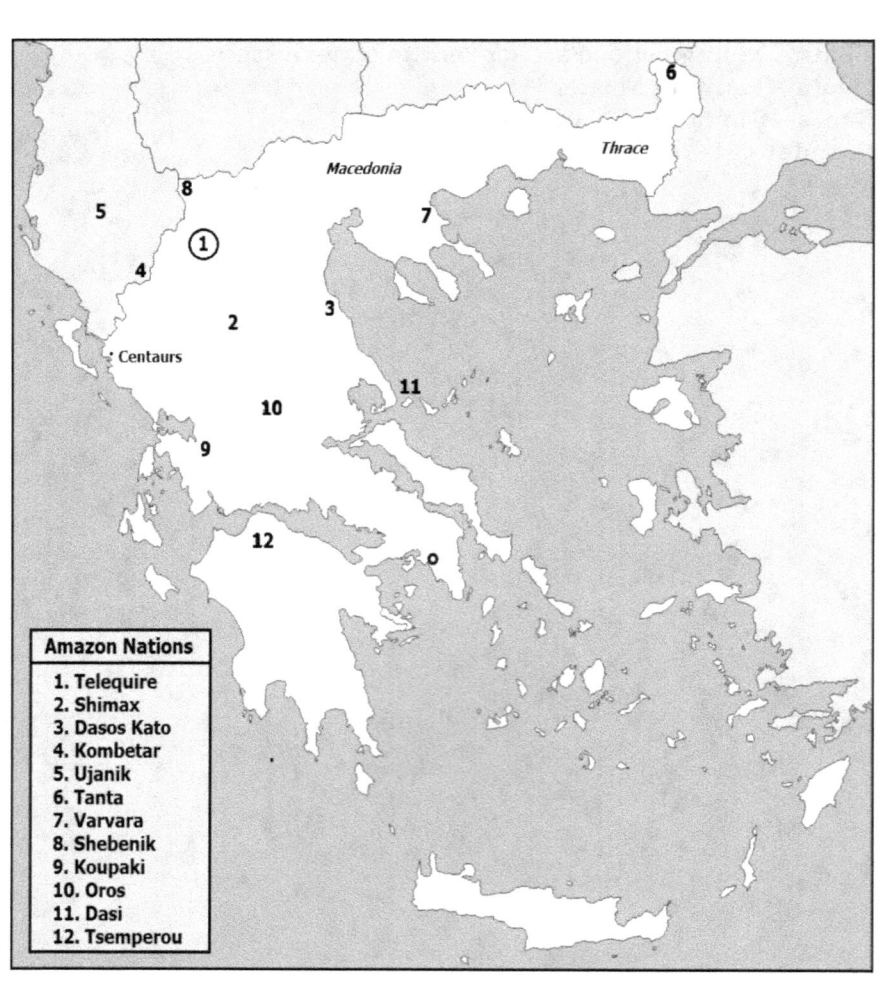

Macedonia

Thrace

Centaurs

Amazon Nations

1. Telequire
2. Shimax
3. Dasos Kato
4. Kombetar
5. Ujanik
6. Tanta
7. Varvara
8. Shebenik
9. Koupaki
10. Oros
11. Dasi
12. Tsemperou

Chapter One

The End of Innocence

MY MIND HAD always been a muddled mess. My mam used to call me a deep thinker and my da would just laugh and agree with her. We lived on our homestead deep within the forest and rarely went to the nearest village or the towns beyond. Because of that I almost never saw kids my own age and I was forced to entertain myself more often than not. The trees became my friends and playmates. Perhaps that was why my da started training me so young, to keep me out of trouble in the woods. Not having any boys, he took me as an apprentice when I was just ten summers old. I think he and my mam always hoped to have a boy at some point but some things were just not meant to be.

There had never been a time when I was not proud of my da. Galen Fletcher was a name well-known as the finest arrow maker for leagues around, not to mention the best archer. He had regular visits from the servants of the local nobles to buy his arrows. Even the king sent his runner once a moon to make a purchase. My da was the best teacher I could have ever asked for. Yet I grieved as I sat on my favorite log. Feet dangling over the stream below, my head remained a tumultuous roil of fear and anger. I often wished that the water could take the burden of my thoughts away but it was a wish that remained unfulfilled.

I tried to understand my sadness, to understand why the fates worked as they did. My da and I did not have a bad life. On the contrary, it was fairly good. We lived on a little parcel of wooded land, one that abutted Lord Esteven's forest. The very stream that I sat above was one of my favorite places and I had spent candle marks of time admiring its beauty. Sometimes I brought a pole to do a little fishing, but other times I would just think about my mam.

She was all sweetness and light. My da would say he did not know what he did to deserve such a smart and beautiful lass. Before she died, mam was a talented cloak maker. Some of my fondest memories were of her showing me how to cut cloth and dye it, then stitch it just right to make it appear as though leaves were strewn across one's shoulders. Her cloaks were truly amazing; some even swore they were created with the gods' help. She showed me everything she knew but I could never duplicate her level of skill and artistry. Perhaps I was too young. One of my most treasured possessions was the cloak she had made for me when I was a child, not long before she died.

My thoughts turned dark as I once again felt the pain of loss. My mam's death by lung fever pierced me through the heart. Six years was no small amount to grieve, for me or my da. I was certain that no matter where I ended up in life, not a day would go by without thinking of her or remembering her smile. The loss of my mam was immeasurable and deep. It meant no more beautiful cloaks, no more candle marks spent showing me how to make the best dough or dye wool to look like sunlight dappling through the forest leaves.

My da was never the same after. I think he only kept going because he knew he could not leave me alone. I was only thirteen at the time and I still needed my protector. He was the one who taught me to hunt and fletch arrows identical to his own. Because that was what we were — we were fletchers. I could feel a tear run down my cheek as I worried the word 'we' like a sore tooth. The fates were known to be unkind. It was not that the day itself was bad to cause me such sorrow. It was a typical one as I threw stones into the water one by one. My chores were finished and dinner had been started earlier, leaving me with a bit of free time. There were some clouds in the sky and a slight breeze that ruffled the wisps of hair sticking out of my braid. I could feel the heat of the sun across my shoulders and every so often the cooling of a cloud as it raced across the sky. That was what my life felt like. After the cloud of my mam's passing, we eventually felt the sun again.

But if there was one thing I learned in life, it was that no sky stayed clear forever. My da had become sick and the local healer was not sure what was wrong with him. My protector was dying. He had been tired for at least a season. He frequently became light-headed and his appetite was nearly gone. The worst of it was the coughing. Sometimes I would lay awake at night listening to him struggle and in my heart I knew that our time left together was running out. His sickness was not like the one my mam had. The healer at least knew what was wrong with her, for all the good it did. It was the darkest part of winter when she got sick and neither the healer's herbs, nor my da's prayers yielded a miracle in the end.

According to the healer, my da was going to die too. I wondered if he would say a prayer for himself or if he would leave it off as a lost cause. My da was not really one to follow the gods but he was a spiritual man. He truly believed that there was an afterlife where he and mam could be together. There were many things that I wished for as I sat on that log over the stream, but none of them would come true. There were no gods to answer his prayers, there was no magical medicine that would heal him. So many times over the years, I had wished for my mam back. Little did I know that my greatest wish would not be for something I had lost, but rather to keep the small amount that remained.

Perhaps it would have been better if I had been born a boy. He would not have been so worried about leaving me behind if I were the son of a fletcher instead of a daughter living in a man's world. But I was not a son and after the death of my mam, nothing seemed to matter but the two of us surviving. On more than one occasion I had overheard him freely admit that perhaps he let me run wild a bit. Because of my apprenticeship, my hunting skills, or maybe just my bold attitude, there were no offers of marriage for me. Not that it mattered because I had never found a boy or man that remotely piqued my interest. Perhaps it was strange but I had never wanted to look too far inside myself for the reason why. It had not made a difference anyway. We were fine with just the two of us.

MOONS WENT BY after we saw the healer for my da and his weakness did nothing but worsen. Between the coughing and shaking hands, he was no longer able to perform our craft. We had a decent store of arrows left but I did not know what would happen if we were to get another noble's order. It was illegal to pass an apprentice's work off as a master, or even to pass one master off as another. I had already considered it but we would lose everything if found out and we could not afford to lose favor with the king and nobles. Late afternoon found us working quietly together. He was plucking the quarry birds I had brought down earlier, preparing them for roasting. I found it heart-wrenching that the man who held so much skill in setting the delicate feathers to shaft could now barely pull them from a dead carcass. Even though I was turned with my back to him, I could sense his eyes.

"Kyri..."

"Yes, Da?"

"I would like to talk to you once you get these roasting." He set the second plucked bird onto a tray.

I mentally cringed, knowing that I did not want to have any more serious conversations. "Sure, Da, just let me finish these up." I took the birds from the tray, stuffed them with wild onions and herbs, and then placed them on the spit over the fire. When I was finished, I cleaned my hands then sat down at the table. "What is on your mind, Da?"

He looked at his hands, probably to collect his thoughts before he met my eyes. It was funny sitting so close to him. I was very aware of our similarities and our differences. I had clearly gotten my height from him and perhaps my blue eyes. But while he had light brown hair, mine was like my mam's. Dark brown almost black, my hair took a whole day to dry after swimming in the creek. My mam also had blue eyes, which was probably why mine were so vivid and deep. There were not a lot of blue eyes in our region so it was the thing that got noticed first besides my height. With both my parents having them, well…I knew enough about animal husbandry that certain traits were more likely to be passed on if both sire and dam have them. When my da remained silent I decided to give him a nudge. "Da?"

He gave a little shake, seeming to come up out of his own thoughts. "Kyri, I have got something to tell you, and it is not going to be pleasant."

I mentally sighed. "I do not want to talk more about your sickness. I do not even want to think about it. You should not waste your time worrying, Da. We will get it figured out. I should be ready to take my test for mastery now, and then we can talk to your regular customers—"

"No daughter, it is not that. I mean, yes, you will take your test for mastery. I have already sent word to another master fletcher to come in and evaluate you. He should be here in a seven day. No, this is about something else."

I could feel a bit of fear creep up the back of my neck. "Well then, what is it, Da?"

"It is about our steading here. You may not remember this, but our steading was given to me by Lord Esteven not long before you were born. I spent nearly ten years in his service and eventually saved his life."

"You did? *How?*"

He patted my hand and smiled. "It was about a year after your mam and I were married. I spent nearly a decade as an archer in our lord's guard and started to develop a reputation as a fletcher as well. When Lord Esteven took notice of my arrows, he began using mine exclusively on his hunts. I was even invited along on the annual boar hunt as a special guest. I think it was mostly to show off his prize fletcher to the other lords." He took a sip of water from his favorite wood cup then continued. "Well, we were hunting wild boar, which you know is as vicious as it is unpredictable. I was on foot, about twenty feet from our lord, when a boar came in and sliced the legs of his mount with its tusks. Lord Esteven was thrown to the ground and lost grip on his spear. I began running in his direction, drawing back my black oak bow as soon as I saw the boar. Just as the boar was a hand span from my lord, I jumped over his fallen mount and while in mid-air, I put an arrow right through the beast's eye. The boar was dead before my feet touched the ground."

Da chuckled to himself. I could not help feeling that familiar glow of hero worship from my childhood. He had done much to be proud of in his life and to take a boar in mid-leap was quite a shot. But then I knew my da was one of the best archers in our kingdom. "Wow! That was a great shot, Da! What happened then?"

"Well, I did not realize at the time, but a handful of guards and at least two other nobles were close enough to see what I had done. After shoving the boar off my lord, I offered my hand and pulled him to his feet. He clapped me on the back and raved about what an amazing shot I had made, then called over the other nobles who were near. He introduced me as his master fletcher and later gifted me this tract of woods as a thank you for saving his life." He took another swallow of his water and both of us ignored his tremulous hands. "With my lord's promotion to master fletcher, I started gaining many customers for my arrows. Between the new customers and the money I had been saving from archery tournaments, I had enough to build our house here and the workshop."

"But that is all good. What has you worried?"

He sighed and looked away. "Kyri, I never thought this would be a problem. I never considered that you may lose me while you were so young."

"Da, please! We will be fine, I promise. Let us just take things one day at—"

"No, Kyri, it is not okay. In this land, steadings can only be held by men or male heirs." He looked at me with sad blue eyes. "Even if you make master rank and gain customers of your own, you will lose the steading if I die. As my daughter and unmarried, there are no options for you where our home is concerned." He closed his eyes and a tear graced his weathered cheek. "I am so sorry, Kyri."

Immediately, my heart seized and my breath caught in my throat. "Everything, Da? So if you die, I lose my home and my last remaining parent?"

He shook his head slowly at me but did not answer.

"How long? How long before I will have to leave?"

Da's mouth turned down and he was close to tears. The way his shoulders hunched told me clearly he felt regret and guilt in equal measures. "You will have time to bury me, Kyri, nothing more."

Suddenly, everything hit home. His illness and the knowledge that I would lose my home when he died, it was all just too much. With a cry of frustration I grabbed my cloak, bow, and quiver, and bolted out the door.

"Kyri, wait!" His voice followed me for about ten footsteps before fading away. I ran through the trees until my breath grew ragged. After crossing the stream, I kept going until I came to my favorite place. Pushing my speed, I ran up the angled trunk of a giant black oak. Scrambling as fast as possible until I got midway up, I settled into a comfortable nook.

I had discovered the place after my mam died, and it had become my private retreat over the years for whenever I needed to cry. The newest tears were not just tears of sadness though, they were laced with a good amount of anger. I did not understand why he failed to tell me of our laws sooner. Maybe I would have tried harder to find a good match. My thoughts stopped before I could traipse any further down a false trail. Would I have tried harder? Searching within myself, I finally faced the truth. No, I would not have tried at all because I had never and would never have any interest in marrying. My hands started to shake. What was wrong with me? Why was I so different when the difference would cause me to lose my home and all that I had ever known?

I sat in the tree so long my backside started going numb. I could hear the rustling of animals in my vicinity along with something else. Quietly I sat forward so I could look around a little more easily. I could hear soldiers, probably patrolling the forest road nearby. I could also hear a woman's voice. Curious, I scrambled down the tree and quietly made my way toward the noise. I approached the road on my belly, their lack of attention and the fact that it was near dusk kept me well hidden. I focused all my will on hearing their conversation.

There were six soldiers, a typical patrol. All carried swords at their hips and two had crossbows. Inferior weapons because while any idiot could shoot one, it took skill and strength to match the distance and accuracy of a long bow. The woman was exceptionally beautiful but dressed strangely in a leather skirt and short-sleeved top. She wore a traveling cloak but I could just make out the pommel of a sword sticking out over her right shoulder. There was also a bow and quiver strapped to her horse. I had never seen anyone like the woman but something about her called to me. She seemed wilder than any woman I had ever seen, freer somehow. I continued to watch as I listened to the conversation.

She dismounted from her horse and spoke with frustration heavily tinging her words. "I told you, my name is Shana. I'm a member of the Telequire Amazon tribe, and I'm traveling to visit another tribe in order to pass news of our new queen."

The patrol leader laughed, joined by his comrades. "Amazon, huh? There are no such things as Amazons! All I see is a woman alone, carrying a sword. Women are not allowed weapons of war in our kingdom." He took a step toward the woman. "You must relinquish your sword and come with us for punishment."

The woman, Shana, stepped back. "I will not give up my sword! I tell you that I'm not from your kingdom and I have an urgent message from our queen. I beg you to please let me pass and you will never see me again."

One of the men with a crossbow spoke up. "Patrol Leader Regan, you want me to put an arrow in her?"

Regan laughed. "No, Camen, there are much better things we can use. Isn't that right, Amazon?"

As soon as he said those words, my heart started pounding in my chest. She turned to get back to her horse and was tackled from behind by two of the soldiers. The Amazon was able to pull a knife and graze the leader's ribs, but another backhanded her across her right cheek. I was torn. I wanted to help but I knew that there was nothing I could do against the soldiers. A third soldier kicked the knife from her grip. While the men had her pinned to the ground, Regan walked up and removed her sword from its sheath. The wound at his side lightly seeped blood. "What a fine blade you have. It's a shame it has the bad luck of being used by a woman. As a matter of fact, I'd say a better sheath would be the dirt of the forest. It can keep company with the skunks and wild pigs." He gave a great heave and threw the sword into the trees. I kept low, as they were facing my direction, but I could hear it stick into something behind me.

Shana had a look of rage on her face as she struggled. "That sword is worth twenty of you, pig!"

The patrol leader laughed. "You hear that boys? She thinks I'm a pig." He turned his menacing stare to the immobilized woman. "Well Amazon, since you think I'm a pig, perhaps you'd like a little taste of my meat. A pretty thing like you shouldn't go hungry now." The men laughed at his crude humor. He turned to one of the crossbowmen. "Kill the horse!"

The crossbow wielder looked confused. "Sir?"

Angrily, Regan pointed at the Amazon's mount. "I said kill the damn horse! That's an order, Jos!"

The man, Jos, put a bolt through the horse's skull, dropping the animal to the ground. Shana gave a grievous cry. "*No!*" I did not want to see what was to come, but I did not know how to stop it. If I ran to get my da it would be too late to help her because our steading was so far away. Not only that, but with dusk fast approaching I would probably break a leg running through the dark. The next half candle mark was the worst I had ever before seen. One by one the men systematically beat the Amazon, punching her in the back and stomach. They kicked and slapped at her, great back-handed blows that left her dazed. She tried to fight but there were just too many. They forced her over the carcass of her dead horse and ripped off her clothing. She thrashed, failing her legs, but after a hard blow to the head from the pommel of a sword, she gave up, dazed and half-conscious, and sobbed. My own tears fell in time with hers. I could feel the rage building, because even sheltered as I had grown up, I knew what was coming.

I fell into a daze as my hands moved in a familiar motion and I quietly strung my black oak bow. Then all my da's training came to the fore and with speed and precision I loosed my arrows upon them. I shot the man that was closest to her first, then both the crossbowmen. In the confusion my first three arrows had caused, I put down the rest. The patrol leader and both men holding the Amazon all fell to my green and blue fletched arrows. I did not think about the fact that I had just killed six men, taking their lives for all eternity. I ran over to the Amazon and dropped to my knees. I looked dismayed at the unmoving body covered in bruises and turned her over. She gave out a pained cry and flinched away from me. "I am here to help, my name is Kyri." In my head, a mantra was repeating, 'please do not die...please stay alive...' I could see she was bleeding from the head. I needed to get her somewhere safe. "Please, Shana, can you stand? I cannot carry you."

Her answer came out as a pained hiss. "Yessssss." With my help, she was able to stand. She motioned toward the packs on her horse. "I've got some supplies in there and a sleeping shift I can use to bind the wound on my head."

I nodded and began working at getting the saddlebags off her dead mount. She seemed disoriented but appeared to recover a bit when she noticed the dead soldiers. Shana stood a little straighter once her head was bound and the skirt re-wrapped. Taking a shaky breath, she asked, "What did you say your name was again?"

I did not hear her at first, my attention was riveted on the men on the road. Men I had killed with my arrows. One was lying in a pool of blood with his eyes still open. When she grabbed me by the arm, I startled. "I am sorry, what?"

She looked at me curiously then back at the men. "I asked what your name is, kid?"

"It is...it is...Kyri." I suddenly felt hot and everything went dark. I woke to find myself lying on the ground. I looked up into the Amazon's face. "What happened?"

She gave me another curious look and then cast a quick glance at the dead men in the road. "Have you never killed before, Kyri?"

I tried to sit up. "Of course I have, I hunt every day!"

She smiled sadly and helped me up. I could not understand why she was helping me when she was the one who had taken the beating. "No, Kyri, have you ever killed a man before?"

"No." I glanced at my beautiful arrows, each quivered in dead flesh. The realization truly hit me. I had killed Lord Esteven's forest patrol and I would be hanged. I was merely a woman and no one would believe my word about the dead soldiers' attack on another woman. I would be held at fault and my family would pay the price. Shana turned toward the woods, and I knew what she wanted. "I heard your sword stick perhaps twenty feet behind me. I can help you search before we lose all the daylight."

She turned back to me with a grateful smile on her face. "Thank you." Then she glanced back at the dead men. "Kyri, are your arrows known in the area?"

I was confused. "What?"

She persisted. "I said, are your arrows known in the area? Would anyone know who killed these men?"

Suddenly my stomach dropped and the blood rushed from my face. I had just enough time to spin around before I got sick, bringing up mostly bile. With a shaking hand, I wiped my mouth and looked at her with tears in my eyes. "Yes! My da is the master fletcher for Lord Esteven and I am his apprentice. My arrows are nearly identical to his, only where he has two blues and a green fletch, I have two greens and a blue. They will know it was me for sure!"

She took me by both shoulders and gave a shake. "Hey, calm down, no they won't! They'll see my horse, because we can't do anything about that. They'll assume the men confronted a traveler and all of them were killed by that person. They will be looking for a stranger to the area, not one of their own."

I protested weakly. "But my arrows..."

"We'll remove them, as well as any identifying tack from my mount. I don't want them to know an Amazon was here."

My stomach flipped at the idea of going anywhere near the dead men. After removing and cleaning my arrows, I grabbed her saddlebags from the ground. This left Shana with her own bow and quiver of arrows. I could tell she was in pain but there was nothing I could do until we got back to the homestead. We kept some herbs and bandages there for emergencies. I could only hope that Da would understand what I had to do. We found her sword stuck in a fallen tree not far from the road.

The trek back to my steading took nearly a candle mark and we arrived in full dark. I knew my da would be worried and I could tell that Shana was fading fast from her trauma and injuries. I tried to keep her talking while we made our way through the trees. She spent the time telling me of her Amazon nation and asking about my life as a fletcher. She even asked for one of my arrows and then told me it was the finest she'd ever seen. This was a great compliment since the Amazons were well known for their archery. Unlike the forest patrol, I was familiar with the tales of Amazons. I would beg my da to take me to the inn in town whenever traveling bards would come through. I soaked up all the tales of comedy and adventure the same way a dry cloth soaks up water. The idea of a nation of all women both fascinated and intrigued me. There was also a pull from deep inside that urged me to find out more. But even the talking could only do so much to keep Shana's mind off her pain. By the time we arrived, I was still carrying the saddlebags but also had an arm around my new Amazon friend, helping her walk. I shouted when we got near the cabin. "Da!"

He was out the door in a bow shot, breathing heavy. The tall man immediately got under Shana's other arm and helped her inside. Once we settled her into my bed, she sagged into herself and her eyes fluttered shut. Da turned to me. "Kyri, what happened?"

I shook my head, rushing around to find the pain killing herbs and some clean wraps. I knew I had to get her cleaned up before I could tell the story. "In a bit Da, can you boil some water for me?"

Seeing Shana's immediate need for attention, he relented. "I already put some on, love. I was going to have a bit of chava while I waited for you to return." Da brought the hot water to my room before making a hasty retreat. He was never good with injuries and healing. That had always been Mam's responsibility. I cleaned her as best as I could. I was able to make a compress for the light gash on her head, and give her some tea that would help prevent pain and fever and help her sleep.

When I left the room and saw my da pacing, I immediately ran to him. "Oh Da, it was horrible!"

He held me tight and whispered reassurances while I sobbed

into his chest. "Shh, daughter, it is okay. She is going to be all right." He rubbed my back and let me cry myself out. Once I calmed down and was able to wipe my tears, he held me away from him by my shoulders. I could see he was inspecting me for any sign of injury.

"I am fine. It was Shana who was hurt."

A very dark and angry look came over his face. It was one I had never seen before. "Who did this, Kyri? Why did they attack that woman?"

I led him to our chairs by the hearth and sat. "I was in my oak when I heard voices coming from the forest road. I could tell it was the king's patrol and I could hear a woman's voice. I was curious so I crept up to the road to see what was going on." I took a shaky breath and continued. "Shana told the soldiers that she was an Amazon and she was taking a message from her queen to another Amazon nation..." Over the next several candle marks, I recalled what had happened for my da. "And then they beat her to the ground. After that... after that..." I could not continue, the images were still too fresh and the memory of her pain brought my tears back in a flood.

Da was patient though and his voice was soft. "What happened then? Did the men just leave her there?"

I shook my head at him and met his worried blue eyes with my own. "No, Da, they were taking turns beating her and they would have killed her. Something inside me snapped and I—"

"Kyri? What did you do?"

I could feel the anguish come over me and I cried out. "I killed them all! Not one of them had a chance against my bow and now they are all dead. Oh, Da, what have I done?" I covered my face in shame and guilt.

Then he said something I never would have expected. "Did you leave your arrows or...or did you take them with you?"

I thought he would be angry with me, or at least disappointed. I looked up in surprise and confusion. "What?"

He grabbed both of my hands. "Daughter, did you bring all your arrows back with you, or leave any there for the next patrol to find?"

"N...no. Shana made me retrieve them all from the dead men. She said people would know who killed the men by the arrows. We also removed any identifying tack from her mare so they would not know an Amazon was in the area. They would assume the men were killed by a traveler or a bandit."

He breathed a sigh of relief. "Your Amazon, she is very bright and absolutely correct. That does not mean the danger is passed. We are still harboring a stranger and will be suspect in the death of those men if we are found out."

"I am so sorry, Da. This would never have happened if I had not run off. And I would have never taken someone else's life. I am a murderer now, Da!"

He looked at me sternly. "No! If you had not run off and if you had not killed those vile beasts, that young woman in there would be dead! You did a service to yourself and your family by doing what you did." He paused and his blue eyes looked very intense in the candlelight. "You did the right thing, Kyri." His face seemed to soften as he leaned over and kissed my cheek. "Despite the danger this brings, I am very proud of you, daughter. Now you should get some sleep. There is naught more you can do for her tonight and morning will come soon enough."

I nodded my head, grateful for his wisdom and understanding. I grabbed a spare blanket and laid it out by the hearth, knowing I would be plenty warm for the night. Da was still sitting in his chair when I drifted off. The nightmares chased me until dawn.

THE NEXT MORNING, Da was already up making breakfast when the dreams turned me loose. I rose quickly and rinsed my face and mouth from the water bucket. I could see his hands shaking and the exhaustion on his face, so I immediately took over and sent him to sit. I finished cutting the bread and fowl from the night before then went to the fire and removed the pot of boiled eggs. "Is Shana awake yet?"

He shook his head. "Not yet. I looked in on her when I got up and mixed up another mug of tea for when she does wake. She is going to hurt for a while, I suspect."

I nodded and swallowed down a lump of emotion before turning to peel the eggs. Once I had a morning meal put together, I took it and the tea to my room. Strange amber-colored eyes looked to me with discomfort when I opened the door. "You are awake, good! I brought you some food and more tea for your pain."

A thankful look crossed her face when I handed over the mug. I set the plate of meat, eggs, and bread on the bed. "Do you think you can eat something? The tea can be hard on your stomach if you do not eat."

"Yes, thank you." She set the tea aside and started on her breakfast. After a few bites she looked at me seriously. "I shouldn't stay here. I'm going to bring trouble to you and your father."

I stopped her. "He...it is okay. My da said he was proud of

me for helping you and I know he will do whatever he can to protect you too. Just focus on healing right now."

The look of fear in her eyes softened and the lines between her brows smoothed a bit with relief. "Thank you, Kyri, for everything." I nodded and smiled.

When she was finished eating, I took the plate and left the room again. I could see her eyes drooping and knew she was headed for another round of healing sleep. As I was cleaning up from our meal, a sudden realization came over me. I went searching for my da in a panic. I found him in the workshop, mixing dye for the fletching. "Da, we are in more danger than I thought!"

He looked up in alarm. "What is it, Kyri? Is Shana okay?"

I quickly shook my head. "Not Shana, us. I forgot everything you taught me about tracking. Our trail will lead them right to our steading. What are we going to do?" I started pacing, wondering how long it would take to find us.

He set down the container of dye and grabbed my shoulders to stop the pacing. "Kyri, settle! I have already taken care of it."

That took me by surprise. "What?"

"I went out before dawn and covered your trail. None of the men that Lord Esteven currently employs will be able to track you."

I took in his exhausted and pale face, his tremulous hands, and I knew what it had cost him to protect us a little longer. "Oh, Da, why did you not let me help you?"

He gave me a smile I failed to understand and sat back down on his stool. "It is fine, daughter. You know I do not have long for this world but I would give every heartbeat I have left to protect you." He patted the other stool next to him. "Come over here for a moment, I want to ask you a favor."

Curious, I made my way around the workbench and sat on the other stool. "What is it, Da? You know I will do whatever you want."

My hands were swallowed by his large calloused ones, and he looked at me with his serious blue eyes. "I want you to leave here."

"What?" I tried to pull my hands away but he held on tight.

"Daughter, listen!" When I calmed down he continued. "You know I do not have long and when I die you will lose all you have here. Kyri, this land has nothing for you and I want you to be safe."

Dismayed, my voice was tinged with desperation. "But, Da, you need me here! All my memories of you and Mam, everything is here."

He shook his head sadly. "I know, love. But all those memories mean nothing if you are dead. I need you alive and happy more than I need you with me. I want you to take those memories and all your skills and start a new life somewhere else." He swallowed and looked around the small workshop. "This place...they will never understand you and never give you your freedom or respect. I want you happy, daughter. Your mam and I always knew you were special, that you had so much to give."

The tears fell again, knowing that he was serious about me leaving and that he would not change his mind. I hated the tears and rubbed them angrily against the sleeve of my tunic. With my world falling out from under me, it seemed as though I had nothing more than the emotions of a small child. But I was not a child any longer and I knew that loss was something I would have to get used to once again. But I grieved, oh how I grieved. The blue eyes that pleaded with me, that begged me, were tired. I knew that once I was gone he would give in to the exhaustion that plagued his days. "But what will I do, where will I go?"

He scratched the stubble on his chin before answering. "You can do whatever you like, Kyri, that is how I raised you. As for where to go, why not travel with Shana? You can either go with her to help complete her quest, or if she chooses to return to her home tribe, maybe you can go there."

I looked at him with bewilderment. "But why would I go to the Amazons? I have nothing to offer them...I am not like them at all!"

My da looked at me with a twinkle in his eye that had long been missing. "Daughter, I think they would be honored by everything you have to offer. Do not lower your own worth, I have taught you too well for that."

I looked at him in surprise and gave a single nod of acknowledgement. "When do you think we should leave?"

The sparkle in his eyes left as quickly as it came. "Soon. As soon as Shana can ride without pain, you need to flee this place. You can start packing a kit now and put together the tools you will need for fletching, as well as your mam's stuff. You can take your mare, Soara, and one of the mules. Probably Dan, he stays calm easiest."

I was confused, not about taking the horse and mule but about taking the supplies. "Da? Would it not be quicker just to make a small pack for the two of us? Why all the fletching supplies, and why mam's stuff?"

"Because, there are many things you can do and do well. And I want you to bring something to your new home. As for your mam's stuff, you may be glad to have it someday." He stood from the stool and rummaged through shelves behind him. "I will put together a kit with arrow making tools and a few other things. You just worry about the rest."

"But what if she says no?"

He glanced over his shoulder at me. "You saved her life." He turned away once again. I knew I had been dismissed so I went back to the cabin to check on Shana and start gathering my memories as best as I could.

That evening, Shana was able to come out and sit with us at our small table. I introduced her to my da before setting the small table for our meal. We ate rabbit stew and the rest of the morning bread. I was happy to see she had a good appetite and that she enjoyed the food. My thoughts were only half in the present as she dragged the last bite of her bread around the bowl in front of her. "This stew is amazing. I haven't had anything this good since I still lived with my second mother."

Da responded proudly. "Kyri does most of the cooking and all the hunting. I have not been able to help as much as I would like since my weakness hit."

Shana looked at my father with sadness and understanding. "Do the healers know what is wrong?"

He shook his head. "No, just that I get weaker each day and it gets harder and harder to breathe." He shoved his half-empty dish away with a shaking hand. I knew he was going to ask her. I sped my way through the last of my own dinner and grabbed our bowls. Sensing he had more to say, the Amazon sat back and waited.

"Shana, I know you are aware of the danger your presence places on our steading." When she started to interrupt, he held up his hand. "No, it is okay. I stand by every decision my daughter makes. I am glad she helped you and brought you back." He sat forward in his chair and took a shaky sip from his mug. In a rare admission of the chest pain he was feeling, it was filled with a tea made from crataegus, basil, cinnamon, and honey. The healer recommended the drink for his worst days. Unfortunately cinnamon was rare and expensive, so he did not make the tea very often. He continued after a few heartbeats of silence. "But now that you are here, I was actually hoping you could help us in return. The thing is, Kyri is not like the people around here. They will never accept her as she is, and when I die she will lose the steading. In this land, only male heirs can inherit. She would have to marry to keep the land or become homeless. I do not wish to see what would become of her in either of those instances."

Shana sat up, catching an inkling of what my da was saying.

"What are you trying to tell me, Galen?"

"I know you have to leave as soon as possible and I would like Kyri to go with you. She is in danger here and I want her to be safe. She needs a home and a family and I will be unable to provide either of those soon." The great man I had worshipped my entire life seemed to shrink before my eyes. He covered his face with a hand and tried to gather himself emotionally. When he looked up again, I could see his blue eyes begging the Amazon warrior across from him. "Please...she means everything to me."

Shana looked at him and then turned to meet my gaze. "And what do you want, Kyri?"

I watched both of them thinking about that very thing. My heart was pounding and my mouth had suddenly gone dry. Reality and realization were colliding in my head. "He...he is right. I have never fit in and I have never wanted to. The only thing I have right now is my da."

She looked at me with compassion and understanding and said, "Let me ask again, what do you want?"

I looked into eyes of dark honey and knew she was searching for a deeper truth. "I want to be a fletcher!"

"And?" she prompted.

I swallowed and glanced at my father then back at her. "And I want to be free to make my own choices, to not be dependent on a husband or father to keep my home and livelihood."

She nodded once, satisfied by my answer. "I understand. Can you be ready to leave by tomorrow?"

Shocked, I stared at her with dismay. "What? You cannot even ride yet. You are not nearly healed enough to travel."

She returned my look with an emotionless mask. "No, but I can walk just fine. I need to continue my journey as soon as possible. My queen is counting on me."

Da broke in. "She can be ready. Most of her things are already packed. She will have her horse and one of the mules. Will that work?"

"But, Da!"

He interrupted me. "No, Kyri, it is time. You know every day you stay will be more dangerous and will be harder for you to leave. Please!"

My eyes tearing up, I took a deep breath, reining in my emotions. It was time to start being strong. It was time to grow up. I sighed. "You are right. I know you are right, Da. I will be ready."

Shana watched me for a candle drop longer. "Okay, we'll leave at first light. But right now I think I need some more rest. Good night to you both."

My father smiled at her. "Goodnight Shana. And thank you from the bottom of my heart. I can never repay you for this."

The Amazon gave him a small smile in return and then glanced at me. "She already has."

I left our cottage then. I had two places to visit before I could let sleep claim me. My first stop was at a beautiful weeping willow set back from the stream. It was the place where we buried my mam six years before. I did not actually believe the dead could hear our thoughts but I wanted to say goodbye anyway. After that, I went to sit for a while on my log. Sunset was not far off, so I knew I would be unable to stay long. But I wanted to say goodbye to the place that brought me so much calm over the years. There was a peace in sitting above the stream that I would sorely miss. There was a part of me that was excited to go on an adventure, to begin another life. But the rest of me was brokenhearted. I knew that in order to find my true place, I had to leave all the rest behind. And I felt a great wrenching sadness at the thought that I would never see my da again. I would have to say goodbye to him just like I did with my mam.

THE NEXT MORNING dawned clear. We were up and fed, and Da had the animals ready to go. There were tears in my eyes when he took me aside but I kept them under control. He wrapped me in his strong arms and held me. I could feel how much he was struggling to breathe with my arms wrapped around him. I wondered how much he had been hiding from me over the past sun-cycle. When he pulled back, I gazed into his blue eyes for the last time. "I am going to miss you so much, Da!"

He smiled and almost seemed as if a weight were lifting from his shoulders. Perhaps it was. "I will miss you too, daughter, but I will die happy knowing you are safe."

"But, Da, how will you live? What happens if your store runs out and you cannot fletch anymore? You need me!"

He shook his head and cupped my cheek. "Kyri, we both know that my stock of arrows will last longer than I will. I can feel it. My time here is almost done." His eyes grew wet with emotion. "I will be so happy to see your mam again. And yes, my daughter, I will always need you. But now is the time to let you go."

"Oh, Da!" I threw myself into his arms and hugged him one last time. "If you do see mam, tell her I love her and miss her every day."

He pulled back. "I will do that for you. And all I want you to do for us in return is to live. I want you to be free and follow your heart. And Kyri, never let anyone bring you down from the trees. You take your heart and your soul and live!"

"I will, Da...I will." My silent tears continued long into our first day. Shana never mentioned them.

Chapter Two

My New Life

THE FIRST FEW days were a bit tense, with both of us learning the other's peculiarities. I knew that Shana was still healing so I had no problem hunting and preparing the meals each day. We took a different way out of the forest and found a northerly road that would take us toward the Amazon nation she was seeking. Because of this different route, we avoided going near the capital and anymore meetings with the king's soldiers. It only took four days to leave the region completely and leave behind retribution for the men I had killed. Shana was well on her way to complete healing by the time we were a seven day out, at least physically. Emotionally, I could tell she suffered each night. I would wake to her nightmares, of her whimpering and crying out in fear and pain. I knew what she dreamed of because I had similar. Only mine always ended with either her, or my da, pierced by my green and blue fletched arrows.

On the ninth day of our journey, Shana remarked that we were only a few days from Tanta tribe lands. A couple candle marks after midday, we met a few rough looking men on the road. We were walking to give my mare a break, simply enjoying comfortable silence. And while we were fairly laid back on the trip, we were not completely unwary. On her suggestion, I always kept my bow strung. The men slowed up as we passed them. A strange tingling ran up my spine and I quickly spun in place, arrow already nocked. Shana turned when I did, sword drawn. Both men had makhairas, which were long knives with a curved cutting edge, and they clearly meant to do us harm. Shana called out to them. "Put your weapons away and keep moving down the road. We want no trouble with you."

The one on the left laughed. "But what if we want trouble with you? Tell you what, you give us your gold and those animals and we promise not to kill you."

Shana shook her head. "I'm afraid that's not an option."

Just then, another man jumped out of the brush to the side of us. He had his crossbow raised as I spun toward him. We fired at the same time, only my arrow slapped his bolt away. Then my second took him through the chest while he was busy reloading. I turned with another arrow nocked to see Shana kicking one man away from her while engaging the other with her sword. I put an arrow through the neck of the man who had fallen as he rushed back into the fray. She quickly dispatched the remaining thief. After cleaning her sword on his dirty clothes, she turned to me. "Are you okay?"

I glanced at the two men dead of my arrows and swallowed the burning liquid that had come up my throat. Nodding, I slung my bow across my shoulders and went to remove my arrows from the dead men. I could not help wondering if I had become nothing more than a murderer. Was that all I was, a killer? While I removed my arrows and wiped them down, she rifled through their meager belongings. After dumping all the money into one pouch, she held it out to me.

"What?"

She looked me in the eye. "Take it, you earned it."

I had no control over the look of disgust on my face. The idea of robbing dead men, men that I had killed, made me feel sick to my stomach again. "No! I do not want money for taking their lives!"

My Amazon friend slowly walked up to me. She grabbed my clenched hands, loosened the fingers of the left one, and wrapped them around the leather pouch. "Kyri, I know you don't have a lot of experience out in the world but they never would have let us go. That is how men like this are. They would have killed us if we hadn't put them down first."

I looked at the pouch in my hand. "But it hardly seems fair. They were no match for my bow."

Shana gently raised my chin until she could look me in the eyes. "And what about the families who have come through here before us? Is it fair to them when these men rape, rob, and kill them? Is it fair to the children who lose mothers and fathers, or to the ones who are taken and sold into slavery?" Releasing my chin, she stepped back. "Kyri, you have a light and these men were nothing but darkness. If you have the ability and the will, it is your responsibility to protect others from that darkness. Amazons defend women and defend the weak. If you want to be an Amazon, you must learn this lesson well and learn to forgive yourself when you are honoring your creed."

She looked at me deeply and for the first time, I think I understood. I nodded and gave a small smile. "Yes, I think I am starting to see that now. Thank you for reminding me that I am still a good person."

She stepped near again and folded me into a strong hug. "You have no choice but to be good, Kyri. It is simply who you are. Never fear on that, little one."

I felt strangely comforted receiving a hug from my new Amazon warrior friend, mere paces from dead bandits. "Thank you." Before we left that section of road behind, we pulled the dead men to the side out of respect for other travelers that would come along behind us.

The rest of the trip was made in relative peace. There were no more encounters with thieves and their like. As we approached Amazon lands, Shana gave me a few pointers about what to do when challenged by the Amazon scouts. Since the day we left my steading, she had been filling me in on all the details of Amazon culture and society. I had already learned a lot about her tribe and the other tribes in general. I was still a little apprehensive about meeting the Tanta tribe though, knowing that they would be mostly strangers to Shana as well. She had no such misgivings.

"You'll be fine," she said.

Ahead of us, I could see the road meander into a thick stand of tall forest. As we entered, the age of the trees seemed to press down on me. All at once, Shana stopped and clasped her hands over her head. Remembering her instructions, I dropped Soara's reins and quickly mimicked her movement. Surprisingly, the animals startled very little when women dropped out of the trees all around us. They were wearing masks and many had arrows nocked in our direction. Fear niggled at my back when one of the Amazons stepped forward and spoke.

"You are trespassing on Amazon land, state your business."

Without lowering her hands, Shana replied. "My name is Shana and I am of the Telequire tribe. I have a message for Queen Myra."

The masked scout turned toward me. "And who are you? You are no Amazon, dressed in men's trousers and lacking feathers in your hair."

I looked the masked challenger in the eye. "You are correct in that I am no Amazon. My name is Kyri and I am traveling with Shana back to her nation."

The authoritative scout turned back to Shana. "Do you vouch for this woman?"

My Amazon friend smiled and then her face became serious. "I stake my feathers and faith in nation, as well as my tribe's name, on the intentions of this outsider. If she disobeys your laws, let me be punished. If she takes the life of a sister, let me die a thousand times in retribution."

Satisfied at Shana's very official sounding pledge, two masked scouts led us toward their village while the rest returned to the trees. I felt like a kidling going to village for the first time as I glanced around in amazement. The scouts acted and dressed so different from what I had always known and I wondered what living with this strange culture of women would be like?

Upon arrival to the village proper, the scouts turned us over to another Amazon. We were shown the stables where we could leave my horse and mule and then we were taken to a guest hut. The new Amazon smiled at us, though her gaze seemed to linger a bit longer on Shana. "You are welcome to freshen up here. The queen will see you shortly. If you need anything, I'm assigned to you for the duration of your stay. My name is Culchee."

Shana grinned at the Amazon's very frank appraisal. "Thank you, Culchee. I'll be sure to keep your offer in mind." Culchee threw another appreciative glance over her shoulder as she walked away.

I may not have had a lot of experience with the sexual interplay between two people, but I certainly recognized it when it was right in front of me. I had witnessed the village girls and their suitors often enough. However, I had never considered the idea of Amazons and their sexuality in a village of all women. Awareness opened up and my mind reeled with the possibilities and implications. When I turned toward Shana, my mouth was open with shock.

She looked at me in concern. "Is everything okay?"

Sudden heat flushed my face and I knew it would be a deep red. I glanced at the retreating Amazon, then back at Shana. "I...uh...I just..."

With one look at my blush, Shana started laughing. "Oh, little one, did you just figure it out?"

I swallowed and nodded my head, still blushing furiously. "Um, yes. I guess I did."

She took pity on me then and did not laugh any more as she led me into our hut. "Come on, sister, let's get ourselves cleaned up so we can meet their queen."

My head jerked up at her words, and my heart was swelled by a flash of affection. "Do you really mean that? Sister?"

She turned back to me while removing her weapons. "Of course I do. Being part of a tribe means we are all sisters. It means we are all family." She smiled shyly at me. "But I confess that I do feel like you are a little sister to me, of blood relation. Perhaps it is all that we have been through together in such a short time."

I really looked at the Amazon in front of me. She could not have been more than five years older but she truly felt like a big sister to me as well. After losing my family and home, it was one more thing I was grateful for. "I feel the same way!"

She chuckled at my obvious joy. "Well then, I can't have any family of mine looking travel worn and dirty in front of Queen

Myra." She waved toward the pitcher of water and bowl that had been provided. "Start washing!"

There was a knock on the door to the hut nearly a candle mark later. Culchee had returned to take us to meet the Tanta queen. We were brought to the center of the village where we were met with a large gathering of Amazons. Some were wearing their everyday garb, others had what looked like full formal leathers and armor. While I was not familiar with their styles, the formal outfits looked a lot fancier than that of the scouts we had seen. Queen Myra looked magnificent sitting on a dais. She had a multitude of feathers in her short mahogany colored hair but her face was hidden by her mask. As we approached the platform, I followed Shana's example and dropped to a knee. I could feel the animosity from some of the Amazons around us and from the masked queen as well. I started to have misgivings as to what I had gotten myself into. In all of our conversations, Shana never mentioned any issues with the Tanta tribe.

Finally the queen spoke. "Messenger of Telequire, you show a lot of bravery coming into Tanta territory, especially with words from your false queen, Lydella! What do you have to say for yourself? Stand and answer."

I remained kneeling and silent. I had no want to involve myself with their affairs.

Shana answered with good grace. "If it pleases you, Queen Myra, I am here to inform you that Queen Lydella is dead. Queen Orianna now rules Telequire in her place."

A commotion rippled through the crowd of Amazons and the queen abruptly sat forward on her throne. Her smile was large and satisfied when she raised her mask to the top of her head. "So the old bitch is finally dead! Tell me, how did she die?"

Shana smirked at her response. "Queen Orianna killed her in a challenge for the queen's mask."

This news caused even more of a commotion through the crowd. The queen stood and motioned us both forward. I got to my feet and followed Shana to the dais as Queen Myra made her way down the steps, followed by her guards. "Come, let us discuss this in my council chamber." I was completely lost, but Shana seemed to expect her reaction. She gave me a reassuring smile as we entered the great lodge that was located just off the village center. My Amazon sister told me a bit about the leadership of a typical Amazon village while we were traveling. There were five council members and one queen. The queen was sometimes referred to having the power of four. The four could be representative of many things, such as four directions, four seasons, the four elements, and the list went on and on. One of the other reasons was that the queen had the power of four council members, meaning that her vote carried the weight of four people. That was why the council had five members, to overrule any queen that exceeded her goddess given authority. I found it all very confusing when Shana explained it to me, but sitting in front of the Tanta queen, much of it was starting to make sense.

We were shown to cushions in the center of the chamber, and the other relevant parties filed in and took their seats as well. The queen called for refreshments then the lodge door was closed. Up close, I could see that Queen Myra was about the age my mam would have been, somewhere between forty and fifty cycles. I had a good feeling about her and was curious about the discussion to come. Surprisingly, the stately woman turned her gaze to me first.

"I have heard from my guards that you are not an Amazon, yet you travel with one and she has vouched for you with the highest oath. Tell me who you are, and how you found yourself accompanying one of our Amazon sisters."

Shana smiled, and patted my knee with reassurance. Suddenly shy, I did not know how to begin. "My name is Kyri, your highness—"

Queen Myra interrupted me. "Please, while we are in this chamber, call me Myra."

I gave her a tremulous smile. "Okay, thank you." I knew she was bestowing an honor on us, allowing us to use her name without the title. I tried to begin again. "I met Shana when she was attacked. My da and I helped her out, but he knew it was going to cause trouble later so he sent me with Shana to see if I could live with her Amazons." I knew my explanation was not the best, and I blew out a frustrated breath.

Shana took pity on me and helped fill out my story. "If I may, Queen Myra, I think I can explain a little better. My friend here may have a lot of height, but none of it seems to be filled with eloquent words." I scowled at that, but everyone in the room chuckled instead.

The queen looked at her and chided. "You may tell her tale, but again, it's just Myra here."

Shana winked at me and then turned back to the queen. "Thank you, Myra. So to start near the beginning, I was one of a dozen messengers sent out by Queen Orianna to bring news of Lydella's death. While I was traveling through the region southwest of here, I was stopped on a forest road by the local king's patrol."

Myra questioned, "Is that King Colmenus?"

I answered. "Yes Myra, he is the king of my region. Lord Esteven holds my local village and lands."

She nodded. "Okay, please continue."

Shana began again. "Apparently, Kyri's region frowns upon women carrying swords or traveling without a male escort. From what I gathered from Kyri and her father Galen, women have very few rights there. They cannot hold property or inherit. Anyway, the soldiers took exception to me and demanded I give up my sword. When I refused, they..."

She faltered, and I knew that my strong warrior friend was still deeply hurt inside despite her tough attitude. I grabbed her hand in mine and continued the story for her. "They threw her sword into the woods and killed her horse. She was beaten repeatedly, then they stripped her and threw her over the back of her dead mount." I could feel my eyes well up at the memory of that day. I glanced at Shana and saw her head bowed but her grip was strong in mine. "I...I had heard the soldiers from where I was in the forest. It was near our steading. So I was able to see it all from the safety of the side of the road."

Suddenly Myra's face looked on mine in fury. "You watched from safety while another woman was being abused? Those are not the actions of a woman who would seek to become an Amazon!"

Shana's head jerked up and she raised a hand palm up toward the queen. "Peace, Myra, let her finish the story."

The Tanta tribe queen gave an abrupt nod, but the look of anger was still there as well as on the faces of all the other women in the council hut. I swallowed past my fear and continued. "I will freely admit that I was afraid. I had never seen anything like the violence I witnessed that day. And when they started abusing her...I..." I cleared my throat. "I just snapped. I had my black oak bow with me and I stood with clear intention and...and I killed them all." I hung my head, still feeling guilt over the men's deaths.

Shana added quietly, "What she's not telling you is that there were six fully armed men, two with crossbows. What she's also not telling you is that she'd never killed anyone before that day. She gave up her blood innocence to save me."

Queen Myra looked back at me. "Is this true?"

I wiped a tear from my eye and nodded. "Yes."

Myra leaned across and took my free hand. "Now that is the action of an Amazon. Thank you for your bravery, sister." She released my hand and sat once again. "Now tell me how you come to travel with Shana. Were you sought out for the deaths of the soldiers?"

"No, we took my arrows from the bodies and removed all other items from Shana's mount that would give them any clues as to the horse's ownership. I led her through the forest to my family's steading and treated her injuries. My da went out after hearing my story and covered all evidence of our passage home." Nervously, I took a drink from the mug someone had set next to me. "It was actually my da who asked me to go with Shana." At the queen's confused look, I continued. "You see, my mam died about six years ago and my da is also dying. He is the master fletcher for Lord Esteven, and I was getting ready to take my mastery test. Unfortunately, only men could hold property or inherit where we live. And when he died I was to lose everything. There was no way I could continue my da's craft even with a Master's Mark. He wanted me to leave and start a new life where I could be free to do as I chose."

The queen looked at me with a new light. "Does your father still live?"

I could feel the pain roll across my face and I closed my blue eyes to hold back a new flood of tears. "His weakness has progressed considerably the past few moons, with every day worse than the one before, so I do not know. I knew when I left that I would probably never see him again."

I opened my eyes in time to catch the queen's sympathetic look as well as mirrored looks around the chamber. She addressed both of us. "I'm truly sorry for all that the two of you have been through. When we leave this chamber, I'd like to extend the utmost hospitality to the two of you until you depart back to the Telequire nation." She turned her attention back to Shana. "Also, Shana, I would like you to spend some time with our healer. She is good with more that the physical injuries." Shana smiled and nodded. "Now, can you tell me more about this challenge and what prompted it? The last I knew, Lydella had the Telequire council pinned under her boot and a nation full of sheep."

A fleeting look of anger crossed Shana's face at the mention of her nation being sheep. She quickly reined in her temper and started her own story. "As I'm sure you are aware, Queen Lydella was quite...harsh. She was very contentious within our nation and over the past few decades she had alienated most of the other Amazon tribes. We were cut off for a long time, but there seemed to be nothing we could do. The council members are old, and I suspect she had threatened them somehow to go along with her policies." Shana scrubbed her hands on her Amazon skirt and took a drink from her mug. "About six moons ago, she started talking about going to war with the neighboring centaurs. No one is really sure why she wanted to do this but it would have meant a massive loss of life on both sides. My friend, Orianna, was the leader of our scouts at the time. We were in the same initiation group together, so we've known each other for many sun-cycles. Her sister happens to be married to one of the centaurs. So she was obviously against such an action, especially since we had lived in peace with the centaurs for decades."

A few of the council members began to whisper to each other with the news that Shana was delivering. I did not know enough about Amazon society, or centaurs, to understand the enormity of the situation. The queen prompted Shana. "Go on, what happened next?"

"Well, a moon ago, the queen and council were getting ready to vote on whether or not we would go to war. I knew Orianna was thinking of challenging the queen and I worried for her. Queen Lydella was known for being very fierce in battle and for killing all other previous challengers." Shana looked straight into Queen Myra's eyes. "We are not all sheep, Myra."

The queen nodded. "I understand. She has always been particularly vicious. Go on."

"Just as the council was getting ready to call a vote, Orianna stood and challenged Lydella for the Queen's Mask. The fight was..." Shana shook her head before continuing. "The fight was amazing and vicious, just as you said. But Orianna is the best sword fighter I've ever seen and she certainly proved it that day. Even though Queen Lydella used dirty tactics, Orianna still won out."

I looked at Shana curiously, as did the rest of the people in the council hut. The queen questioned, "Dirty tactics?"

"No one is sure when she did it, but Queen Lydella coated all the challenge weapons with the fire weed juice." A few people looked dismayed but I remained confused. When Shana saw my face she elaborated. "Fire weed juice causes intense burning wherever it touches the skin and eventually causes blisters. Anyway, no one thought it strange that Lydella fought with wrapped hands. It was only after that we discovered why. And yet through the entire fight, despite the pain Orianna must have been in, she never said a word. Even when Lydella threw a handful of dirt into her eyes, she still never said a word. Despite all Queen Lydella's tactics, she still fell to Orianna's sword that day. And the nation breathed a sigh of relief."

Myra sat back, having unconsciously leaned forward during Shana's tale. "Well, that is quite a story. And I'll be the first to admit that I'm not sad to see that woman dead. And Queen Orianna? How is she?"

Shana's face was transformed by a broad smile. "Queen Orianna is like a breath of fresh air for our nation! I know you may think I'm saying this because she was my friend before, but I'm really not. We already have treaties with two neighboring villages and a peace accord with the centaur nation. She's...goddess! She's all fire and wind, swirling around the nation with change, burning away all the dead brush. It is truly an honor to call her queen."

Myra smiled at her descriptive enthusiasm. "If you'll excuse me for saying so, but you seem young. How old is Queen Orianna?"

Shana smirked. "She is my age. She just celebrated her twenty-fourth sun-cycle this summer. She may be young but she's one of the wisest people I have ever met and she always puts the nation first. Despite the fact that she's the youngest queen Telequire has ever had wear the Monarch's Mask."

The Tanta queen shook her head in amazement. "Not only that, she is the youngest I've ever heard of. Younger even than the famed Hypolyta! So with the changing of queens, does this mean your nation will once again be joining the festival of nations?"

Shana grinned. "Yes, it does. Her instructions to her messengers were to spread the word of Lydella's death and let the other nations know that we would like to be welcomed back into the fold, so to speak. She wishes to start a fostering program between nations to encourage communication and learning between the tribes."

The queen looked pleasantly surprised. She spared a raised eyebrow for the rest of the council before once again addressing Shana. "Do you need to take anything back to your queen from me?"

The Telequire Amazon smiled once again and reached into the small satchel at her side. She pulled out two scrolls, each with a wax seal comprised of a leaf and feather. "Actually, I've brought the fostering agreement with me as well as a list of Telequire resources that would be available for trade. She would also like to start trading more with the other nations since we all have different specialties. Trading could happen twice a sun-cycle, when the fosterlings are being exchanged. Tribes would meet at the halfway point between their nations. It's all in the second trade resource scroll."

I looked at the woman next to me and abruptly realized that the fierce Amazon warrior I had been traveling with was a lot deeper than I first thought. She was intelligent, and diplomatic, and I was in awe of her. When I glanced back at Queen Myra, I could see a dawning respect in her eyes as well. "Well, you've definitely brought me a lot to think about. I'm afraid I can't have your answer right away. If you spare me a few days to discuss everything with my council, I can have answers for you then."

Shana nodded her head. "Of course, Myra. The need my queen has for answers far outstrips my want to be home with friends and family. I will take whatever decision you reach, when you are ready."

Myra slapped her hands to her thighs. "Okay then!" She turned to one of the runners. "Send word to Berrenta that we have guests for the next few days, and I'd like a celebration tonight to honor the good news they bring." She turned back to us. "In the meantime, Culchee will show you back to your huts and then give you a tour of the village."

Culchee stepped forward. "My queen, they are both in the same hut."

The queen shot her a look that was both irritated and slightly embarrassed. "Honored guests, Culchee! Give them separate huts. Don't pack them in like field mice on those little beds." But before Culchee to could leave to follow orders, Myra's eyebrows went up as if she had a sudden thought. She held up her hand to stay Culchee and addressed us again. "Unless you two...are you together? If so, we can keep you in the same hut..."

Shana laughed at the Tanta queen's changed demeanor. "No, Queen Myra, we are fine in separate huts. I'll look forward to sleeping on a real bed again. I forgot how rough traveling is on the backside."

One of the council members, and older woman, cackled. "You should try it when you've passed fifty winters!" The rest of the room broke up laughing at that and we filed out into the sunshine.

Culchee came up between us. "Since you're going to be here for a couple days, is there anything you need from your pack animal? Spare clothes for the celebration, or any other items you may need?"

Shana nodded. "I would like to get my saddlebags. I've got my dress leathers in there, and my decorative jewelry. Plus a lavender soap I picked up on my way here. I'm certainly ready for a bath."

I looked down at my trousers and travel-stained shirt and felt my face redden. I did not own anything nice or fancy for the celebration. Both women stopped at my sudden silence. Culchee asked, "What about you? Is there anything you need?"

I shot Shana a quick glance and then I looked back at our Amazon guide. "I, uh...well I do not really have anything nice to wear, just another pair of trousers and a long-sleeved shirt."

Culchee reached across and gently tugged my shirtsleeve. "No worries, Kyri, I can help with garments. We keep a community hut stocked with supplies. So if there is something you need, don't hesitate to ask, okay?"

I returned her smile, tentatively. "I have money, I can pay—"

"You are a guest here and it would dishonor us to accept your money."

Shana nudged me. "Say thank you, Kyri."

I grinned at her, knowing my blue eyes were twinkling. "Thank you, Kyri."

Both women started laughing and Shana slapped my arm. "Smart one!"

After dropping off the gathered pack and saddlebags to our huts, Culchee continued the tour. She took us by the food hut, the Temple of Artemis, and the baths. When Shana saw the bathing huts, she burst out, "Goddess, I'm going to soak for an hour when we're done."

I looked at them in confusion. "I do not understand. What is so special about bathing in a little tub that can barely fit a full grown adult?"

Shana stared at me incredulously and Culchee started laughing. "We don't have little tubs! Come here." She took me by the arm and led me to one of the unoccupied huts. When I looked inside, I felt shock down to my toes. It was no little tub rolled in to sit by a hearth fire. Gods, the bathing tub was half the size of the entire hut!

When I pulled my head back out of the doorway, Culchee shook her head at the look on my face. Shana reached over and gently pushed my mouth closed with her finger. "Are you excited for a bath now?" I just nodded.

After the bathing huts, she took us through the center of the village. People were going every which way with many of the women preparing for the evening's festivities. I could see a large bonfire being set up and a few deer roasting over cooking fires off to the side. Large logs were scattered around the area, providing plenty of seating. The next stop on the list was the training fields. There I saw women practicing with a variety of weapons, staves, swords, knives, some sort of short sticks, and even a few women working on unarmed combat. I was impressed at the display of skill. But what truly caught my attention was the archery field. Culchee noticed the interested look in my eye. "Are you an archer, as well as fletcher, Kyri?"

Shana answered for me in a serious voice. "She's the best I've ever seen." I scowled at her exaggeration before making my way toward the field.

Seeing us approach, the instructor greeted our guide. "Ho, Culchee, who are your friends?"

The Tanta Amazon smiled back at her. "Heyla, Deata. This is Shana. She is the ambassador from the Telequire tribe." Shana startled at the description of ambassador. "Her tall friend is Kyri. She is traveling back to Telequire to join their nation. I'm just giving them a tour of Tanta, as requested by Queen Myra." Looking at us, she said, "This is the Tanta training master, Deata."

Deata gave us both a big grin. "Welcome sisters! Is there anything that I can do for you? You are free to use the target range while you're here."

Culchee chuckled at the hopeful look in my eye. "Actually, Shana says Kyri here is the best archer she's ever seen. I'm sure she is especially interested in a little practice on your field."

I blushed at Shana's foolish boast. "My skills are not so fine as that. I am nearly a master fletcher so I just have to know how to shoot what I make."

The training master noticed my bow and arrows. "May I see your gear?"

"Sure." I nodded and removed my bow and quiver of arrows, handing them to her.

She immediately looked at my bow. Noticing the loose string, she looked up at me in question. Knowing she wanted to string it tight, I gave my consent. "Go ahead but be warned, it's a tough one. To string and to draw."

Deata got it strung with some effort and then drew it back. "Deh, you're right, that is a strong draw. Is that black oak?" I nodded and she handed it back to me. Next she removed one of my arrows and whistled. Holding the arrow up, she looked at me. "This is your work?"

I nodded again. "Yes, ma'am."

"Nice, very nice!" Suddenly she put the arrow back and handed me the quiver. "I want to see you shoot."

I looked at her curiously and then glanced at Shana. I wondered if this was normal, asking guests to perform their skills. She nodded in encouragement. "Go ahead, Kyri, have a little fun."

"Okay."

As Deata led us over to one of the stations, I could hear Shana and Culchee whispering behind us. "How good is she?"

"I watched her shoot a crossbow bolt out of the air."

Deata pointed at the furthest target. "All right, if you're as good as your friend says, you should have no problem shooting the center of that target."

Before she could say another word, I quickly grabbed an arrow, nocked it, drew, and fired, all in one smooth motion. The training master did not say a word, simply nodded. I heard more whispering behind us. "I told you so."

Deata chuckled. "Clearly that was too easy. Let's see how you do with our advanced targets. She called out to a short blond Amazon that was a few paces away. "Tyra set up an advanced target, will you?"

The blonde nodded and took off down the field. From behind the first target, she pulled out another. This one was smaller and it featured a pole lashed to the top. The pole was pointed at me, sticking out maybe an arm span from the target. Hanging from the end of the pole was what looked like a length of twine and a wooden ring. Based on the size of the blond Amazon moving the target, the ring looked like it was a little bigger than a hand span across. I could see it gently swaying in the breeze. I grunted and knew that their advanced target would not be so easy. I looked at the training master. "Did you say advanced, or impossible?"

She laughed at my trepidation and clapped me on the shoulder. "Come on, kid, let's see what you're made of."

I was disconcerted to notice that my time with Deata had started to draw a crowd. Out of the corner of my eye, I noticed what looked like wagering going on between some of the Amazons. I stepped up to the rope that was strung across the station. There would be no quick draw for such a difficult target. I had to time the wind and my breathing just right in order not only hit the center of the target, but also put the arrow through the swinging ring. I watched as the breeze picked up and it gave a little twirl. Taking a deep breath, I pulled and nocked an arrow. I was comforted by my blue and green fletching. It was familiar. I let out the breath and took in another deep one, sighting and waiting for just the right moment. I felt the wind still and released my breath just before I released the arrow. I think everyone froze, me included, until my arrow appeared as if by magic in the center of the target down the field. The ring swung slightly back and forth, unable to spin completely due to the shaft that held it in place. Behind me I could hear a chorus of cheers and whistles. I blushed when I realized just how many people had been watching.

I looked back at Deata and she was giving me a curious look. Then she smiled. "Come on, kid, walk with me to get your arrows." I slung my bow across my shoulders and followed her downfield. I knew I had made a hard shot and that my da would have been proud. A few paces into our walk, she started questioning me. "So who taught you to shoot?"

"My da. He is Lord Esteven's master fletcher and the best archer in our kingdom."

She looked at me and then at the target that was rapidly approaching. "I'm not so sure I believe that."

Could she show so little respect to a visitor? I felt my face grow hot and I started to defend my father. "He is too! Everyone has said so!"

Deata turned suddenly and put her hand on my arm. "Peace, kid. I only meant that I think you may have taken that mantle from him." I looked skeptical. We arrived at the target and she pointed at the ring. "I'm the only one who has ever caught the ring from that distance. And the day I did it was completely calm with no wind." She carefully removed my arrow. "You've got skill, girl, and I hope the Telequire tribe appreciates every bit of it."

Suddenly we heard someone cry out. "No!" The familiar tingling sensation crawled up my spine again. I heard a faint rustling and at the last possible heartbeat I reached down and caught an arrow in front of the training master's belly. We both looked at the arrow in surprise then back toward the archery stations. I could see a young girl crying at the station next to mine. Deata stormed back down the field as I hastily grabbed my first arrow from the easy target. I could hear her clearly before I even caught up. "Tisha! What do you think you were doing drawing on a target when there were people downfield the next one over?"

The girl continued to cry. She could not have been more than fifteen summers. "I'm sorry, Training Master, I didn't see you."

"Tisha, this is the third time you've almost injured someone because you weren't paying attention. I think you need to go back to the basics for more rudimentary training."

"But, Training Master!"

Deata slashed her hand through the air. "No, end of discussion! Turn in your bow and quiver and report to Gorla."

Tisha hung her head in shame. "Yes, Training Master."

Once the girl was gone, Deata turned back to me. "Now, how did you do that?"

I was confused at first and then my feat of speed with the wayward arrow came back to me. "I...I really do not know." I felt relieved when Shana walked up.

"Are you okay?"

"Yes, I am fine. I was not the one that was almost hit, it was Deata."

The training master gave me a curious look, as if she were

trying to figure out some mystery. "Yes, I was, and it would have been a slow and painful death had the arrow made it to its destination. You say you didn't know how you did it, but tell me how it felt."

I looked at her curiously and really thought about it. "Well, I heard the yell, and then I felt a tingling up my spine. It was the rustle of the arrow through the air that I heard. That was why I reached out my hand to grab it. I guess I just got lucky."

The Tanta training master stared at me then down field at the advanced target. "Lucky, huh?" She grinned and shook her head before walking away. She called over her shoulder, "Come back and visit me again before you leave, and I'll find something even more challenging for you."

I smiled, sensing I had won the training master's respect. Once she was gone, Culchee felt safe enough to approach again. "Wow. That was truly incredible, Kyri! I haven't seen anyone shoot like that other than Deata. And I've never seen anyone grab an arrow out of the air before."

I glanced at Shana to see her reaction. "I have to agree with her, Kyri. You have developed a little fan club with this demonstration." She smirked. "Better watch yourself at the celebration tonight."

When I looked at the girls gathered behind the archery range, two of them waved. I looked back at her in confusion. "W...what?" She winked at me and I felt my face heat up with realization.

Culchee giggled at the entire exchange. "Come on, let's go find you some proper Amazon leathers then you can each bathe." I went along easily enough until I saw what was in store for me in the supply hut.

"No."

Culchee stared at me wide-eyed. "What?"

I shook my head and backed away from the table. "I said no, I cannot wear that."

The Tanta guide was indignant. "Just what exactly is wrong with these? These are quality Amazon leathers and linens!"

Shana took one look at my red face and placed a hand on the ranting Amazon's arm. "Culchee..." Once she got the other woman's attention, she continued. "She's embarrassed. Remember, she didn't grow up like us. I'd wager she's never worn anything but men's trousers and a shirt." They looked at me and I nodded my head, feeling shameful and unsure why. Once again, my Amazon sister came to my rescue. "Why don't you let me look through here and see if I can find something that will make her feel comfortable?"

Culchee appraised my current outfit seriously. "Sure, and maybe I can help a bit."

In the end, we found a girdle that had a wide decorative belt and a separate skirt made of long thin strips of leather. It looked like grass hanging around me. When I moved, I could feel the grass-like skirt swirling around my bare legs. But over all, it was better than the skimpy skirts most of the others were wearing. As for my top, I had a wrap that seemed complicated at first. It was made from soft cloth that was dyed in a multitude of greens. The wrap draped over my neck down the front of me and crisscrossed over my small breasts before circling my waist twice and tucking into the wide belt of my girdle. My supple brown boots were pronounced 'Amazon worthy.' By the time we exited the supply hut it was late afternoon. Since there was only one bathing hut available by that time, I agreed to share with Shana. She could see the shyness skittering across my face and rushed to reassure me. "It will be fine, Kyri. We can wash each other's backs."

By the time I was fully immersed in the hot water, I had completely forgotten about my other cares of the moment. "Oh, gods, this is bliss!"

Shana splashed a little water at me and smirked. "I told you so." She grabbed her personal soap and started lathering her hair. "Unfortunately we don't have much time due to someone taking so long in the supply hut. So get washing, kid!"

I laughed, knowing she was not really angry with me.

Chapter Three

Coming of Age

THE CELEBRATION WAS like none I had ever experienced. I had been to harvest festival, equinox, solstice, May Day, and a multitude of others, back in my home village. But this was so very different. Before the feasting began, the queen called us both up to her dais. Then, in a voice guaranteed to be heard by the assembled Tanta nation, she announced us. "Hear me, Tanta Amazons! Our celebration tonight is to welcome two visitors." She gestured to Shana. "This is a Telequire messenger, an ambassador, bringing us news of a new Telequire queen. Queen Orianna has extended an invitation to trade and has asked us to participate in a fostering program, along with the other Amazon tribes. Please extend your best Amazon welcome to our fellow Amazon, Shana." A roar of cheers swelled above the village center. I smiled and clapped along with everyone else until I realized I was next. When she turned to me, I started to sweat. "Next, we have Amazon friend, Kyri. She has already saved the life of two Amazons, Shana and our own Training Master, Deata. With her skills I'm sure she would make any nation proud, should she choose to join with one." The raucous cheer rose and I blushed nearly purple. I could see Shana laughing at my discomfort. I shrugged and smiled, knowing I would get over it eventually. We were given the honor of eating with the queen so there was no reprieve from being the center of attention. It was not until the meal was passed around the table that I realized some of the Amazon foods were completely foreign to me. I asked a lot of questions and tried many different things. I was unsure what we were drinking, but it burned a little going down. It also made my belly feel warm and my head fuzzy. After a while I asked for water from one of the women serving the queen's table.

Shana leaned over and quietly spoke into my ear. "Is something wrong, Kyri?"

I could not stop the giggle that emerged and then quickly clapped my hand over my mouth. "Uh, no!"

My Amazon sister raised an eyebrow. "You're tipsy, aren't you?"

"I *am*? Am I tipsy? I have never drank anything but water or tea. Da did not keep wine or ale. He said it dulled the senses." I cocked my head at her and evaluated my physical state. "So far I only have a warm belly and my head is a bit dizzy. I feel...strange."

Shana slapped a hand over her face. "Oh Goddess, help me." She finally looked up and chuckled. "It's okay, Kyri, you're already doing what you need to do to feel better. Keep drinking water and eat some more food. You'll feel better soon." She pushed my mug toward me. "Stick with the water though, and don't go back to the Amazon wine. Even I think Tanta wine is a bit strong. Woo!"

After dinner was done, we were left to wander through the crowd to see the sites. I found a few women doing acrobatics with tumbling, juggling, and flips. Two more women were having a bawdy rhyming contest a short distance from the acrobats. Everyone was laughing uproariously. Eventually I found my way to the drum circle and dancers. I sat down on one of the nearby logs and watched the graceful women flow around the packed dirt that circled the central fire. I found myself, subconsciously, swaying to the beat of the drums.

It was not long before a woman about my age approached me. She was smaller with long blond hair and looked vaguely familiar, but I had seen so many faces that I really could not be sure. She sat on the log next to me and offered her water skin. "Would you like a drink? My name is Baeza."

"Yes, thank you. I have not drank anything since dinner." I realized the mistake immediately as I upended the skin. I coughed and sputtered, thinking for a heartbeat I was going to die. My throat was on fire, and it shot like an arrow down to my belly. "Wh...what was that!" I hastily handed the skin back and tried to wipe some of the spilled liquid from my face.

She looked dismayed. "Oh, I'm so sorry! I thought you realized that our red skins were spirits."

I stopped brushing. "Spirits? Like my soul and the stuff that priests and priestesses speak of?"

She giggled and put a hand on my knee. "No, spirits, like wine but stronger. We boil and ferment fruit juices, and then distill them down. Amazon sister Brandel makes this one. She calls it Brandy." A little scowl crossed her cute face, and she frowned. "You didn't like it?"

I put my hand on hers. I really did not want to make her unhappy, she seemed so nice. "No, it is all right. It just took me by surprise. Maybe I should try a little more." A little voice in my head, which sounded suspiciously like Shana, was telling me to stick with water. But I thought, what could it hurt?

She beamed and handed the skin back to me. I took a small

amount in my mouth and rolled it around my tongue to get the flavor of it. It was...horrible. Maybe I just was not made for drinking spirits. It took every bit of my willpower to swallow the liquid and not make a face.

I handed the skin back and she took her own swallow. "It's good, right?"

I simply nodded and fought the urge not to gag. And to think Shana was worried about the wine. Their brandy was much worse. I could feel my head spinning and I felt flush. Then I noticed something new. Her hand was casually rubbing my leg above the knee where the strips of my skirt had fallen away to reveal bare skin. When I looked up at her, Baeza's smile held a different quality. "I think you're really attractive, Kyri. Do you have a partner, or a lover?"

Butterflies erupted in my stomach. Part of me was terrified, screaming 'what are you doing?' But the other part of me soothed with things like 'she is pretty' and 'I like her hand there.' The voice that came from my lips did not feel like mine, and it certainly did not sound like mine. It was nervously high, and breathy. "N...no."

She leaned close to me and whispered with lips against the edge of my ear, "Good." When she pulled away and saw my panicked face, she laughed and handed me the red skin. "Here, have some more brandy."

I accepted the skin and with only slightly shaking hands took another swallow. It was...smooth. "Hey, that is not so bad now."

She looked at me curiously. "You haven't had a lot of alcohol, have you?"

I shook my head and stared at my hands in my lap. There was no way I would admit to her that Tanta wine was the first that had ever passed my lips. I looked up when she reached over and placed her hand on mine. I could see her eyes were a warm brown in the firelight. "Hey, it's okay. That's the way alcohol works. The more you drink, the more relaxed you feel. Your body gets used to it and you just feel nice all over." I smiled back at her. I liked the way she was so reassuring. I felt comfortable with her, which did not happen with a lot of people.

After a few more swallows, she set the skin on the ground. She stood and held out a hand to me. "Would you like to dance?"

I nodded shyly. "I am not very good though and I do not know your dances here."

She grinned and pulled me up. "That's okay, we'll teach you. Come on!" Laughing, we stumbled into the circle where Baeza and five of her friends taught me their dance. I had never felt so free before, so light and happy. It was as if I belonged. More red skins made the rounds and I took a swallow every once in a while.

When it started getting late, I could see some of Baeza's friends cajoling her about something. My hearing had always been keen and I could just make out some of their whispers.

"Come on, Baeza, just ask her."

"Gelna, I don't even know her that well. She seems very shy."

"What can it hurt, sister?"

"Yeah, just ask already."

I was back on my original log, taking a much-needed breather. When Baeza and her friends approached. Baeza gave me a broad smile. "Kyri, after dancing in the celebrations, a lot of us like to go soak in the large bathing hut. Would you like to join us?"

I looked at her in surprise. "You mean there are larger ones than what I was in earlier?" She nodded, and the rest of the group smiled. Then I realized what that meant. "Wait, you mean we all take a bath together?" All of us, without clothes. Suddenly the butterflies were back and I took another swig from a nearby red skin. That seemed to settle them.

Baeza giggled. "Well, we don't actually bathe, unless you really want to. We just go to soak and relax, and get to know each other. So, would you like to join us?"

One more swig of brandy and I gave her a smile and a nod. I wondered if I should tell Shana where I was going. I glanced around and saw her sitting with a group of women, a few years older than my group. She seemed in deep conversation so I did not want to bother her. I stood and looked at my new friends. "Okay, lead the way."

Baeza locked her arm with mine for the entirety of the walk. In the large bathing hut, I found myself amazed once again. There was room for almost twice as many as our little group. I wondered how they heated the water because it seemed like a lot of work. I could only assume that some of them filled it ahead of time knowing they would come back after dancing. I quickly undressed and got into the enormous tub, the brandy definitely helping with my shyness. I tried really hard not to look at the nude Amazons getting in with me. I tried. Before coming to the Tanta nation, I had not seen a nude woman other than my mam when I was a child, and that was not the same. The water was warm but I did not think that was why my face felt so hot. Baeza called out to one of her friends. "Mesha, did you bring them?"

A darker skinned brunette answered. "Of course I did. Here, pass these around." She held out a red skin and another traditional tanned leather skin.

Baeza leaned in close. "You know what the red one is, and the regular skin is just water." When I looked at her in confusion she pointed to the two flaming hearths. "It gets very hot in here, so it's important to drink lots of water so we don't get sick."

I nodded weakly. "Okay." When the brandy was passed around, I did take another few swallows. And when the water made it around a little later, I gulped down a good amount. The girls were a lot of fun. It was a little awkward because they spent a lot of time asking me about myself. But conversation was a flowing thing, like water, and we never stayed on a topic for long. We had been in the tub for nearly a candle mark when I felt the first touch on my upper thigh. I tried hard to stay calm and not show how startled I was. My eyes widened and I started to blush when I realized whose hand it was. I turned my head slowly and looked at Baeza. She winked in return. Before I could say anything, someone else was asking me a question and I had to focus hard to answer.

When the conversation turned elsewhere again, Baeza leaned over and whispered in my ear. "I still think you're very attractive, Kyri." She followed her statement with a series of kisses that went from my ear down along my neck and jawline. My body got hot and I shivered even as my hands clenched under the water. When I felt the touch of her tongue on my neck, I gave a little gasp and closed my eyes. I could not help the quiet sound that escaped my lips. I had never felt any of those sensations before. Was I experiencing desire? When she pulled away, I opened my eyes and looked at her. She must have seen how I felt written hotly over my face because that's when she kissed me. Oh sweet softness! Her lips were like rose petals and hot honey. The taste of brandy on her tongue was intoxicating and I could only follow her lead when she entered my mouth. I think I moaned when her hand inched higher on my leg.

Suddenly, a wash of cold air flooded the hut, and we all looked to see the cause. In the doorway stood Shana and the training master. I felt a pang of guilt, wondering if Shana had been looking for me. The training master was the one that spoke to the group of us. "All right ladies, it is well into moonlight and time for everyone to disperse the public areas." We all rose to get dressed though some of the girls were grumbling good-naturedly.

The training master approached me after I was clothed again. I could see Shana approaching Baeza in the same way. "Kyri, I was looking for you earlier tonight. I wanted to ask if you and Shana could report to me after breakfast tomorrow. I have some more questions about your technique and your fletching skill."

I nodded numbly. "Sure, I would be happy to help." She walked away and I could hear the end of Shana and Baeza's whispered conversation.

Shana looked angry and worried, though I was not sure why. "I'm telling you, she's an innocent and she walks in the footsteps of the goddess. Tread carefully with my sister."

Baeza paled. "I'm sorry, I swear I didn't know. I just thought she was shy."

"She is shy. That's partly why I'm protective of her."

I did not understand what Shana had told her and felt bad for eavesdropping so I quickly followed Deata out of the hut. I missed the rest of the conversation, but I suspected there was not much because they were right behind me. I bid goodnight to everyone and Shana walked me to my hut. I was surprised when she entered behind me. "How do you feel? Did you have fun?"

I could see she was still concerned. "Yeah, I had fun. But my head is pretty fuzzy now and the room is kind of...spinney."

She grinned at me. "I thought as much. I noticed a red skin in the bathing hut. Did you try their brandy?"

I scrunched up my face. "Oh yes. Although, it was not bad after I drank it for a while."

My Amazon friend laughed at me. "You must have drunk a lot then. Better hope it doesn't come back up later." I paled, and she took pity on me. "Here, get some water into you and I'll make you some tea that will help with the headache and sick stomach tomorrow. I'll also leave you more that you can make for yourself in the morning."

I grabbed the water skin she handed to me and drank it down. When she finished with the tea, I drank that as well. She went to the door and turned back toward me. "Get some sleep, Kyri and I'll see you in the morning. If you skip breakfast, I'll just see you at the archery grounds."

I nodded as I slid into my bed. Just before the door shut I called out to her. "Shana!" She looked back at me curiously. "Thank you. For everything."

She gave me a gentle smile. "No problem. Now get some rest."

AS THE GODS were my witness, the next morning there was a small part of me that wanted to die. I groaned at the thought of putting anything into my roiling stomach. I did get sick into the pot that sat in the corner of my hut. I wiped my face and neck with a cool cloth and then I diligently set out to make the tea

Shana left for me. I did not want to put it in my mouth. I did not want to put anything in my mouth. My head was throbbing and I just wanted to go back to sleep. But I had a commitment to keep with Deata. I only hoped that my actions the previous night would not cause me to embarrass myself in whatever the training master needed from me. I sighed and sipped the steeped tea. I was amazed that it only took about a quarter candle mark for my head to feel better and my stomach to settle. Maybe the coming day would not be so bad after all. Feeling refreshed, I dressed and set off for the food lodge. I could see Shana sitting with a few others, including Culchee.

Shana glanced up when I made my way over. "Hey, you made it. How do you feel?"

I gave her a weak smile. "Eh, better now that I have had your tea. I thought maybe I would try to eat something." I looked at their plates. "What are you eating?"

Culchee responded. "Pan cooked chicken eggs. They're great." I thought them strange looking since I had only eaten boiled eggs with my da. Then I watched her cut into the egg with a knife and a runny yellow yolk came oozing out. She ran a hunk of morning bread through the yellowish slime and popped it into her mouth.

It only took a heartbeat before I found myself bolting toward the door. I made it a little way into the trees before I lost the meager contents of my stomach once again. I cautiously made my way back only to have Shana meet me outside. She held out a large piece of bread and a skin of water. "Here, you need something in you or you'll be weak and shaky all day. Eat slowly."

I flashed her the most grateful look I could muster. "Thank you. That was just so..." I shuddered, remembering the mess on the plate. She gently patted my back sympathetically.

Everything was fairly settled again by the time we made it to the archery range though I still felt a bit shaky. Deata took one look at me and had us follow her back to her office in the training hut. She gave me a sly smile. "Last night finally caught up with you, hmm?" I nodded miserably. "First time drinking, kid?"

I cleared my throat, my voice hoarse with sick. "And last." Both women laughed. Clearly they did not think I was serious.

She poured us some water and settled back in her chair. "So, tell me more about your training with your father."

I explained all about Da's training, about how he taught me to hunt from trees, and how to adjust my aim for moving targets and to compensate for the wind. I shared the first time he showed me the obstacle course. I was meant to go through it running while he counted aloud. I had to hit every target, some from trees, and make it back to him before he reached one hundred. Both women seemed impressed.

"So he taught you to climb trees?"

"Well, not exactly. He told me what I should do and gave me pointers, but I had to teach myself. I can hunt and skin just about anything, and I am not afraid of heights." I turned to Shana my heart full of self-doubt. "I know I am not good with people and I am shy, but do you really think your tribe will want me?"

Shana smiled at me and patted my knee. "Kyri, you would be a valuable addition anywhere you choose to settle. And I have no doubt that my tribe will love you."

Deata chimed in. "The Tanta tribe would love to have you as well. You know, in case you're tired of traveling already." She winked in good humor.

I looked at both of them and smiled. "Thank you."

The training master became serious again. "What age did you apprentice as a fletcher, and what age did your father start training you to shoot?"

I thought for a beat. "I apprenticed at ten summers and started learning to shoot at the same time. But I did not start running the obstacle course until I was twelve. Each year after my twelfth, he would change the shooting course to make it more difficult."

"So, tell me about the last time you missed a target." Deata cocked her head at me. "Have you ever missed a target since you were old enough to string your own bow?"

I thought about it and nodded my head. "It was after my mam died, when I was about thirteen. I was really sad for a long time and finally Da told me to get my bow and go outside." I took a sip of my water. "He started counting and I took off through the woods. When I returned, he was on one hundred and seventy-two. We went out and looked at all the targets. I hit every one, but not a center shot. Then he told me I could not be sad forever because my mam would not have wanted that. I told him that I *would* be sad forever because she was my mam. We argued back and forth, with me just a kidling. He did everything he could to make me madder and madder. Finally he stopped and handed my arrows back. Then he started counting again."

Deata interrupted. "And you were only thirteen?" I nodded and she asked, "How old are you now?"

"I'll be twenty on equinox eve, in a moon or so." She shook her head but did not say any more.

"So I took off again and on my second pass I made it back in my fastest time. He was only on seventy-nine when I stopped in front of him." I took another deep swallow of water, vividly remembering the lesson of that day. "That time when we walked the woods, I saw I had missed all the targets, every single one. Completely missed. We collected all my arrows and then he led me to a big log and sat down. I remember word for word what he told me. He put his arm around me and said, 'Kyri, your emotions will always control how you fly. Sadness will make you slow and imprecise. Anger will make you fast and careless. Never aim an arrow when you do not have complete control.'"

Shana nodded. "That's great advice but I'm surprised he was imparting it on such a young child."

"Da always taught me what he thought I should know, when he thought I should know it. But he had one more thing to say that day. He told me that I could use good emotions to help guide my arrows. Passion, love, and loyalty would give me the truest shots of all."

The training master's eyes went unfocused as she gazed at someplace on the opposite wall. "Well that explains a lot about your skill and mature mindset. Now, can you two tell me about the attack near Kyri's steading? Were there any other problems on your way here?"

Shana answered. "There were six armed men when I was attacked. I had my eyes shut trying to...block it all out until I heard a woman scream in fury." She looked at me, but I could not bear her gaze. I still felt a lot of guilt for not stopping the men sooner. "I know she shot the man on top of me first, I felt him slump and die. I was able to look up in time to see both men with crossbows going down with an arrow to the throat. The two holding my arms barely had time to react before I saw her green and blue fletching sprouting from their chests. Finally, the patrol leader turned to run. That was the man I had stabbed earlier, so he wasn't running very fast. He only made it two steps before falling to the ground."

Deata leaned toward her. "How many candle drops did this take? Were they so poorly organized they couldn't defend against a single archer?"

Shana glanced at me again, then back at the training master. "Not candle drops, heartbeats. I'd wager she pulled six arrows in a row from her quiver, and each man fell that fast."

My stomach rolled listening to her description. Hearing it described aloud made my actions and their consequences seem even more real. I was angry at myself for not finding another solution. I was angry at myself for not acting sooner. My heart hurt from the dichotomy of such thoughts. The training master whistled at Shana's description. "That's pretty impressive, kid."

I could feel anger set my eyes ablaze. My hands clenched when I spoke. "I am not a kid. I am a murderer! And you say *impressive* like it is a good thing. I never wanted to impress anyone by taking a life. Those men are dead and it is my fault. The other men on the road later met the same fate. I did that and nothing I can do will return them to their families." I leapt to my feet to run out because I could not contain the pain and anger anymore. I needed to get away, to find a tree to hide in.

Shana jumped up and grabbed my arm. My whole body quivered with suppressed rage. But Deata stopped her. "Let her go. She'll be back, won't you, Kyri?" I nodded once and ran as soon as Shana dropped her arm. I bolted out the door and took off across the training field. I found the shortest path possible to the forest and ran until I found a tree that looked like my tree. I leaped over some brush and launched myself off a fallen log, grabbing the lowest hanging branch of the great oak. Pulling myself up, I quickly climbed until I found a comfortable spot. It was only then that I let the tears fall. Losing my da, and my home, was hard. But I had not stopped to reconcile who I was now, the new Kyri who was a killer. Taking a human life was not like hunting. My mam and my da taught me to revere life, to always give back to the forest whenever I had to take. But how do you give back when you take the life of a man? How was there balance? What would my mam think of the person I had become?

I sat there for a while and only looked up when I heard low whistling echoing through the trees. It did not belong to any kind of bird I knew so I dried my eyes and looked around from my perch. Immediately, my gaze was drawn to movement in the treetops. There was a group of Amazons running the branches, heading in my direction. I did not want to startle them so I mimicked the whistle I had just heard. Instantly, the one in the lead pulled up short and gave a hand signal for the rest to follow. I could see that it was Baeza but I did not recognize the ones with her. I assumed they were on patrol so I raised my hand and waved.

Once they got a little closer, Baeza stopped. "Ho there, Kyri, what brings you to our neck of the woods?" She peered down the length of my tree. "And how did you get up there?"

I decided to tease her a bit, which she deserved after getting me drunk on brandy the night before. "Oh, it was easy enough. Why? Do you need some pointers, Amazon?"

I could hear sniggers coming from the women in her group. Baeza glanced back down the length of my great oak and joined in their laughter. "Maybe I do." She turned to her group with a quick word, they began to move away while she came closer.

Climbing a little higher on the tree next to mine, she stopped when she was a few strides from me. Taking in my tear streaked face, she asked, "So what brings you out here? It's not about last night is it?"

"No, last night was fun except for the brandy. I just have some heavy thoughts weighing on my mind right now. I feel like..." I struggled to find the words. "Well...I do not feel like I know who I am anymore and my heart is carrying the weight of it."

She looked at me softly. "I know we don't know each other that well but you can talk to me if you want. Who knows, I just might understand."

I looked back at her warm brown eyes, from high in the treetops. Maybe she would. "Have you ever killed anyone, Baeza?" At first her gaze looked pained but then softened.

"Yes, once. I was on patrol and a large group of bandits was harassing a family on the edge of Tanta land. My patrol group decided to come down out of the trees and help the family. My sword was responsible for two of the dead men." She cocked her head at me. "Have you lost your blood innocence, Kyri? Is that what troubles you?"

I hung my head. "Yes, I killed the six men who attacked Shana near my steading. Then on the way here, I killed two more that were attacking us. Eight men. *Eight.* That is how many lives I have ended. How do I find my balance after that? I was raised in the forest, and there was always a way to give back what you take. But how do you give back when you take someone's life?"

The Amazon scout smiled tenderly. "I'm going to tell you what my older sister told me. When you take the life of a good person, there is no balance. You can never properly give back what you have taken." I nodded sadly and opened my mouth but she cut me off. "No, let me finish, Kyri. Have you ever grown a beet?"

Startled by the question, I stammered, "S...sure. My mam started a little garden before I was born and my da and I kept it up after she died. Why?"

"You asked about balance. You know that a beet only has some useless greens above ground, right?" I nodded. "And you also know that the best part of the beet, you can't see at all." Another nod. "When you take the life of a bad person, someone who takes the lives of good people, your balance is a lot like the beet. All you see is that you cut the top off that beet. But what you don't see is the countless other lives you saved. Those are hidden in the soil of that person's future."

I started to feel something in the pit of my stomach, a

tightening at hearing her words. There was a part of me that knew understanding was coming. We were more than just the direction of our future, we were also a sum of our pasts. I never stopped to think about what those men had done before they attacked on the road, or what they would have done after.

She continued. "Do you think that was the first time those six soldiers ever attacked a woman?"

I thought about the way they worked together to hold her down. I thought about how they knew to kill the horse to lay her body over and how two men stood guard. I could feel the rage start to well up again. In a low voice, I hissed, "No."

"Do you think that would have been the last time they ever attacked someone?"

My fists clenched in my lap. "No!"

"That is your balance. Each life that they have harmed and each person you save is your balance for taking the life of those men. Even the most majestic creature needs to be put down when it is no longer right in the head."

I could feel the weight in my chest melting away. "Baeza, you are right! That is exactly it!" I stood from my perch and ran along a branch until I could leap to her tree. When I got there, I pulled her into the biggest hug I could manage. "Thank you so much!"

I released her when I remembered there was someplace I had to be. As I scrambled down the trunk of her tree she called out to me, "Where are you going?"

I yelled back as I took off running. "I have to go see Deata!"

WHEN I GOT back to the training grounds, I found Shana drilling with the Training Master. They looked like they had been at it for a while, both dirty and covered in sweat. Deata signaled to stop when she saw me. "Look who's returned. Did you work through some things?"

I looked at her and Shana, and smiled. "Yes I did, with a little help from a bird."

The two women sheathed their knives and wiped themselves down to get rid of some of the accumulated sweat and grime. Deata turned to me when she was finished. "So Shana told me about the second batch of raiders, the ones just outside Tanta territory." She started walking us toward the archery range. "She said you shot a crossbow bolt out of the air."

She stared at me and I suddenly felt uncomfortable. My words came out stammering and unsure. "Kind of, I mean...I did. But it was just chance really, an accident. I accidently hit the bolt when I was shooting at the brigand."

She stopped abruptly and put her hand on my arm. "Kyri, were you shooting at the brigand or were you aiming for that crossbow bolt?"

"I...I..." I sighed because there was no way I could avoid the truth of my miraculous seeming shot. "I was aiming for the bolt, though I was not sure if I would actually hit it. I knew he was shooting at me, and he would not be able to reload fast, so I took a chance on his bolt first. Then I killed him."

Shana poked me in the ribs. "See, I told you she was amazing. No one I've ever met could have made that shot."

I grumbled. I certainly did not need her help. "I am telling you, I just got lucky!"

Deata resumed walking and we had no choice but to follow. I got nervous when she replied, "I don't think you did." We arrived near the weapons hut moments later and she ducked inside. A few candle drops went by before she returned with a crossbow and whistled for two of her instructors. One took off toward the trees and the other followed behind us. The nervous feeling blossomed into full-on anxiety when she walked us away to a secluded area.

"What is going on, Deata? Why are we out here?" I briefly wondered if this was an Amazon ritual I was unfamiliar with. I glanced at my sister but found no answers.

Even Shana looked at her with concern. "Deata?"

She turned back to us when we finally arrived at our destination, as her instructor walked about forty paces away. "I don't believe your shot was luck. I've seen you do the impossible twice, and I've heard the tale of your training since childhood. The problem is that you don't believe in your own skill. And that will get you, or someone who relies on you, hurt. Though you are not part of any tribe yet, consider this your first lesson in being an Amazon."

Shana stepped in. "Whoa, you can't do this, she could be seriously hurt. You can't just have your instructor shoot a crossbow at her, that's insane!"

The training master glanced from me to Shana. "I'm not. She's going to shoot at me. String your bow, Kyri, I don't want to die today."

Shana threw up her hands and paced away, cursing in Greek, and Latin, and something I did not recognize. I quickly strung my bow. I nocked an arrow and without warning I heard the crossbow fire. Just as fast, I released my forest fletch and the crossbow bolt was dashed to the ground. The tingling up my spine returned and I heard a rustle in the breeze. I quickly spun my bow around and knocked another standard arrow out of the sky before it could find a home in Deata's back.

I stood in shock while Deata looked calmly back at me. Shana furiously ran over and shoved the training master to the ground. "What the hades was that. You could have been killed! She would have had that on her conscience as well."

Deata slowly stood up and held her hand out, palm up. "Peace, Shana, there was no danger." I could see the Amazon with the crossbow approach and another appeared from the trees carrying her bow. When I looked back at Deata, she was removing her leather shirt. Underneath were thick blocks of wood across her chest and back, connected at the top by leather strips.

My mouth dropped open. "But...you..."

Shana shook her head and rolled her eyes.

Deata removed the blocks and put her shirt back on. She placed a warm hand on my shoulder and looked into my eyes. "Now do you believe in yourself? Do you believe in the power and strength of your bow, the speed of your reaction, and the instinct that marches down your spine?"

I stared at her in awe. How she could know what I felt? "Yes, but how do you know about that?"

She smiled and winked. "It's what all the best have. It is the knowledge of all the things around them and the ability to know when something doesn't belong. This is the gift that you have, may you always use it wisely."

The training master started walking back with the other two Tanta women. I could hear them excitedly talking amongst themselves. Shana approached me. "Are you okay?"

I looked at her, feeling strange. "I do not know."

She helped me retrieve my arrow then put an arm around my shoulder as we walked back. "Do you think you're ready to eat something yet?" My stomach growled loudly and she laughed. "I guess that's a yes."

"Hey!" I protested. "My mam always told me if I do not eat I will stunt my growth."

She gave me a wide smirk. "Uh huh, let's go, sprout."

WE WERE JUST finishing up our midday meal when a messenger from Queen Myra came in. Shana's presence was requested at the council hut. Since their talks did not involve me, I decided to go back to my hut for a nap. With all the excitement, I felt pretty drained. I woke a few candle marks later feeling refreshed and decided to take another bath. I could easily get used to the hot soaks and sincerely hoped the Telequire tribe had something similar. I was not looking forward to bathing in small buckets or cold streams again. Shana found me after I had sufficiently pruned. She wore her dress leathers again, apparently having brushed them before she went to bed the previous night. I was glad they had given me two identical outfits the day before. At least I would not have to put on dirty clothes again, or the outfit that I had darkened with sweat while dancing and not had a chance to clean. I thought briefly that I should burn the stained trousers and heavy shirt. Shana was sinking into the tub as I finished getting dressed. "So did the queen finally make a decision? Do you know when we are leaving to go back to your tribe?"

She smiled while she rubbed a cake of soap into her hair. "Yes and yes. She has two scrolls that I'm to take back to Queen Orianna. And we will be leaving at first light." I grinned at the news, excited to be moving on again. She laughed at the look on my face. "I thought you'd be sad to leave so soon. Don't you like it here?"

I nodded my head excitedly. "Oh, I love it here. It is so much more than I imagined, being part of an Amazon tribe. But..." I stopped and chewed my lip. I was not sure how to explain it when I did not fully understand the feeling.

"You're ready to move on to the next adventure."

I whipped my head up and met her eyes. "Yes. That is it exactly. Well, not all of it. I really want to get back to the Telequire nation." I waved my hands for emphasis. "I want to meet Queen Orianna and ask to join your tribe. I want to train, and I want to be an Amazon with you. I want to contribute and help others..."

Shana splashed me to interrupt. "Okay, stop already, I get it. I'm glad you're so excited to meet my tribe and queen. I'm very excited to bring you back with me as well."

I swallowed the lump in my throat. "Really?"

She looked back seriously. "Really. I just have this feeling in my gut...Kyri, you're going to be one of the best. And I can't wait for Orianna to meet you." She laughed and splashed my way again. "Now go! We are having another big dinner tonight as a send-off. You get a chance to say goodbye to all your new friends." She winked at me and I blushed before hastily making my way out of the bathing hut.

Dinner that evening was great. I even got to sit with Baeza and her friends though I did not drink more alcohol. After the meal, the village bard stood up. The pictures she painted with her words had us all laughing one instant and in tears the next. On top of my wish for massive bathing tubs, I also hoped the

Telequire nation had a bard. I was about to find Shana to say good night when the training master caught up to me. She pulled me aside. I looked around nervously.

"No worries, kid, no more tests for you." I breathed a sigh of relief and she continued in a more serious tone. "Kyri, I believe you have a tall tree to climb before your end days but I have all confidence that you'll make it to the top. I just wanted to take a moment to thank you for my life."

I looked at her in confusion. "I do not understand."

"That wayward arrow, it would have ended my life as sure as any brigand. And there is no way I can ever repay you for that." She took off the hammered bronze armband that she wore around her left bicep. Where it once was plain, I noticed she had added the scribed image of an arrow. The fletching grooves were even filled in with green and blue dye, and the excess wiped away. My eyes watered and I did not know what to say. I was shocked when she dropped down to a knee and held it out to me. "My sword, my bow, my heart, and my soul, should you need any of these things they are yours. I pledge to you and my goddess, I will answer your debt of death should you find yourself without coin."

I took her armband, my mind reeling from her pledge. With her help, I placed it around my own left bicep. "Thank you, Deata. I am honored to consider you one of my first Amazon friends and I would save you over and over if I could."

She smiled and clasped my forearm like we were both warriors, though I knew I was not. I still appreciated the respect she was paying me. We said our goodbyes and Shana walked with me back to the guest huts. She could tell I had a lot on my mind so there was no talking until we bid each other goodnight.

Our leave-taking was a quiet affair the next morning. We had said our farewells the night before. Queen Myra and Deata were there to see us off and Culchee led us to the edge of Tanta lands. I was sad because I knew I had made some true friends amongst the Tanta nation. But I was also eager and excited to travel again. As much as I would have liked to go back through my home region to check on my da, I knew it was too risky. Shana and I had discussed it the day before and decided to take a more southerly route. Besides, I had already said goodbye in my heart. There was nothing left to say.

Chapter Four

The Bronze Arrow

WE HAD MORE than a fortnight of quiet travel, sleeping in the woods each night. The Tanta nation had given Shana another horse to replace the one killed when she was attacked. That sped our journey immeasurably. Since we were about halfway back to her home, Shana suggested we treat ourselves and spend the night at an inn. It was late afternoon when we rode into the town of Kozani. It was easy enough to find our way to the local establishment. We left the horses in front and entered through a sturdy oak door. I saw a man and woman at a table in the corner, but other than that the place was empty. We were just starting to wonder where the innkeeper was when he came through a doorway wiping his hands.

"What can I do for you ladies?" I could see him taking note of Shana's feathers and our Amazon garb, but he did not acknowledge either.

Shana held up her coin purse. "We'd like a room for a night, two beds if you have them, and stabling for our horses and mule." I poked her in the arm and she added to her request. "And a bath." Another poke and she sighed before speaking again. "And dinner." I grinned in triumph.

He shook his head at our antics. "The cost is one gold and two coppers. Meal will be ready at sundown." He motioned his head toward the door. "Just lead your beasts around to the boy, and he'll take care of them for you."

I stepped forward hesitantly. "Excuse me..."

He grinned in surprise. "Oh ho, she does talk."

I blushed and Shana laughed. "Yes, I talk. Can you tell me if there is a market near here?"

"Sure. Just head out the door to your left and keep going to the village center. You'll see the banners they hang. But you ladies better hurry, they close down at dusk."

"Okay, thanks."

He started to walk away, then turned back to us. "I'll have the boy fill a bath for you after dinner." Shana nodded in response.

WHEN WE FINALLY arrived at the market, I was stunned by the sights and sounds. The town was a lot bigger than the village near my homestead. I could not believe the level of noise and all the different odors. When I saw a vendor nearby with delicious smelling roast meat on sticks I turned to Shana. "We could have had our dinner here."

My Amazon sister took my arm and led me further into the marketplace away from the vendor. She leaned in close. "Do you know what that meat was?" When I shook my head no, she continued. "Neither do I. There is no way I'm touching that. Some vendors are known for using rats."

I scrunched up my face in disgust. "Ugh, that is awful!" I shuddered and did not mention the mystery meat vendor again. I looked in a lot of the stalls but nothing really caught my attention until I got to the bow maker's tent.

Shana saw that she had lost me for the time being so she pointed vaguely toward a weapon seller. "I'm going to be over here."

I nodded and walked in to look at the archery equipment. There were at least twenty different types of fletched arrows at differing lengths and selections of arrowheads in small baskets. I could see a few other customers in the tent, and the practitioner was busy with one of them. I made my way around the space, looking at the variety of bows he had on display. I saw one with a multicolored wood grain. I could pick out red, green, blue, and yellow amongst the colors but could not puzzle out how it was made. It was gorgeous but I was particularly fond of my own bow. It was a present from my da when I turned sixteen.

The man must have finished up with his customer because he approached me while I studied the strangely colored weapon. His gruff voice startled me. "See something you like, lass? My name's Torrel and this is my shop."

I pointed at the beautiful bow. "Can you tell me how you did that, or is it a secret?"

He looked up and smiled. "Ah, well it's no secret, but not a lot want to go through the effort. It's painstaking, that type of stain is." When I looked at him curiously he continued. "The only thing to it is patience. You have to paint each grain with a different dye and keep repeating until enough soaks in to make it bright. Then I have to go over the entire thing with olive oil, and lastly, a layer of wax."

I nodded, understanding his description. "How long does the staining take?"

He looked thoughtful. "I'd say to cut, shape, stain, and seal this entire bow took me about a moon. Most of that was the staining. Are you interested?" He looked at the bow and quiver strung across my back. "You have a pretty nice bow yourself, black oak?"

I nodded. "Yeah, my da made it for me when I was sixteen."

He squinted and looked a little closer at my quiver. "Can I see one of those arrows?"

I shrugged and drew one for him. "Sure."

Torrel whistled as he sighted down the length of it. "This is master quality. It looks really familiar to me, but the fletching's not quite right." He squinted at me. "Who made this arrow?"

Curious as to why he wanted to know, I was honest. "I did, sir. Why?"

"Ah, well it looks like my old friend Galen's work. I believe he was the master fletcher somewhere north of here, I think in Colmenus's kingdom."

My face brightened. "Yes, sir. That is my da. His arrows differ in that he uses two blue and a green, while I use two green and a blue."

"Well I'll be! How is your old da anyway?"

My face darkened and I swallowed the lump in my throat. "He was dying when I last saw him. He had a weakness that kept progressing and even the healer did not know how to help. He...he sent me off to make a new life with the Amazons."

Torrel handed back my arrow with a deep look of sorrow crossing his face. "I'm really sorry to hear that. He was a great man and the best archer I'd ever seen. Tell me, did he teach you to shoot?"

At that point, Shana walked in and heard his question. "She's better than any you could put against her."

I felt my face grow warm. She ignored me when I spun around to glare at her, embarrassed once again by her bragging. "Shana!"

Torrel chuckled at my red face. "Nah, s'okay, lass. I know Galen from way back, and I believe that anyone he saw fit to train could be nothing less than the best." He cocked his head. "There is an archery tournament tomorrow. The prize for first place would be more than enough to buy this bow. You should think about entering. It would be interesting to see how Galen's protégé would shake up the locals." He winked at me and turned away to help another customer.

Shana looked at me, then at the bow I had been admiring. "It certainly is beautiful."

I stared at it wistfully. "Yeah..."

"Why don't you enter?"

I whipped around and gaped, surprised that she would make

the suggestion. "Because we have to go. I know how important it is to get those scrolls to your queen so we should not delay." I chewed my lower lip for a beat or two and sighed. "Besides, there will be dozens that enter the contest. There is no way I could best them all."

"The scrolls can wait one more day. I think you need to do this. Besides, I'll even make an interesting wager with you."

I looked at her curiously. "What?"

She smirked. "If you win, I'll give you one of my matched daggers and teach you to fight with it. And if you lose, you owe me two dozen of your fancy green and blue fletched arrows."

I thought about her wager and nodded my head slowly. It seemed like a fair deal. All that was left was to find out where to enter.

TORREL ACTUALLY SUBMITTED my name to the contest with the entry fee I provided. Shana thought it was a fitting use for the money taken from the dead brigands. The next morning came early on the heels of a night of restless sleep. The tourney had arrived with the rising sun and I was a bundle of nerves. Shana reminded me of my demonstration while we were with the Tanta nation and I tried to explain to her that it was not the same.

"How isn't it the same? What you did there was amazing. You should have no problems at this little competition."

As we approached the field where the tournament was to be held, I could see dozens of men entered to compete. They were all carrying their bows and had a white strip of cloth tied around the upper part of their left arms. I pointed to the milling archers. "*That* is the difference. Look how many people are here to compete." Then I caught a glimpse of the crowd that was there to watch and paled. I let out a curse that I had heard my da say many times before. "Bent arrows and broken string! Look at all those people, I cannot do this."

Shana pulled me to a stop and I looked at her curiously. "When you shoot your bow, what are you looking at?"

I thought her foolish and it plainly showed on my face. "The target, of course. Why?"

She pointed at the field, packed with archers and spectators. "Where is your target?" I squinted and pointed in the direction of the few targets I could see. They were at the far end of the field. She nodded at me. "Good. Now don't lose sight of your target and remember that the rest of the people here are just trees in the wood. Now I want you to take two deep breaths and let them out slowly."

I shut my eyes and complied with her instruction, then opened them again. My friend looked into my blue eyes. "Now, are you ready?" I nodded. "Good, because I want to see you with a new bow by the end of the day."

I grinned and we went to the table to check in. They did not give us any details about what each challenge was. Though I suppose that was normal, I had never seen a contest of such a size before. Once we were lined up on the field two men to a target, the crowd quieted. It was not all men though at the target pairs. Surprisingly there were a few women other than me shooting. There was only the lightest of breezes, nothing that would cause a major problem hitting the simple targets at the end of the field. The rules were easy enough, each person was allowed two shots and the closest shot to the center of the target would move on to the next round. The man I was shooting against was short and stocky. He had sandy blond hair and a well-kempt beard of the same color.

He held out his hand to me. "Huzzah, my name's Lagus. Are you an Amazon?"

I clasped his arm and smiled. "I am Kyri, and not yet. I was hoping to join my friend's nation soon. This town was just a quick stop on the way there."

He laughed good-naturedly. "Ah, well good luck to you then. And I suspect good luck to me since everyone knows the Amazons have some of the best archers." He waved off my protest of not being an Amazon. "Oh I know you're not one yet, but I don't think you'd enter this contest nor would your friend take you back if you were a lost cause."

I nodded and laughed. "Thanks, and good luck to you too."

Someone yelled out at the opposite end of the field. "Archers, on your ready!" When we were paired up, we drew straws to see who would shoot first. Lagus had lost so he had an arrow nocked and ready. The same person called out, "Begin!"

Lagus loosed his first arrow, and we immediately switched spots. I could see he was slightly off center when I pulled, nocked, and loosed my own. My arrow went in next to his, but still slightly off. We switched again, only the second time his was dead on. I was suddenly aware of the roaring crowd and the butterflies tumbling around my stomach. "You are pretty good yourself," I commented as we switched places for the last time. I pulled my second forest fletch arrow from my quiver and nocked it, then closed my eyes. After two deeps breaths, I opened my eyes, sighted, and released on the exhale. Despite the sudden gust of wind that swept through the field as I shot, I found myself grinning at the result. My arrow had perfectly split the wood of his, taking over the center of the target.

I could hear Shana cheering somewhere behind me as Lagus gave a whistle. "That was some shot, friend. Good luck, Kyri." He clapped my shoulder once, then turned and walked away.

I noticed half the archers were gone, so I followed the rest when they gathered as a group. We were waiting on instruction for the next round. When I glanced to Shana, she held her closed fist in the air. 'To victory!' she was saying. I grinned and shrugged my shoulders.

The next round was explained and I raised an eyebrow. There were twenty archers left, and we all had our own target. Each archer was allowed six arrows in their quiver. The announcer would count up to five, starting with 'one archer.' We had to shoot all six arrows within the red circle before the announcer yelled out 'time.' To ensure honesty, there would be a volunteer watching each person, making sure all six arrows had been shot before time was called. I grinned, finally feeling the confidence that Deata had tried to instill in me. This was a challenge I could do and do well.

Everyone had one hand holding their bow and one hand grasping the nock of their arrow, but the arrow had to remain in the quiver until the announcer started counting. When he yelled "begin," I smoothly pulled and shot all six arrows. I smiled when I heard, "Five archer" yelled out after my last shot was released.

"Time!"

All archers lowered their bows. At least a half dozen had failed to shoot all six arrows in time so they were immediately eliminated. After the volunteers checked our targets, another six were eliminated. Only eight of us remained. I was actually surprised, I thought the second round was quite easy.

For the third round, they returned our arrows and split us into pairs again. I noticed there were no other women left, just me. After the explanation for the third challenge, I knew it was going to be much more difficult. Each archer would be assigned a color, either red or blue. Five painted wooden disks of each color would be thrown high into the air, one after another. The archer to shoot the most of his or her assigned color disks would advance to the next round. I was in the last pair to do the challenge. The flying disks would be just like shooting ducks from the sky. It was over almost as soon as it began. As the volunteers rapidly tossed the disks high into the air, we released our arrows. Unfortunately for my opponent, he had hit only three while all five of mine met their mark. Since one of the pairs had neither man hit a wood disc, there were now only three of us left.

I found Shana's face in the crowd again. She winked back at

me, and repeated the victory sign. While standing next to the other two archers, I looked on curiously as the final challenge was drawn onto the field by a pair of horses. It looked like a giant round tabletop, only the top was facing us. The end of an axle stuck out of the middle so I assumed the entire thing would turn like a wheel. There were two red circles painted on it, opposite sides to each other. We were allowed to approach the spinning disk, to see how it worked while they explained the challenge. We were only allowed three arrows but we had to hit both circles. And we could not release our arrows until the wheel started spinning. I swallowed, feeling the butterflies return. This was at least as hard as any challenge my da ever gave me. We were given about five candle drops to study the contraption, and then we had to draw straws again to see the order to shoot. Unfortunately I drew the short straw and had to go first. One thing I noticed about the wheel was that there was a small keyhole near the axle, I suspect this was to lock the wheel when necessary. I decided I could use that. The spinning target was taken out about thirty paces and I lined up my shot. They started it spinning and called out. "Ready!"

My first arrow hit the keyhole perfectly, stopping the wheel. My second and third arrows hit the center of the two red circles, just as I had planned. Immediately the crowd exploded and the other two contestants' faces grew red with anger. The announcer struggled to get control. "Hold, hold, hold!" He looked at the stationary target, then back at me. With consternation he said loudly, "You're supposed to hit the red circles while it is spinning."

I looked him straight in the eye and responded in just as loud a voice. "You never said it had to be spinning. You merely stated we could only use three arrows and two of them had to be in the red circle, and that we could not shoot until the wheel was started."

The crowd roared and cheered at my response while the announcer scrubbed his face with a hand. Finally he looked back at me and in a much quieter voice responded to my logical explanation. "Please, it really is in the rules that the target has to be spinning while you shoot each arrow. I didn't mention it because we've held this contest so long that we just thought everyone knew. Will you shoot again?"

I looked at his weary face and finally conceded. "Fine, but I want to redraw straws."

Luckily, I had the better draw the second time around and was slotted to shoot last. I watched as each man lined up and released arrows. Of the six they shot between them, I could only see one that had caught the edge of a red circle. I smiled and held out hope. The crowd actually quieted when I lined up, perhaps sensing something in the air. My first forest fletch landed a good finger's width into the red circle. It was not at all a center shot, but it was still quite good considering the nature of the challenge. I drew back and sighted again. I followed the speed of the wheel, sensed the rhythm of it, exhaled and released. My other arrow hit just off center of the second red circle. The crowd started cheering when I drew my third arrow and released. With my last shot, I once again hit the keyhole and stopped the wheel.

The announcer just shook his head at my rebellious antics and clasped my shoulder good-naturedly in honor of my win. Loud enough for the crowd to hear he asked, "Why don't you tell everyone the name of the archer that has defeated the spinning wheel."

Once again raising my voice to match his, I answered. "I am no archer. I am Kyri, daughter of Galen the Master Fletcher." Swallowing the lump in my throat, I added, "This win was done in his honor, and his memory. May the spirit of his fletchings live on."

For my win, I was awarded a purse of gold and a small bronze arrow. I knew I would treasure the arrow because it would always remind me of my da. Shana ran up and wrapped me in a big hug, pounding my back in excitement. "You did it, you show off! I knew you would, Kyri."

"I am glad someone did. Now come on, let us go find Torrel and buy a new bow." As we made our way through the crowd to the village market, I was stopped by quite a few well-wishers. Everyone seemed to be in awe of my win though I just thought they were easily entertained.

Torrel arrived at his tent right after us. "Kyri. I knew any kid of Galen's would take that tournament. Congratulations, girl!" He opened the flap and bid us to enter.

There was a young man inside watching the wares while the bow maker was away. I looked for the bow and panicked when I could not find it. "Torrel, you did not sell the bow already did you?"

He chuckled. "Nope. I told you I knew you were going to win, so I wrapped it up and set it aside until you could come buy it." He walked to one of the many crates stacked along the wall and opened it. Inside, wrapped in sheepskin, was the multi-colored bow.

I must have sighed aloud because Shana laughed quietly behind me. As soon as I had the beautifully carved and stained bow in my hand, I knew I was in love. I ran my fingers along the smooth oiled and waxed grain and smiled with pleasure. It was almost too pretty to shoot. Almost. "Can I try it out now?"

"Sure." He handed me a freshly waxed string and led me to a small shooting gallery behind the tent.

I strung the bow and drew back the string to test it out. "Deh, it is a strong one...but really springy. What kind of wood is this?"

"Well the traders said it was something called Madagascar Rosewood. It's from across the southern sea, well beyond the land of pharaohs. The man said he wouldn't go down there himself because it was nothing but savages, but he met another trader coming north that had a bundle of stave-length wood. I cut a good deal with him to get a few lengths." He smiled proudly, watching me pull and shoot. After only sinking six arrows into the target, I was impressed. He could tell. "Nice huh?"

I beamed and caressed the wood again. "It is amazing."

Shana just mumbled, "Someone needs to get out more..."

Along with the bow, I was given a lump of wax and a couple extra strings. Then Torrel wished us luck and bid us farewell. Even though it was midafternoon, Shana really wanted to get underway again. So after a quick restock of some supplies, we mounted the horses and led Dan out of town. My old bow was carefully wrapped and strapped to Dan's packs. My new one was across my back, crisscrossed against my quiver. I even had some of the gold left from my winnings. I felt rich in goods and in spirit as we rode out of town.

THE EVENING WE left Kozani, Shana made good on her wager. She pulled one of her matching daggers and its sheath from her left boot and handed it to me. She told me I could wear it on my belt, thigh, or boot. I chose my boot, the same way she wore hers. She said that she would begin my instruction on the next night. After dinner I sat on my bedroll inspecting my new knife. It was longer and wider than my skinning knife. Its total length was about that of my forearm, and it had a leather wrapped handle. The pommel was shaped like a circle but came to a slight point at the end. I assumed this was to do the most damage to the top of a man's head, but I did not ask. There was something quite appealing in its simplicity, and I could tell it was well made.

Shana watched me inspect the blade. "The pair was a gift from my second mother, when I went through the Ilio Choroú. That is our rite of adulthood in the nation."

"What? I cannot take this if it was a gift to you!" I tried to hand it back, only to have her push my hand down.

"No, it's okay. By giving you that blade, I'm honoring the Amazon I see inside you. I truly feel like you are a sister and I know that it's the right thing to give you my second dagger." She paused for a heartbeat. "We are much the same, you and I."

I looked at her curiously. "How do you mean?"

"Less than a cycle after I took up my duties in the Amazon nation, I lost my own parents. The previous queen frequently sent our warriors and scouts to battle the surrounding nations of men. It mattered not that we were often outnumbered and unprepared for some of the war tactics used." She paused to take a drink from her nearby water skin and stared into the fire while she continued. "Anyway, my mothers were sent on the same futile mission, a needless raid to the east that resulted in the entire group being slaughtered."

She drew in a shuddering breath as she watched the flickering flames. "After Combe and Sikara died with ten other women, the council voted unanimously that both members of a bonded pair with children could not be sent off to battle. Without my friends, Queen Orianna and Basha, I don't know what I would have done."

I didn't know what to say, but I did understand her pain. "I'm sorry for your loss."

Shana shrugged, but I had come to recognize when she pushed difficult things away from her. "It was a handful of years ago now, not so fresh in my memory. But I'm telling you because I want you to understand why I feel such kinship with you. We share a bond of loss."

Her words wrapped me with respect and understanding. I finally nodded and swallowed the lump that had lodged in my throat. After stowing the dagger into my right boot, I stared into the fire for a few candle drops. When I thought I was in control of my emotions, I turned my gaze back to her. "Once I am settled into your Telequire nation, I would like to make some arrows for you in return."

She smiled and nodded. "It's a deal. Now, get some sleep. We have a long way to go tomorrow, and your first knife lesson is at the end of the day."

That night I dreamed that I was running the woods at the homestead. I could hear my da counting as I shot my new bow. Each arrow I loosed found its target. The obstacle course seemed to go on forever, but Da kept counting. By the time I made it back to him though, he was only on eight. Confused, I looked down at my beautiful new bow. I could hear him saying, 'eight lives Kyri, eight lives you have taken.' Then he kept repeating, 'Where is your balance, Kyri...where is your balance, Kyri...,' over and over again. I woke to the sound of my name, only it was Shana calling me.

"Kyri, it is dawn. Time to go." I grumbled at my dreams, and at the early hour. Though I was no stranger to sunrise, having gotten up early my entire life, I had also hated it my entire life. Shana just smirked at me and handed me a chunk of bread with some cured ham.

The next several days went by fast. I was actually enjoying the knife instruction. Shana told me that with my agility and size, I was a natural. Apparently I had a fearsome reach with my long arms. Trouble found us once again while on a long stretch of hot road. We heard the thunder of hooves and could see a cloud of dust approaching in the distance. As a gesture of respect and wariness, we moved the horses and mule to the side to get out of the way. A band of riders came into view and slowed up when they got near. The eight mounted men that stopped near us were dirty, their gear in disrepair. I had a gut feeling on their approach so I had an arrow nocked but kept it alongside my horse out of their view.

The lead rider moved a little forward of the rest. "Ho there, boys, what do we have here? What are you two supposed to be, a couple of Amazons or something?" His men laughed and I worked to calm my racing heart.

Shana remained calm. "We *are* Amazons, traveling back to our home nation. Let us pass in peace."

Her words were met with a chorus of jeers from the men. Their leader held up a hand for quiet. "I've heard Amazons were a fierce and feisty bunch. I bet we could have a lot more fun keeping you here than we would if we let you pass, right boys?" The group of unsavory men hooted and leered at us, clearly interested in what their leader was implying.

Shana subtly dropped her reins, preparing to draw a sword. In the same calm voice she repeated her previous statement. "We are Amazons, traveling back to our home nation. Let us pass in peace…and you will remain unharmed."

A look of anger clouded their leader's face. "You don't threaten me and my men you Amazon bitch! I think it's time you were put in your place."

As soon as I saw Shana's hand signal I lifted my bow. As fast as I could draw, men fell from their horses. Unfortunately, I only dropped four of them before my gentle mare became spooked by the noise and confusion. She spun me away from the action, so I leaped from the saddle and once again took aim. Shana was busy fighting the leader and another man from horseback while the other two aimed their horses in my direction. I dropped one more before the last man was on me. I ducked the swing of his sword and moved under his horse's head to the other side, drawing the dagger from my boot. Before he could reorient, I slashed the saddle strap and he was dumped on the ground. While he recovered, I put the handle of the dagger between my teeth and put an arrow in the brigand who was circling around behind Shana. By the time my opponent had regained his feet, I had tossed my bow aside and took the dagger firmly back in hand. He looked at me and laughed.

Perhaps I seemed comical with a dagger in one hand and one of my forest fletch arrows in the other. Or maybe it was the circumstance of me facing a man with a sword holding the most meager of weapons. I did not care either way. I kept my breathing even, just as Shana had taught me. I knew I only had one good shot against this sword-wielding man, and I had to make it count.

We circled each other, both wary. He had watched me take down his comrades with my bow. I could tell he was angry and perhaps worried that I may be just as proficient with this new weapon. I watched his eyes, waiting for them to give away his actions. I had a droplet of sweat running down the side of my face when he attacked. Sword held high, he came in with a very basic overhand swing. With my reach and strength, I was able to block the sword low on the blade of my dagger while my arrow found a home in his chest the hard way. It was over before that same sweat dripped from my jaw.

I turned to Shana and saw her wiping her sword on the dead leader's cloak. She smiled and held up her fist. I smiled back and did the same. She helped me remove and clean the arrows that were good. Three had been broken when the raiders fell from their horses. As for the horses, she found a rope and put them on two strings to be led with Dan. Each of us took a string of horses. We were not sure what we would do with them, but there was no sense letting them go to waste. Though I did not want to, she said we had to move the bodies off the road to the trees. I knew it was a courtesy to other travelers but the dead men were particularly foul. When we were finished, Shana approached me with a concerned look. "Are you all right?"

I thought for a heartbeat and nodded. "Yes, I am okay."

"You're sure? I know how hard it has been to kill, and it seems like you've had to defend yourself a lot since you left home."

I smiled reassuringly. "Actually, Baeza helped me understand a few things that day I ran from the training master's office." Shana raised an eyebrow so I continued. "I think I struggled most because I could not find my balance for the lives I had taken. I was raised in the forest, to give back for every life I take. But I could not find a balance when taking human lives. She made me realize that my balance was in the people I saved by killing those that had turned to the darkness, that each murderer and brigand I killed saved numerous people in the future, and probably avenged numerous people in the past."

Shana clasped my shoulder. "She's right about that, and I'm very glad she helped you find your balance." She grinned at me slyly. "So...did she help you find anything else while you were out in the trees?"

I blushed deep red and scowled as we mounted our horses. "No, you interrupted the only thing she was trying to show me in the bathing hut."

Shana moved her horse closer to mine. Her voice took on a serious quality when she spoke. "And were you ready for that?" I thought for a heartbeat and then shook my head no. "I thought not. Don't worry, it will happen soon enough." She gave her horse a little kick and her string of animals fell in behind her. "Come on, kid, let's go home."

THE NIGHT BEFORE we were due to reach Telequire lands, Shana found a nice campsite near a small waterfall. We worked diligently to picket the horses then I went off to hunt for fresh game. We were both tired of trail rations over the past few days, so I thought I would bring back a few rabbits. Or maybe woodcocks...or both. My mouth watered at the thought of fresh meat. Once I got far enough away from the animals and our camp, I ran up a big maple tree. It was taller than other maples I had seen and seemed to really thrive in the woods near Shana's nation.

I let the quiet overtake me as I patiently waited. Maybe half a candle mark went by before I heard some noise in the brush. I smiled and pulled back my arrow. Taking a slow deep breath, I released my forest fletch on the exhale and took the rabbit clean through the head. I quickly made my way down the tree to clean and skin it. I had just removed its head and hung it from a low tree branch to drain and skin when I felt the familiar tingling running up my spine. I heard a low growl from somewhere above me and grabbed for my bow. I pulled, nocked, and released my arrow just as a furred shape gave out a roar that sounded like a saw on wood and dove at me from above. My arrow was true, but the great cat still had some fight in him. I felt claws rake down my right thigh as the weight of the beast brought me to the ground. I knew it was trying to claw my belly as big cats were known to do with their prey, so I stayed hunched beneath it. As quickly as I could, I drew my dagger and slit the spotted cat's throat but unfortunately not before taking another lighter claw hit to my left shoulder. I winced at the pain of the two injuries but still managed to shove the dying cat off me. Panting, I made it to my hands and knees and took a few heartbeats to catch my breath. I could see my leg was bleeding a lot, so I tore off one of the leather strips that made up my skirt and tied it around my thigh above the wound. I could not do anything for my shoulder but it was not bleeding as much.

I looked around to collect my bearings and knew I needed help, so I cupped my hands and loudly yelled for my travel companion, though I was surprised she had not heard the roar when the cat attacked me. I called a few more times before gathering my dropped bow and skinning knife. Just as I was about to call again, I heard a rustling from the opposite direction of the camp and immediately nocked another arrow. Wounded as I was, I could not afford to take any chances. I only hoped it was not another leopard coming to investigate the noise and blood smell.

I quietly stalked the sound until I came to a large hollow log lying on the ground. When I knelt down I could see little eyes gleaming from inside. The tiny growl and swiping paw had me scrambling back heartbeats before losing my nose. Pain throbbed sickeningly through my thigh. Cautiously, I tried again. I only got a scratched hand for my efforts. Clearly the little bugger was vicious and not coming out easily. But I also knew that without its mother the little beast would die. Something inside me could not let that happen. With a burst of inspiration, I gingerly stood and limped over to the strung rabbit. I carefully cut a bit off and brought it back to the hollow log. This time I was able to coax the cub out from its hiding place. I was even able to run my hand across its back. I wondered briefly if I had gotten its mother's scent all over me when she attacked.

With more of the leather strips from my skirt, I was able to fasten a harness of sorts for the little cub. After a massive fit of acrobatic rebelliousness, it finally calmed down. The calm was probably aided by the fact that I put the rest of the rabbit down for it to eat. Leaving it tied to the log, I went back to the dead leopard. I had just started skinning the animal when Shana finally arrived.

She took in the dead leopard, my injuries, and the small cub tied to the log. With each new sight, her eyebrows rose higher. "I really can't leave you alone for a single heartbeat, can I?" She shook her head in amazement. "Well that explains why the horses were so spooked. I was trying to calm them when I thought I heard my name. Once I re-tied the picket line, I started looking for your trail. "

I smirked. "And you just now found me? Is this where I make fun of your poor tracking skills, Amazon?"

She smirked back. "Is this where I make fun of your ability to draw trouble like bees to honey?" I started laughing, but it changed to a hiss of pain when I shifted my weight to the injured leg. Shana winced at the claw marks on my leg. "Yeah, she got you good. Okay, let's get rid of that cub and get you back to camp. I can come back and skin the dead leopard once I've treated your leg."

Shana drew her knife and moved toward the little cub I had tied to the log. It started growling and tried to back away. I grabbed her knife arm. "No! We cannot kill it. I took its mother, now I am responsible for it."

"Kyri, it's just an animal. That's the way nature works. You can't raise a wild animal."

I moved between her and the cub. "No, this is my duty now and I will not let you kill this cub. And if that means I cannot join your tribe, so be it." I stubbornly refused to move, standing firm in my convictions. At least I stood firm until a wave of dizziness overtook me and my body rushed to meet the ground.

It was dark when I woke again. I was back in the camp on my bedroll and my wounds had been treated. I panicked for a beat remembering the cub but I felt a rumbling warmth against my side. I slowly sat up and saw Shana on a log nearby. Opposite the fire was the leopard skin, stretched out to dry. I looked at her, taking in the bandages on her hands and arms and the look of consternation on her face. "How long was I out?"

"You mean now long did you nap after you decided to lose half a skin of blood?" I nodded. "Oh, about three candle marks." She pointed to the water skin next to me. "I suggest you drink the entire thing. Fish should be done shortly."

My stomach suddenly growled since I was out looking for dinner when I was attacked. I laughed when the cub growled back in its sleep.

Shana looked at me, then down at the cub. "Did that just...answer you?"

I smiled at the little ball of spotted fur. "I think it did." I looked around the camp then back to my friend. "How did you..."

Shana snorted. "It wasn't easy. I went back for a horse so I could get you to the camp. Once I was able to treat your injuries, I came back for the leopard skin. I fleshed and brained the pelt then made a frame and set it out to dry by the fire. I saved the rest of the brain mash so I can give it another coat tomorrow. Unfortunately, you won't be able to stretch and smoke it until we return to my village. Finally, there was your little friend." She held up both bandaged hands and I stifled a laugh at the pained look on her face. "That adorable little ball of fluff is the most vicious and mean little son of a Bacchae that I have ever had the displeasure of knowing."

I could not hold the laughter back any more. "Oh gods, I am sorry but it is really funny." After a candle drop, she started laughing too. We took a good amount of time to relieve the stress and tension then calmed down. I sobered and glanced at my leg. "How bad is it?"

Shana moved over by me, careful not to disturb my new friend. "It's actually not that bad. Mostly superficial. There are two deep spots that should heal without too much trouble if you keep it clean. I was going to ask if you wanted an ash rub to stain them when I change the bandages later."

I thought about it, contemplating the idea of coloring the claw marks with black ash. One of the things I had learned when we were with the Tanta nation was that ash staining was a common practice among the Amazons. Sometimes warriors would stain their wounds after a great battle to highlight their deeds of bravery. And sometimes they would make decorative cuts on themselves to stain, in honor of a loved one or an event. "How about we just stain the shoulder mark? I will leave the leg alone. If it is deep, I do not want to irritate the wound any more than necessary."

"That makes sense. I've got some black charcoal that I pulled from the fire and ground up earlier. I'll do it after we eat. If your leg looks hot tomorrow, we'll stay here another day so you can heal." Shana moved to the fire and removed two of the sticks that she had used to spit the fish. She handed one to me then pulled two rock cakes off a hot stone by the fire. Tossing a cake in my direction, she once again took a seat on the log. "So what are you going to do with it?"

I looked down at the little cub that was waking up at the smell of fish. I was content to ignore it until I heard the plaintive little mew. Sighing, I broke off a bit of fish and gave it to the fuzz ball. "I do not know. I mean…it seems to be eating meat just fine, and it is behaving…"

Shana snorted. "Yeah, for you." She mumbled a few curse words before trailing off.

I finished eating my fish and rock cake and pulled the little cub into my lap. It protested the abrupt movement then protested even more when I lifted its tail. I was forced to make a mental correction at the lack of extra bits...*her* tail. I pulled her close to my chest and she settled down again. When I looked back at Shana, her face held a mix of affection and irritation. "The question is, can I bring her with me or is this where we part ways?" The thought of not being able to continue on to the Telequire nation with my Amazon sister caused my chest to ache. I could feel tears prickling so I looked down, not wanting her to see my pain when she said that the little cub would not be welcome.

She tapped her foot for a candle drop before giving me an answer I did not expect. "Truthfully, Kyri, I don't really know. Nothing like this has ever come up in the nation. The only thing you can do at this point is show up with her and see what they decide. And though it hurts my heart to say it, you can always leave again if they won't let her stay."

"It would hurt my heart too, so I really hope they let us stay."

"And you won't change your mind about the little beast?"

I looked at the sleeping cub, so innocent and alone. On some deeper level I related to her. "I cannot."

After we finished eating, Shana wrapped the leftover fish and checked my wounds again. It stung when she rubbed ashes into the claw marks on my shoulder, but it was not anything like the original injury.

Shana smiled while winding another length of material around my shoulder and arm. "And am I to keep calling her the 'vicious little beast,' or will you give her a name?"

I ran my hand through the little cub's soft fur. "Gata Anatoli."

My Amazon sister shook her head. "Okay, that seems like a mouthful though..."

I shrugged and felt my eyes slipping shut. "So just call her Gata."

Chapter Five

Settling on the Edge

ONCE AGAIN, THE morning intruded way too soon. I woke to angry mewing. The little cub was on my face batting at my mouth. When I did not respond fast enough she moved around to my ear and clamped sharp little teeth around its lobe. I sat up yelling and slapped my hand over the newly throbbing ear. "By all that is holy, you little daemon!"

Shana was already awake and warming some bread and leftover fish by the fire. She cracked up laughing at Gata's action. "You wanted her!"

I grumbled and silently analyzed how my body was feeling. My upper arm ached but was manageable. I would still be able to shoot my bow if I had to, though not with my normal level of skill. The leg was pretty sore, but not alarmingly so and it did not feel hot through the bandage. "My leg does not feel too bad today. We should be able to head out soon. I would like to wash up by the stream first though. I wish I could jump in and bathe but I probably should not until this scabs over a bit more."

Shana handed me the warm fish and flat bread. My little charge started immediately sniffing at the food in my hand. I sighed and gave her some. "Clearly I am going to have my hands full just feeding this little beggar."

The Amazon across from the fire chuckled. "Think of all the hunting practice you'll get."

My mouth dropped open and I shot her an indignant look. "I do not need the practice, thank you very much." She just laughed and finished her morning meal.

After bathing and taking care of Gata, we worked out the logistics of traveling with her. Or rather, I worked it out. Shana told me that as my responsibility, I had to take care of her. Soara was nervous at first when I introduced the little cat. And the cub just hissed at the animal that was so much larger than her. Once they settled down I gingerly mounted the gentle mare and Shana risked more scratches to hand the cub up to me. I think we were both surprised when the little cat did not protest or unsheathe her claws.

After breaking camp, we rode for a few candle marks with Gata in front of me on the saddle. She fell asleep easily to the swaying of the horse. However, once she woke again she got restless. Finally tired of her squirming to see around me and the horse's head, I twisted and deposited her on the bedroll lashed behind my saddle. I watched as her little claws dug in, and then she settled down.

Shana rode behind me since we had transferred the entire string of horses to her. The only one behind me now was Dan the mule, and he probably would not care if I had an adult leopard on the back of my saddle. I think that was why Da sent him with me. Just the fleeting memory of him brought the familiar heaviness back to my heart.

"You know, she actually seems to like riding up there."

I turned to watch the curious little cat. She was looking all around, spending most of her time facing backwards. Her little head would look at the horses behind Shana, then back at Dan, then it would whip around and watch a bird flit through the treetops.

Around midday, my leg started to throb. Shana decided to stop and build a small fire so she could make another poultice from her limited supplies and steep me some painkilling tea. As much as I wanted to reach our destination, I was grateful for the break. I even shared a bit of my cured meat with Gata since she had a penchant for begging. I knew that I probably should not have given in because it was sure to cause bad habits down the road.

It was afternoon and the sun was starting to slant through the trees when Shana said we were nearly to Telequire lands. I was suddenly struck with butterflies and a multitude of emotions. I was excited and relieved to finally arrive. I was also sore and tired, and worried. And what if they would not let me keep little Gata Anatoli? What if they did not want me at all? Did I really have enough to offer the nation for them to honor me as an Amazon?

Shana reassured me as best she could. "Kyri...sister, it's going to be all right."

I gripped Soara's reins in a tightly clenched fist and chewed my bottom lip as my fears rose again to plague me. "But what if they judge me for not helping you sooner? I know you have nightmares every night and it is my fault."

She rode as close as her string of horses would allow. "Whose knife is in your boot?"

I stared ahead and answered. "Yours, Shana."

"No." I tilted my head and my brows drew together as I stared back at her with confusion. Once she successfully captured my eyes, she continued. "That is *your* knife in your boot. Look around you, Kyri. That is *your* horse and pack mule, *your* bow, *your* leopard skin, *your* gods-be-damned cat cub. Half this string of horses is yours, as is my life." I startled when she shouted the last few words. "Those arrows that killed my attackers were yours. You, and you alone, are the one responsible for all the lives your actions may have saved. You are the one whose arrows brought justice for me and countless others. There is a debt between us just as there is a debt between you and Deata. Do not belittle that with your what ifs. We both suffer the scars of that day, and thanks to you we will both heal."

Her words lifted an unseen weight from my shoulders and I felt curiously light. It was during that time of quiet contemplation that I felt a subtle change around me. I stopped my horse, and just as Shana glanced at me puzzled, I raised clasped hands above my head. Only then did my sister notice the rustling in the trees above. Eight women dropped from the lush canopy. I heard a little growl come from behind me but Gata remained unnoticed.

One of the masked women stepped forward. "Shana, you've returned! With good news for the queen I hope." She pushed up her mask, a move that was copied by the rest of the scouts.

Shana put her hands down so I followed suit. "Of course I have good news Deka. Do you think I'd bring back any other kind?"

The Amazon called Deka smirked at her. "Tell me, is it the menagerie you have strung to your mount that made you miss your sisters flying through the trees? Why, even your Amazon companion felt us before you did." The others laughed at the woman's good-natured ribbing.

Shana joined in their laughter. "Ah, but Deka, this is no Amazon who felt you in the trees. She is merely a petitioner seeking membership to the tribe." Her words caused a rumble through the group of scouts.

"What do you mean she's not an Amazon? How did she feel us then? No outsider sees us when we run the trees."

My companion could not resist poking the lead scout's pride. "Perhaps you all need to relearn to fly like hawks instead of waddling through the branches like a parade of ducks."

The group of scouts roared with laughter. I heard a least one say, "Good one, Shana."

Deka simply shook her head before walking to my mounted companion and clasping her forearm as warriors do. "Welcome back, friend." She turned to me. "And do we get your petitioner's name?"

I cleared my throat and rode forward a pace. "My name is Kyri, and I'm very pleased to meet you all." Between all the commotion and the fact that we had stopped moving, Gata had become displeased. She let out a growl and a little hiss of distemper from behind me on Soara.

One of the scouts off to the side nocked an arrow and pointed at her. "What in the goddess's name is that?"

I immediately brought the cub around in front of me, protecting her. "Do not shoot her!"

Deka raised an eyebrow. "Shana?"

My sister-friend shook her head resignedly. "It's a long story, and one best told to the queen first."

Deka took in the sight of the little cub, my injuries, the leopard skin stretched across Dan's pack, and the string of eight saddled horses. "Perhaps you're right." She sent the rest of the scouts back into the trees and took us the rest of the way in herself. As we clopped along, I gnawed my lower lip and kept Gata in front of me on the saddle. The journey through the forest to the village gave me plenty of time to think and worry.

MY FIRST IMPRESSION of the Telequire nation was its vast size. It was a lot bigger than the Tanta tribe. Everywhere I looked there were women in constant motion, going from one place to the next. Shana walked with Deka and I had stayed mounted in deference to my leg injury. But the amount of stares I was getting made me wish I was on the ground blending in with the beasts. Thankfully, Gata stayed quiet and close. The afternoon scout leader called to me when we were a little ways into the village. "I'm going to take you to one of the guest huts. We can leave your saddlebags and pack from the mule with you. You can stay there, and I'll send a healer to look at your leg. Or you can come with Shana and me to take care of the horses."

Shana looked up at me. "Kyri, you should probably lie down for a while." She then glanced at the ball of fur in my lap. "And there's that…"

I was torn because I wanted to take care of my horse and see more of the village, but my leg throbbed in time with my heartbeats. I finally sighed. "I guess I will stay in the hut and wait for the healer."

Shana smiled. "Don't worry, Kyri, you'll get a full tour of the Telequire nation when your leg is better. I also have to speak with the queen as soon as possible and she'll probably want to meet you after, so rest up." I frowned and nodded, knowing my eyes would be nearly gray with the apprehension I felt. Mam always said it was through my eyes that my emotions shown the brightest.

A few candle drops later I found myself sitting on a bed in a guest hut with a leopard cub in my lap and all my earthly belongings in the corner. I leaned back and closed my heavy eyes, trying to ignore my pained thigh. I was almost asleep when knocking on the door startled me. "Yes?"

The door opened and an older woman entered. She had long dark hair turned mostly gray, and a large leather satchel hanging from her shoulders. When she saw me she smiled. "Ah, caught you napping did I?"

I squinted at her. "You did?"

"Well I knocked a few times before you answered."

"Some would-be Amazon I am..."

The elder chuckled and set the bag down. "As you can guess, I'm here to check your injuries. I'm sure Shana did a fine job patching you up, but I'll look at them too. Let me just get a fire started so I can make some tea. My name is Thera."

Gata chose that moment to stand up in my lap and stretch. Thera was startled for a heartbeat or two then exclaimed delightedly, "Oh ho, who is this? I thought it was part of your clothes."

I became anxious and sweat gathered on my skin even as my heart raced in fear of judgement. A healer was an important person in a community and I knew that moment was to be my first test with Gata. I swallowed back my butterflies and stroked the cub to settle her again. "This is Gata Anatoli. I killed her mother on the trip here and I could not bear the thought of leaving her alone and defenseless. And my name is Kyri."

Thera smiled. "Ah, you're a tenderhearted one, aren't you?" I just nodded, still apprehensive. Curious once the cub had shown herself, the healer approached the bed, the fire forgotten. "Is she friendly? Will she let me touch her?"

Curiosity was good, right? "Truthfully, I do not know. I have only had her a day, and she was pretty wild at first. But she seems to have calmed down a lot now." I sent a silent prayer to the little cub, 'Please behave, please behave...' I wanted the healer to like her. I wanted Gata to be friendly and something the tribe would not mind keeping around. But I was also well aware that she was a wild animal.

The little cub lay there while Thera stretched out her hand. Tentatively, the healer made contact and her face lit up. "Oh, she's so soft." Gata was very good, even giving the strange hand a lick. I slowly began to breathe again. Then the other woman started excitedly tossing questions at me. "Do you know how old she is? Was she still suckling, or does she eat meat? What are you going to do with her?"

At first I was taken aback by her sudden barrage of questions. I answered what I could. "She eats meat because that is what I have been feeding her." I thought for a several heartbeats. "She is probably more than a few moons old, but I have no way of knowing for certain because I do not know when leopards wean their young. And I am not really sure what I am going to do with her. I figured I could just raise her and take her back to the wild when she was old enough to survive on her own."

Thera raised an eyebrow. "I don't think that little one is going to follow your plans."

"What do you mean?" I looked at the cub who was purring in my lap.

The healer grinned. "Well I don't know a whole lot about wild things but it looks to me like she is already bonding with you. I don't know that you'll be able to get rid of her so easily when the time comes." She returned to the fire.

I had not considered the possibility that I might end up with a permanent charge when I had decided to take care of Gata. I had certainly never raised anything like a wild animal before. The only creatures I had previously taken care of all ended up in the stew pot. In that handful of heartbeats I feared that my sense of right would complicate things for me more than I had originally surmised. All at once, I felt a lot more responsibility for my little charge. I ran my hand through her soft fur. "I was worried enough when I thought I would have her with me for a few moons. Now I find out she may not want to leave me." I looked into the healer's kind eyes. "Oh gods, what if they won't let me stay? Then what?" I closed my eyes tight, fear and worry battling inside my chest. I whispered, "But I...I have to stay. This is where I belong."

Thera walked over and placed a gentle touch on my hand. "Easy, little one. Why don't you think we'll let you stay?"

I looked at her, my blue eyes shining with unshed tears. "Because of Gata...because of all the things I have done and have not done." Making up my mind, I picked up the cub and set her on the bed next to me. "I have to speak with the queen, to explain everything."

Thera stilled me again with just a look and a simple touch. "Kyri, you will speak with the queen when she's ready. Until then, stop worrying. There are no rules against having a pet; I think Odella even has a pet rabbit."

I let the information filter in. "But Gata is a predator, what if she eats Odella's rabbit."

She chuckled at me. "You're looking for river trouble before it even rains. Patience, little one, I'm sure all will be fine. Now drink this tea and let me look at your wounds." She inspected both injuries while I continued to sip my tea. "Oh, this looks really good. How long ago did this happen?"

I shut my eyes, letting the tea do its work. "Just yesterday, late afternoon. I was out hunting for our meal when she took me from above."

She clucked her teeth. "That's pretty impressive. Not just living to tell about it, but in that you're healing so fast."

"I have always been a fast healer. My da said I must have a touch of the gods, but I think him and my mam just had a lot of good stuff to make me."

She patted my knee. "I think you're both right." She worked quickly, making a poultice for my thigh and wrapping it back up. When she unwrapped my shoulder, she leaned in to scrutinize my injury. "Did Shana stain you?" When I nodded she smiled. "I thought so. This is going to look really good when it heals up." I craned my neck around to see the outside of my shoulder, just above my bicep. There were four jagged cuts in my skin, raw looking, but I could see the black stain. I knew some of the black would come out by the time it was done healing. But for the most part it would stay dark. Despite the pain, I decided it was a good reminder of that moment. I could feel my eyes growing heavy as she was bandaging the shoulder and I tried to fight it. I knew I had to be ready to meet the queen.

Thera startled me awake again. "There, all set!" She stood and began putting all her things away, leaving a small satchel of herbs on the table. "Now, the tea is going to make you sleepy so don't fight it. I'll be by later to check you again and bring you something to eat. I'll even bring some scraps for your little friend."

As she made for the door, I called out to her. "Wait. I am supposed to meet the queen."

She paused in the doorway. "No worries, little one, the queen knows you've been injured. She'll meet with you tomorrow and hear your story then. Until later, Kyri, get some rest."

In the next heartbeat she was gone, leaving me sore and sleepy and very alone with my thoughts. I whispered to the empty room. "But I want to meet her…" And then I just drifted off.

I WOKE THE next morning feeling sore but overall a lot better. I vaguely remembered Thera returning the night before with food for me and Gata. That was probably why I did not wake with a cub chewing on my ear. Leaving the beast on the bed, I limped over to build up the fire and start water heating for tea. Once I had some pain relieving drink in me, the leg was manageable and I started to get restless. I checked the little leather harness on Gata and finding it still in place I attached a cord to it and decided to teach her to walk with me. After ten candle drops of dragging the cub back and forth across the floor on her side, I gave up. I blew out a frustrated breath. It was not working and I was worried that she probably had to go out to eliminate. I looked around the hut, searching for inspiration of some kind when I noticed a new addition. Assuming that Thera left it the night before, I carried Gata over to the good size basket of sand. Not wasting a heartbeat, I dropped the cub into the basket where she sniffed around curiously, then peed. I wrinkled my nose at the smell and was pleasantly surprised when she buried the urine under more sand. I smiled at Thera's ingenuity until I remembered how big the cat-cub was going to grow. I would have to find another solution when she outgrew the basket. I also found it exasperating that the cub started following me without prompt as soon as I removed the lead.

With that taken care of, I had discovered another problem. I was getting hungry and restless, but I did not know if I was allowed to leave. Even if I was allowed, I had no idea where to go. I did not see a point in unpacking the bags that Da had sent with me because I doubted they would keep me in a guest hut for very long one way or another. I wished Shana would come. Since my leg was feeling better with the night's sleep and Thera's tea, I dressed in my second Amazon outfit since it was clean and did not have pieces missing from the skirt. I slipped the dagger into my boot and slung my bow and quiver onto my back. I had never idled well, oft times driving my mam and da crazy as a child stuck inside during the coldest parts of winter. Feeling confined in the guest hut, I worked off some impatience by pacing back and forth, limping along. I actually laughed aloud as the little cat paced along with me. She was silly at times and had really begun to grow on me.

A sudden rap at the door stilled my clumsy pacing and whirling thoughts, and I spun in place. "Kyri, are you awake?"

Gata and I rushed over and I threw open the door even as my leg protested the sudden movement. "Shana! Where have you been? Can I meet the queen now? Did you talk with her? Will she let me stay?"

Shana held up her hands and started laughing at my barrage. Surprisingly, Gata chose that moment to rub up against her legs and give a loud rumble. Shana looked down at the cub in shock. "I thought that little daemon hated me."

I grinned. "Well, Thera said she has bonded with me, so maybe she considers you family too since our scents are all over each other from traveling together." I scooped the cub up before she could wander out the door and Shana came inside. "So, when do I get to meet Queen Orianna? What did she say to you?"

My sister-friend waved toward the table and we sat down. "Well, I spoke with her at length last night. I gave her the scrolls and conveyed my impression of the Tanta tribe. We also spoke about my trip and you."

I leaned forward in eager anticipation. "And?"

"She really wants to meet you and hear your story in person. She's also the one who will take your pledge as an Amazon initiate. Unfortunately, she left at dawn with a band of warriors. The centaurs have a petty warlord on their northern border, and she took fifty fighters to help them out." At my puzzled look she added, "It is part of our alliance to help each other when in need."

"But..." My face fell. I could not explain why I felt so sad. I felt as if I was teetering on the edge of my new life and I was waiting for something or someone in order to step over. The queen was the one that would make everything happen and I found myself discontent with waiting. I felt like one of those ships on the southern sea with all the wind out of my sails. I was going nowhere. "So I am stuck here then?"

She laughed at my agonized look. "No, not at all. We're going to get you set up in your permanent hut and give you a tour of the village. I'm going to introduce you to a few people you will need to know, then I'm going to introduce you to my friends." She winked. "How does that sound?"

I felt all the clouds roll away and I could not prevent the smile from splitting my face. "That sounds great, I am ready now."

She grabbed my arm when I stood up. "Whoa there, kid, halt that horse of yours. What do we do about Gata?" She glanced around the hut. "We could probably leave her here. I'm just concerned about what she'll do when you're gone."

I looked down at the little cat-cub. "Could she...come with me?" Shana gave me a skeptical look. "No, really. Watch this." I paced back and forth across the length of the hut. I gave Gata a low whistle and she started pacing alongside me.

My Amazon sister clapped. "Okay, that is really cute but will she do it outside with all the distractions of the village?"

I stopped walking and the cub stopped with me. "Well, there is only one way to find out."

We started toward the healer's hut and if anything, Gata

stayed too close to me. Numerous times I had to stutter step to avoid her tripping me and the wrenching motion aggravated my leg. She seemed especially wary of the noise and confusion around us and I think that was what kept her so close. The healer's hut was a much larger structure, similar to the Tanta nation council chambers. It was a long building with solid log walls forming the lodge. All the cracks and openings were sealed with clay. There were plenty of windows to let in light and two hearths. Thera came through a doorway at the opposite end of the entrance. "Look who came to visit. How's the leg?" She waved me over to a chair and I sat down. Gata prowled around curiously, occasionally batting at something hanging down.

"It is surprisingly good, all things considering. The soreness is causing a bit of a limp, but it does not feel warm. And while my arm is a little tender, it is nothing that causes problems with mobility."

Thera nodded and sat in front of me, unwrapping my bandages. "Good, good..."

When she was finished, she pronounced me fit enough. She also handed me a small leather sack containing salve, bandages, and another little pouch of herbs for tea. Clearly she trusted me to take care of myself going forward. My stomach growled when we were saying our goodbyes. Thera chuckled. "It looks like the meal house is your next stop." Little Gata chose that moment to answer my growling stomach with a little growl of her own. The healer shook her head. "Now that's pretty funny."

I looked down in dismay. "Shana, I do not think we can take her in there. People might be strange about it."

Shana considered the little cub, rubbing her chin with her finger. "I think you may be right. It's probably too soon for that. How about I run in and get us our morning meal and some scraps for Gata? We can take it outside to eat."

Outside the food hall I found a weatherworn table and benches. I took a seat with the little cub curled up between my boots while Shana ran inside. She had only been gone a few candle drops when a group of women approached, most likely heading in to break their fast. They came over to my table when they noticed me sitting outside. An attractive blonde stopped nearest to me and I found her smile unnerving. I looked up into her hazel eyes and was startled to realize that she was probably as tall as me. "Heyla sister. You must be the visitor that came in with Shana yesterday. What's your name?"

She was incredibly attractive. My palms started sweating in the face of the curious strangers and my tongue grew dry. "Um...my name is Kyri. Wh...who are you?"

The engaging woman seemed to be the leader of the small group and she grinned at my nervousness. "My name is Coryn, and this is Shela, Petrice, and Deima." She pointed to each woman as she said their name and I did my best to remember their faces. There were so many people in the Telequire tribe that I knew it was going to be hard.

"It is very nice to meet you." I gave them all a little wave. It felt very much like they were inspecting me, trying to figure me out, and I did not know what to say.

"So why are you sitting out here? Do you want to come in and get some food with us?"

Before I could answer Shana returned and saved me. She had a woven basket of bread, cheese, cured meat, and a few hard-cooked eggs. She also had leather pouch hanging from the other hand. I suspected that was for Gata. "Heyla, Coryn, you're not out here pestering my friend are you?"

Coryn and the others laughed. The blonde responded with good nature. "Of course not. We just saw a beautiful woman over here all alone and asked if she wanted to eat with us." With her last word she flashed a salacious wink at me. I blushed scarlet, not completely understanding her interest.

Shela, Petrice, and Deima snickered behind her. Shana sighed and in a low voice said, "Coryn..." It sounded like a warning to me, but the taller woman clearly did not care.

"Oh come on, Shana, don't be like that. Unless you two are..." She glanced back and forth between us and I think I turned from scarlet to a deep shade of purple.

"Watch it, Coryn. Kyri is like my sister...my younger sister...and I'm very protective of my family. So leave it be. You will all see her and get to know her at the celebration when the queen returns. Until then she has some settling and mending to do."

When Shana's last few words sank in, Coryn took in my appearance again. I could see exactly when she noticed my bandages. Her face took on a chastised look. "My apologies, Kyri. I look forward to learning more about you in a few days. Until then I hope you feel better."

I smiled at the woman who failed miserably at completely scrubbing the cocky look from her face. "No problem, Coryn, I am certain we will talk again soon." I looked at her friends behind her and their demeanor had turned decided uncomfortable. "And it was nice meeting you all too. I look forward to chatting with you again."

As they walked away, I could hear them whispering to each other. Shana sat the basket of food on the table in front of me.

Noticing the way my gaze followed the little group, she sighed. "Don't worry about them, Kyri, they're just curious." She knelt and opened the little pouch of scraps, and I heard Gata mewl from between my feet.

"Oh, I figured they were curious. But, Coryn, she seemed...almost predatory." I slapped my hand over my face. "Broken string and bent arrow! I made a complete fool out of myself, blushing at every word."

The unhelpful Amazon across the table just chuckled at me. "Well, she certainly is easy on the eyes. But don't go there, Kyri. It's definitely not worth it."

I peeked between my fingers to see an irritated look on her face. "Oh? And how do you know this, big sister?"

"Oh, I've had my share of playmates in the tribe. I'm much older and wiser now. Ha. Trust me though, she's definitely not one for you to mess around with."

Maybe it was because I had no experience in such things, but I failed to truly understand why she was warning me. "I do not get it, what is wrong with her?"

She mumbled something under her breath that I barely heard. "Oh Artemis, give me patience..." She set down the bread and cheese and looked me straight in the eye. "Kyri, how much relationship experience do you have with women?"

Thinking of my lifetime spent running wild through the woods, I blushed and mumbled. "None."

"With men? Anyone?"

I looked down at the rough wood table and my voice dropped to a whisper. "None." I was embarrassed that I had never been interested. I figured that growing up in the woods with my da had to have some downfalls, and my personal experience with people was what suffered over the years. I knew I was shy, but I was sincerely trying to change that. From what I had seen in my time with the Tanta Amazons, then with Shana's tribe, Amazons were a very social group. And very sexual. And right at that moment I felt very much like an outsider. Was there anywhere I would truly fit in? There was a great amount of emotion inside me and I knew that someday it would come out. I just assumed that once I found my calling as a master fletcher it would show itself in my work. But what if that was not it? I had definitely learned a few things about myself since leaving the homestead and I knew I would continue to learn. But I was also changing, and I no longer knew where my path was going to take me. The Amazon nation was a divergent place, with people different from all I had known before. Maybe they had no need of a master fletcher. Maybe they needed me to be the archer that everyone already thought I was.

I felt a light touch on my hand and looked up. Shana smiled and I was once again reminded of how lucky I had become to call her friend. "Kyri, just be yourself."

My eyes grew wide. How could she have known my thoughts? "But..."

"No, just be you. Have patience with the world but don't lose your curiosity. Learn, explore, and get to know people. You are not the only one to walk in the footsteps of the goddess, nor are you the oldest. Things will happen in their own time, don't rush yourself through life. Your purpose will find you." She took a deep breath. "There are many things and people you'll be drawn to. But while the beauty and peace of an old oak will calm the soul, the flickering flames of a fire will surely burn. People like Coryn are fire. They burn hot and beautiful but soon move on to consume someone new. Do you understand?"

I did not want to be anyone's fuel. I did not want to be burned. But the tree...yes, I would not mind finding my tree. I finally smiled and picked up one of my eggs. "I do understand, and thank you. I am not looking to get burned right now and I have no want to get too personal with anyone while my future is still uncertain. I want to be an Amazon first, and then I will see where life takes me."

After eating, Shana took me on a tour of the village. It was similar to Tanta in the types of buildings and the societal structure. I got to meet the council members, the priestess, master of supplies, and the training master. I was most nervous about the last. Shana told me that the training master was at her debriefing the day before, so she heard everything Shana had to say about me. Her name was Kylani and she was rumored to be the best at swords after Queen Orianna.

When we got to the training field, she took one look at my shoulder. "Are you fit enough to give me a demonstration?"

I was slightly taken aback at her brusque manner. "Y...yes ma'am, I think so." I looked down at my shadow then back at the training master. "Do you have a length of cord I could borrow?"

Curiously, she looked back at me then the cub at my feet. "Whatever for? Are you going to tie that thing up?"

"No ma'am, she already has a harness. But I can put a thong on it and let Shana hold the thong so she does not follow me. I do not want her to get hurt."

Kylani stared at me for a heartbeat or two then turned on her heels. "Follow me. I think I have something that will work."

When I had Gata properly secured and responsibility handed off to Shana, I was able to follow Kylani to the archery field. Once we were in place she turned to me and only then did her face soften a bit. "May I see your bow, Kyri?" She was near my height but more muscular so the fit and draw would be comparable if she chose to shoot it.

I slid the bow off my shoulders and handed it to her. She whistled and ran her hands over the colorful wood grain. "This is beautiful. Where did you get it?"

I explained meeting Torrel, the master fletcher and bow maker, on our journey and described the tournament and my prizes. "Torrel said it was called Madagascar Rosewood from far beyond the southern sea, in a land of savages. It is the strongest, most flexible wood he has ever worked with."

With my permission she strung it and drew the string back. "Deh, you're right, it's strong and flexible. And you pull this back with ease?" Kylani eyed my lanky frame with skepticism but she had no idea that I had been pulling back such a draw for years. My muscles were used to it.

I nodded. "Yeah, my other bow was pretty similar and I had that for almost four years now. Though I am not sure how it will feel with the claw marks dug into my skin."

Kylani looked at my bandaged left shoulder. "Well the good thing is, it's not your draw arm but I bet it will still sting. Are you willing to give it a try?"

"Sure."

She pointed downfield at what I thought was a standard target with a red center. She started walking toward it and I followed. "So Shana has told us all about your skill with the bow, and I know what the Tanta tribe's advanced target looks like. I'm going to show you our version. This is a three tier skill level target."

Once we were standing next to the target, I could see that the red circle, about a forearm in diameter, was actually a wood pendulum. There was a hole in the center, about three fingers wide, and another red target behind the pendulum. I was unsure if I was supposed to hit the pendulum, or the red target behind it. I looked at her quizzically and she explained.

"An advanced level Amazon archer will hit the red target behind the pendulum without their arrow being dashed away by the pendulum. A master level archer will hit the red pendulum itself. However, only the best archer can hit the red target through the hole in the pendulum. This will obviously stop it from swinging."

Each level she explained had my dark brows crawling up to my hairline. I had hit the small keyhole during the archery tournament, but it was not moving at the time. Granted, the hole was a little bigger but it still seemed an insurmountable challenge. "That is an impossible shot."

She smirked at me. "I hear you're good at those. Unless you don't think you're up for it, if that arm of yours is giving you trouble..." She trailed off but I knew somehow that she would think less of me if I did not try.

"Fine, I will try it."

She grinned and set the pendulum in motion, and then we went back down the field to the shooting line. I drew an arrow and she stopped me. "Can I see that?" I nodded and handed it to her. She did a thorough inspection, checking the fletching, the arrowhead, and sighting down the shaft. "This is nice. Your work?"

"Yes ma'am. I was going to try for my Master's Mark when I had to leave with Shana."

"And your father, he was the one who taught you?"

"Yes. He was a master fletcher and archer for Lord Esteven back in my home territory. He was the best archer around and used to win tournaments every year. But he stopped traveling to them when my mam died."

Kylani smiled and handed the arrow back. "Well, I suspect you picked up more than the art of arrow making from him. Why don't you show me what you can do?"

I nocked the arrow and drew it back, immediately wincing and letting off my draw. Kylani did not say anything about my obvious pain. Taking a few deep breaths, I once again drew and sighted. I watched the pendulum for a few heartbeats to get a feel for the rhythm of it. My arm shook from the strain of holding the draw. When I felt like I had it timed, I released my forest fletch. It sailed downfield and embedded itself into the swinging red pendulum just to the right of the center hole. I knew it was a good shot but I was still disappointed. I wanted the impossible.

I startled when I heard the training master clap behind me. I narrowed my eyes, thinking she was making fun. But she was not, she looked genuinely impressed. I still found it necessary to apologize. "I am sorry, I could not hit the hole to stop it."

She looked at me incredulously and started belly laughing. She turned to Shana. "Can you believe this one? Just a day after surviving a leopard attack, and with a shoulder injury to boot, and she apologizes for only shooting at a master level."

Shana laughed with her. "Now you are starting to understand Kyri."

I felt my face flush. Not hitting what I was aiming at pricked my pride and I did not like it. I had something to prove, if only to myself. "You are probably right." I turned and looked at them both. "But know this though, on my twentieth birthday I will hit that hole!"

Kylani's eyes widened. "Oh? And when is your birthday?"

"Equinox eve."

She grinned and clapped me on the good shoulder. "Well then, I look forward to seeing you do the impossible in about a moon and a half."

When Shana and I were walking back to my hut, I asked what had been top of my mind since seeing the target. "Has anyone ever hit through the pendulum into the center of the red circle behind?"

Shana stopped, deadly serious. "No. No one has ever done it, though a few have come close. There is a rumor that Artemis comes down in the light of the full moon and hits it once a sun-cycle."

I snorted at her tale. There were no gods and goddesses. I learned that a long time ago. "Well then maybe I will have to give her the year off."

Chapter Six

Queen and Conscience

EVEN THOUGH I was on the mend, I found myself getting bored shortly after my archery lesson with the training master. When Shana insisted that I would be staying in my assigned hut for a while, I decided to unpack the things that my da had sent with me. Shana found me near mealtime that evening, sitting on my bed with red-rimmed tear-filled eyes. He had written me a letter, knowing we would never see each other again. I read it three times before I could no longer see through my blurred vision. Gata simply curled up in my lap and purred. When Shana saw me, crying eyes with letter in hand, she pulled me into the longest hug. I did not know what I would ever do without her because she had become my rock and foundation with all that I had gone through. She also forced me to go to dinner with her after deciding that Gata would be fine on her own for a short while. I never actually got to the unpacking part because of the letter. Over dinner I mentioned that I was getting bored sitting idle. But all the things I would normally do to keep myself entertained were not possible with my shoulder and leg injuries.

Shana suggested I take the leopard skin to the tanner and see if I could finish it with her help or find out if it was a lost cause. I knew I would have to soak and treat it with brains again to finish tanning the fur. If it was salvageable, I would make a simple bed throw for when the weather turned colder. I briefly wondered if it would be weird for Gata to sleep on the skin of her own mam then figured she would neither know nor care. And that was the majority of my third day in the nation.

On the fourth day I finally unpacked everything. My da was very thorough in the tools and fletching materials he sent. I even found a few other surprises. Wrapped in a leather pouch, I found a couple odds and ends that must have belonged to my mam and da. There was the wood comb that smelled like cedar that mam used to wear in her hair. Her little carved bird that Da won for her at the fair the year after I was born. My da also put in his bronze salpinx, a delicately carved arrow he wore on a thong around his neck, and the knife his own da had given him. All the pieces of mine and my parents' life threatened to make me cry again but I held back my tears. I was tired of crying over the past,

I wanted all of my mementos to be happy memories. As for the items, I set the bird and bronze horn on a shelf in my hut. I contemplated wearing the comb, but it was pointless with my braid so I left that on the shelf as well. His knife I put into my left boot, and I decided to wear the arrow around my own neck. The arrow was all I had ever known and I never wanted to forget where I came from. After all, I was a fletcher. The last item I found was a cloak wrapped in a large piece of scrap leather to keep it protected. I knew as soon as I unfolded it that the cloak had been made by my mam. I was dumbfounded. How had Da kept it from me all the years since my mam's death? It was a fall cloak and clearly meant for me. Instead of the usual multitude of green leaf-shaped pieces of fabric dappled across the shoulders, they were in colors of fall. Greens, yellows, reds, maroon, and oranges. It was perfect for blending in to the changing trees. Inside the cloak I found another shorter note. That one *did* make me cry because it was written by my mam. She made the cloak many years before, knowing that I would grow tall like her and my da. It was meant to be a birthday present since my birthday was the day before fall equinox. I held it to my face, and I swore that it still smelled like her. It was an interesting design, besides the coloring. It could be left long so that it fell to mid-calf. Or it could be shortened into a half-length, but twice thick, cloak. I thought perhaps the shorter cloak would be good for running in the trees. Knowing my mam, that was probably her intention. All the unpacking was interspersed with meals, attempting to train Gata, and more knife lessons from Shana. They were still pretty basic, which was a good thing considering my claw wound. The healer suggested I did not do any archery or running until I could do both without pain. I did not tell her about the knife lessons.

On the fifth day, I start hunting down shaft wood for arrows. I wanted to make some for Shana in exchange for my lessons. I spent the remaining days before the queen's return working hard on my gift. I also wanted to replenish some of the ones I lost or broke during my travels. That was what I was busy with when the queen and all the warriors returned to Telequire. I actually missed seeing their arrival since it was late, but I heard the commotion. I stepped outside my hut with Gata in my arms but it was too dark to see anyone clearly.

The next morning I took stock of myself. My shoulder was pretty much healed and my leg was no longer sore unless I poked at it. Shana explained that the Amazons always had a celebration on the evening following the warriors' return. Also, any necessary funeral pyres would be lit for the sisters who died in the battle to the north. I was both nervous and excited to finally meet the queen. She seemed to be all that people would talk about. I suppose it was because she had done so much for the nation in such a short time.

Not long after my morning tea, Shana came to find me for breakfast. "Did you see that Queen Orianna returned last night?"

I nodded. "I heard them, but it was too dark to seen anyone. Do you think she will want to meet with me today?"

My sister and friend grinned at me. "Oh yes, she will definitely want to meet with you today. You already met Steffi, the queen's Left Hand, when you took the tour. Margoli is the queen's Right Hand, and she was with the queen and warriors in the battle up north. You'll get to meet her too. Once you're confirmed as an initiate, it's possible that she will be one of your instructors during your initiation. She is the overall head of the warriors and the scouts."

I knew some of the structure already because all Amazon tribes followed it and Shana had been instructing me. That was how I knew that Steffi, the queen's Left Hand, was her economic advisor and Margoli was the queen's Right Hand and military advisor. Besides the advisors, there was the queen's council and the conference of elders. I suspected the conference of elders was simply a place to send old Amazons who had too much mouth and stamina to settle in to carding wool and raising grandbabies. I also knew that whenever the queen had to go outside Telequire lands, she would leave a regent in charge. Her regent was Basha, another one of Shana's childhood friends. I thought perhaps Queen Orianna was guilty of nepotism, however no one seemed to complain and all her appointments were quite capable.

I looked over at Shana before we arrived at the meal hut. "You never told me why Queen Orianna sent you to the Tanta nation. I know you told Queen Myra that she sent out runners to all the Amazons, but you never said why she sent you personally to the tribe that hated the old queen the most."

"Truthfully, I think she sent me because she knew I'd need more persuasion to my words than the other messengers possessed. We've known each other since we were little-uns. I've always been more interested in talking my way out of a fight than fighting. I'm the first one to introduce myself at gatherings and I always talk the vendors down on their prices."

"So you really were an ambassador of sorts. Perhaps you will be Telequire's first diplomat."

Shana shoved me away. "Bite your tongue woman." Once we arrived at the meal hut, I stayed outside as usual with Gata nestled between my feet while Shana went in to get us some food. Gata was getting really good at listening to basic commands, but I still did not trust her in a room full of food and strangers. My da did not raise a fool. Over the past seven days or so, I had many people stop and say hi while I waited for my meals. I would probably always be painfully shy but at least I was getting used to the sociability of the tribe. Everyone I met seemed nice and only a few showed more than friendship interest like Coryn. I was getting better at deflecting those advances too. As I told Shana, I was not interested in burning myself on someone's flame. I just wanted to be an Amazon, hunt, and fletch my arrows.

The morning had started out beautiful with only a slight chill to the air and I decided to wear my new fall cloak to morning meal. I was deep in thought about my upcoming initiation and Amazon trial when a voice broke through. "What a beautiful cloak."

When I looked up, I swear my heart stuttered for a beat. I knew it was rude to stare but I could not help it. My hands started to sweat and I could feel my face get red. The woman was...there was no other way to put it...a goddess. She was shorter than me with short blond hair, and she looked very athletic. We were probably close in age. She looked young but she had an air of maturity about her. Physically she was nearly the opposite of me — light to my dark, shorter to my tall. But it was her eyes that froze me in place. They were the color of the dappled green of my mam's cloaks. I stammered, turned redder, and stammered some more. "I...uh, I..."

She laughed. "People usually just say thank you." She held out her hand. "You must be Kyri. How are you settling in?"

Taking a deep breath, I clasped her hand in my own sweaty one. "Yes, I am so sorry. Thank you. It was made by my mam many years ago. And I am settling in fine. I really enjoy it here. Uh, what is *your* name?"

She smiled and to her credit she did not wipe my sweat off her palm. "I'm Ori, and I'm really glad you like it here." She looked down between my feet and noticed Gata. "Who's your friend?"

I bent down, barely avoiding knocking myself silly on the table, and lifted her to my lap. "This is Gata Anatoli. She is a leopard cub I saved on my way here. You can touch her if you like."

Ori cautiously held her hand out and let the little cub sniff it. When nothing untoward happened she ran her fingers through Gata's soft fur. "That is really amazing, she's so soft!"

"Yes she is. And though I have only had her a short time, she is really well behaved. I have been worried sick all week that the queen will not let me keep her. I really like it here and I do not want to move again after everything that has happened over the past few moons. But I am responsible for her now. I killed her mam and I could not bear to leave her to die in the wild." I stopped talking and blushed again.

"Oh, I think you'll be fine. I don't think the queen will turn you away because of this adorable little gal."

I know my face beamed hopefully back at her. "Really?"

Ori winked. "Yes, really. Well I have to go now, Kyri, but we'll talk again later, okay?"

"Okay. And thank you, Ori, for helping bury some of my fears."

"Anytime." With that, she went off and disappeared into the meal lodge.

I had no idea what direction to steer my thoughts. Sure, Coryn was beautiful but she did not make me feel anything like what went through my body in that moment. Those eyes, and the rest of course. And Ori was so nice. The feelings did leave me a little scared. I did not want to lose focus, I wanted to be an Amazon more than anything. But maybe, just maybe, Ori would like to be my friend. Shana returned with our food and startled me. "Heyla, sorry that took so long. They forgot to put together some scraps for Gata." She must have noticed a strange look on my face. "What's up, kid, did I catch you day dreaming?"

I blushed again remembering Ori. "Uh, maybe. I had another visitor this morning, and she even saw Gata and wanted to pet her. She was so nice, Shana." The image of Ori's smile and those green eyes flashed through my head and I sighed.

"Sounds like she was a lot more than nice. Did you finally meet someone that got you hot and bothered?"

"She was *beautiful*."

I could tell Shana was trying her best to stifle her laughter but I could not help myself. "Go on, did you get her name?"

"Her eyes were the color of sunlight dappled on the leaves of my oak, back in the homestead..."

Shana leaned across the table and poked my right arm. "And her name?"

"Oh, yeah. She said her name is Ori, and she also said she did not think the queen would make me leave the nation because of Gata. She seemed to really like my cub."

Out of nowhere, Shana started laughing, great rolling laughter. She slapped the table, tears in her eyes. I sat patiently, if irritated, while she wiped the tears away. "Oh goddess, Kyri." This only seemed to set her off again. "Well, kid, I'm glad you liked Ori. She seems really nice."

I looked at her skeptically. "You are not making fun of me, are you?"

Shana smiled and started eating her food. "No, sister, I'm really glad you made a new friend."

"Do you know her then?"

"Oh yes, Ori is a good friend of mine." Shana gave one last chuckle. "I have some news for you. The queen wants to meet in a couple candle marks. That gives you time to eat and clean up, maybe even do a little shooting on the archery range. You can get in some practice for your wager with the training master."

"I think I *will* go shoot a quiversful. That might help get rid of the butterflies that have suddenly taken up residence in my belly."

After eating, we walked to my hut. I was doing my best not to trip on the little cub. Just outside my door, I turned to Shana. "It was not a wager."

Shana looked confused. "What are you talking about?"

"It was not a wager with the training master. It was a statement. I will stop that pendulum on my birthday, impossible or no!"

Shana smiled. "I never thought you wouldn't. I'll be back in a few candle marks to take you to the queen. And remember, just be you."

THE ARCHERY RANGE was no challenge. I ended up splitting my own arrows twice. It was a good thing I had been making more. After unstringing my bow, I ran the trees around the training area. They were a large mixed variety with branches that slightly overlapped each other high above the ground, perfect for running. After a good portion of my nervous energy was depleted and my leg was left aching slightly, I headed to the bathing area. Oh bow and branch, their bathing huts! I remember wishing the Telequire nation had bathing huts as nice as Tanta. When Shana finally showed me the ones in her home I was shocked. The surrounding forest and lands around the Telequire nation was full of caves and hot springs. There were a few that no one used because of the pungent smell but the rest were practically fit for a king. They had a curious contraption that brought water from the nearby stream. You could stand under it and it felt as though it was raining on your head. One of the scouts said the water supply was modeled after the Roman aqueduct system. Whoever made it was a genius.

It did not take long to wash away the dirt and grime. I looked curiously at my shoulder while I was soaking. I was glad that

Shana blackened it for me because it looked quite fierce. I was proud of my shot that day, though not happy that I had to kill Gata's mam. I traced the jagged black marks on my arm. "Great leopardess, I swear that I am doing my best by her."

Shortly after I finished changing into my best leathers, Shana returned to my hut. About to leave, I shoved Gata back from the door but Shana stopped me. "Queen Orianna requested that you bring the cub with you."

I cast a worried look at her. "Did she say why?"

"She just said that you were a pair and should be seen together."

I swallowed and let Gata follow me through the door. "So what is she like, the queen I mean?"

Shana smirked. "Oh, Queen Orianna...I hear she's nice." She cracked up again, and I couldn't get another word out of her. She was wiping tears away when we entered the council lodge. It was similar to the Tanta tribe's in size but the layout was completely different. Instead of cushions on the floor, there was a great table occupying the center with long benches on all sides. I slowly looked around the table, taking in the familiar faces of the council members, the training master, and the queen's Left Hand, Steffi. It was then that I took in the new faces. There was a tall woman with short dark hair wearing a stern look on her face. She reminded me of Queen Myra and I wondered if she smiled as easy. The next person sitting at the head of the table...oh broken string and bent arrow! "Ori," I whispered. I paled and stared with my mouth open.

Shana chuckled yet again and gave me a little nudge forward. She then whispered into my ear. "That's Queen Orianna to you." Fear and anxiety blossomed in my chest and I felt my breathing speed up. Shana dropped to a knee in deference and pulled me down with her. "Calm down, relax." She pulled me back up when she stood again. I could only stare down toward the end of that council table. Appraising green eyes stared back at me with perhaps a hint of humor.

I concealed a jab to Shana's ribs and side whispered, "Why did you not tell me?"

Shana whispered back. "It's funnier this way."

The queen gave me a few heartbeats to get over the shock then stood and walked toward me. Taking both my hands into her own, she turned those dangerous green eyes to mine. "Hello, Kyri, it's good to see you again."

I answered with as much grace as I could muster. "Hello again Or...um, Queen Orianna. It is nice to officially meet you."

"Come and have a seat." She glanced down. "Oh good, I see

you brought Gata. Do you think she'd let me hold her?"

"You could try. She is pretty friendly. And she is always open to a little dried meat."

The queen scooped up the little cub, who to her credit only gave a slight mew of protest. She waved me to an empty seat between the training master and the military advisor. I felt like a mouse in the eyes of two hawks while she sat pleasantly back in her seat holding my cat-cub. Shana took a seat farther down the table. "Shana has told us your story, Kyri, with some of your deeds and history. I've also been told that you want to join the Telequire nation. Is this still true?" I swallowed and nodded my head. "We don't see a lot of adult women who wish to join the tribe because it's a pretty big adjustment for most. Tell me, how do you find it so far? Give me the first word you can think of to describe your experience here, just one word."

It seemed like a strange question but my only choice was to accept her words with complete seriousness. I thought for a candle drop about all the things I had done and the people I had met. Then I thought about my old life and where it was headed. "Freeing."

She nodded. "Good. Now, give me another one word answer. What do you think of the people here, and all the other Amazons you've met?"

I only spent a few breaths thinking of the answer. "Family."

"Interesting. You were raised mostly by your father right?" When I nodded she continued. "Spending most of your life with your father, a man, why do you think you're so comfortable in an all-woman environment? Why do we feel like family to you?"

That one was a harder question and I had to look deep inside for the answer. "I loved my mam and my da very much, and I had a good childhood. I ran through the trees, hunted, learned my craft, and cherished my family. But even they knew I did not fit in, that I was different from the others in my area. While my heart has always been with my family, my soul has always run the trees. I have lived my life by the leaf and the arrow and I respect the trees and the animals they shelter. It was the forest that gave me freedom for a long time. It was not until I came out of the trees that I saw the truth of the world and what was in store for me if I did not leave my home. My da sent me away because he loved me, but I left because I needed to find my soul. Here with the Amazons I finally feel as if I have found people that share my dreams. I have found women who respect each other and the forest, and who are respected in their freedom."

I saw a lot of heads nod around the table. The queen spoke again while continuing to stroke Gata's soft head. I noticed someone had brought some dried meat and she was feeding little bits of it to the spoiled cub. "So you feel like you fit in here?"

I smirked, hoping to steal back a little bit of my honor for her joke on me. "Well, Queen Orianna, back home I was like an almond tree growing in an orchard of apples. But here...everybody is nuts!"

There was a surprised gasp from one of the seats, and then everyone burst into laughter. "I'll take that as a yes then." The queen looked at me as if to say 'touché'. Once the table settled again, the queen Orianna continued. "During tonight's celebration, we will officially make you an Amazon initiate. Over the next few moons, you will be instructed in the different parts of Amazon culture. You will learn about the society, duties to the nation, economics, war, history, basic healing, scouting, and weapons training. Once all your instructors tell me you are ready, you will be allowed to go through the Amazon trial."

She paused, seeming to wait for an answer from me. "Thank you, Queen Orianna. May I ask what the trial will be?"

She cocked her head and for the first time I noticed the feathers in her hair. I saw two birds of prey and one that looked like a peacock feather. "The first trial will be to run the trees around the entire Amazon nation in one day. The second trial will entail hunting and bringing back an animal capable of feeding twenty warriors. The third and final trial will be to prove your worth to the tribe. There will be one day rest between each trial."

"Prove my worth? How am I to do that?"

"That is why it is a trial, Kyri, and also why it is a challenge only you can answer. Some seek proof in the divine, others show a skill or perhaps have money they can donate to the nation's coffers. I suggest spending a lot of time thinking about that topic specifically as it will surely shape your future with the nation." I thought for a beat and nodded. "Now for your assignments. They are as follows: Basha will instruct you in Amazon society and your duties to the nation, Steffi will instruct you on Telequire economics, Margoli, will assign someone to instruct you in war and history..."

She was interrupted by Margoli, the queen's Right Hand and military advisor. "Actually, my queen, I'd like to instruct her personally."

Queen Orianna looked at her for a heartbeat and then nodded. "That's fine. You will learn about basic healing from Thera, scouting from Coryn, and you will take weapons training with Kylani." She paused to observe my reaction to the assignments. "Do you have any questions?"

"What about Gata Anatoli? What is to happen to her?"

The queen looked down at the cub sitting in her lap. "I don't see that anything has to happen to her provided she remains well behaved and doesn't interfere with your training." I breathed a sigh of relief and she added one last thing. "See? I told you the queen was nice." A few chuckles went around the table and I joined them. My internal thoughts were whirling through the trees though as I stared at my queen's beautiful green eyes. I thought to myself that Ori was more than nice. As quickly as it came I stuffed the vague disappointment back into its cage. No, not Ori...Queen Orianna. She was going to be my queen and I doubted very much we could ever be the friends I had hoped for. At least she would be a good queen.

Everyone stood and I knew the council session was finished. Some council members filed out, while others milled around engaged in conversation. The queen approached me and held out Gata and I shivered as our fingers met on the exchange. She did not say a word about the goose bumps racing up her own arm but I saw her eyes widen in reaction. Did she feel the...? I searched for the word within my head and came up empty. I did not know what it was that I felt, but I knew it was something. Once the cub was safely in my arms again, she spoke. "Thank you for the privilege of letting me hold her. Should you ever find yourself in need of someone to watch Gata, I would be more than honored. She is very sweet."

"You say that now because you clearly have not had the joy of her chewing the feathers off your arrows or dragging your tools around the hut. But thank you. I just may take you up on your offer from time to time."

"Anytime, Kyri." Queen Orianna exited then, taking some of the air from the lodge with her. I was left to make my way around the room to reintroduce myself to my new instructors. My anxiety lessened when I saw they already had a schedule complete. I was to have weapons practice every morning after first meal, for two candle marks a day. The rest of the time before midday meal would go to Margoli for my war and history lessons. After lunch I would have two candle marks with the scout leader Coryn, and a candle mark with Thera. Then, in the bit of time before evening meal, I would have a candle mark with Basha for society and duties, and a half candle mark with Steffi to learn economics. I was allowed two days off, every quarter moon and I suspected I would use it to sleep. When I said as much to Shana later she laughed and told me I was probably right. She also told me not to worry about Coryn, that she was a good scout and I would learn a lot. But she stressed that if I had any problems with the attractive woman, I should not be afraid to speak up. I hoped there would be no problems with anyone.

THE CELEBRATION THAT night was at times sad and overwhelming. It far surpassed the Tanta tribe, partly because the Telequire nation was bigger and also because of the added ceremonies. Along with funeral pyres, there were also bead and eagle feather honors presented to different warriors who showed exceptional bravery. I heard someone say that the queen should have gotten the biggest acknowledgement for her role in northern battle. It was said that she personally took down the invading warlord. However, I imagined as queen, Ori only ever gave the honors and no longer received them. That thought made me sad. It should not be that way but who was I to say different?

By the time my introduction to the tribe and the announcement of my initiation rolled around, I was sweating. My stomach roiled and I felt as though I were going to be sick. Gata stayed nearly attached to my boots the entire time, and Shana stood reassuringly by my side. Then the moment came when the queen called me to the dais near the great bonfire. I knelt before her, the leopard cub hid in the folds of my cloak. In a voice loud enough to be heard by all, she called out to the nation. "Kneeling before me is Kyri, daughter of Mira and Galen Fletcher. A guest to our nation, she wishes to seek sisterhood with the Telequire Amazons. Who gives the first honor for her pledge?"

My good friend and near-sister called out from the crowd below. "I, Shana, daughter of Combe and Sikara, give first honor in support of this one's pledge to sisterhood!"

The crowd roared, and the queen held up a hand. "Who will give second honor to Kyri, the skilled fletcher of Colmenus's Kingdom?"

I was surprised when the weapons master stepped forward. "I, Kylani, daughter of Tamar and Sheryn, give second honor to support this one's pledge to sisterhood!"

Again, the crowd roared. The queen let them calm on their own before continuing. In the silence that followed, she truly shocked me. "I, Orianna, daughter of Korleena and Malcom, give third honor to support this one's pledge to sisterhood. And I welcome her companion Gata Anatoli as well."

The crowd, also surprised by the queen's personal support, swelled in noise. The queen signaled for me to rise. Sensing the little cub's fear, I quickly picked her up, tucking her under my left arm before standing. The assembled Amazons quieted once more to let me speak, curiosity slowly stilling their voices and cheers. I raised my right fist and placed it over my heart. I was told I did not have to say much, just acknowledge the nation and my pledge. I took a deep breath, then looked at the crowd. I then took another deep breath to prevent falling off the raised dais. "Telequire nation, I am deeply honored by being allowed the opportunity to join with you. Once I am an Amazon, I will spend the rest of my days returning that honor." I paused for a few heartbeats and swore I could feel the queen's green-eyed gaze burning into my back. "I recently said that while my heart will always be with my family, my soul will forever run through the trees. I am hoping that you will be my family now and that I can find my tree again in your forest. I pledge to you all, to Queen Orianna, and to the trees around us, by leaf and arrow, I will honor and protect the nation with my very life. By leaf and by arrow, my creed and my heart, I promise to maintain the balance and for everything I take from this world I will return something of equal value. This is my pledge to you."

The crowd cheered once again and drums started on the other side of the fire. I turned to the queen and knelt at her feet with my head bowed. She lightly touched my shoulder so I looked up and was struck by the way her eyes reflected the dancing flames of the bonfire. Her voice was just loud enough for me alone to hear. "You have much honor, Kyri Fletcher. I look forward to see how your tree grows in our woods." I swallowed when she gave me a heart-stopping smile. "Now, I believe Shana is looking for you. Go...go have fun and make some friends." I smiled shyly before making my way off the dais.

When I found my way to Shana again, she reached up to touch my head. "Funny, you don't feel sick hot. That was quite a speech you made up there."

I blushed and held the squirming cub a little tighter in the jostling crowd. I suggested we walk Gata to my hut, then return to the celebration. Many women came up and introduced themselves. I knew I was not going to remember any of their names and I would surely have to work on that in the days and moons to come.

I had a great time that night. I tried a little dancing, and it was okay. I remembered some of the steps I learned with the Tanta Amazons. I tried my hand at drumming...I was not good. There were many foods that I sampled and I liked most of them. I was offered both wine and ale but I turned them down. I knew neither would have been as strong as the brandy I had drank with the Tanta tribe but I simply did not care for it so I stuck with fruit juice and water. If my da could have only seen me dancing, nibbling figs, and laughing with complete strangers, he would have smiled. I could feel my heart being dragged kicking and screaming out of its leafy shell and it felt...it felt nice. And throughout the night, every single candle mark, I was aware of the queen, of Ori. Every so often I would let my gaze wander to the dais where she lounged with a cup of wine, speaking with her friends and councilors. And on every occasion I would find those eyes starting back at me. It was unnerving, and something deep inside told me to keep that knowledge and feeling to myself.

BECAUSE OF THE lateness and level of revelry, the next day was considered a day of rest. There was a big hunt planned but not much else. It would help replenish the stores of food used for the celebration. The hunt was not mandatory. Usually just the Queen and some of the more proficient hunters would attend. Many chose to stay at the village to rest and help clean up after the feast. Shana talked me into going the night before. While she was not the most proficient of archers, she said she would usually go with her friends before Orianna became queen. Other people I recognized were Basha, Kylani, Margoli, Coryn, and her scout friends Shela, Petrice, and Deima.

Coryn walked over when she saw me. "Heyla, Kyri Fletcher! We've heard much of your skill with a bow. I hope you can impress us today. It would be a shame if your legend turns out to be more clouds than rain." Her friends laughed, as did I. After weeks of her flirting and witty jibes I had a good handle on Coryn. She would not be unnerving me again no matter how attractive her face.

"Oh I never claimed to be a legend, Coryn. But legend or no, even a cloud can still block your sun." More laughter followed and I knew I had maintained my honor. It was then that a horn sounded and most of the women took to the trees, including the queen. Shana and I followed her.

We ran for half a candle mark until we came to a spot of woods with known boar activity. There were marks in the soil and on the bark of the trees. Another group of hunters went even farther, hoping to bring down a few roe or a red deer. The queen, Shana, and Basha dropped to the ground below me, hooting and clamoring in hopes of driving the boars from the thick underbrush. The Amazons were spread out, most waving spears back and forth. The spears themselves were shortened to make it easier to run the trees yet still long enough to be good for hunting boar. Suddenly, despite the hooting, I heard a sound. Tingling ran up my spine and I took off toward the queen. Everything seemed to happen in slow motion as a great long-tusked boar burst from the brush behind the queen. It knocked her to the ground, tearing a gash in her side with its hand span length tusks. Before it could come at her again I flipped from the tree above and landed between them. Then with a racing heart I put a forest fletch straight into its eye. The beast was dead before it hit the ground. It took a candle drop for the others to reach us through the underbrush and I had already started tending to her wound. It was not life-threatening but I could see in her eyes that it hurt. I pulled a piece of cloth from my waist pouch, folded it twice, and held it firmly over her left side as she lay on the ground at my feet. She placed a hand on my wrist. "Thank you, Kyri." I simply nodded at her.

Once the others arrived, I was gently pushed aside while a second level healer tended to her wound. The rest crowded around the boar lying on the ground. I watched them drag it toward a nearby tree to be cleaned and skinned. Shana, who had been gathered around the queen, spun around and grabbed my arm. She looked me up and down. "Are you all right?"

Though my heart was still racing I managed a nod. "I am fine. It did not even touch me." I dropped my head. All I could think about was the fact that I had not been fast enough. I should have just shot the boar from the trees. But I did not and the queen got hurt. "I am sorry, Shana."

"What?" She exclaimed.

I knew the guilt showed clearly in my eyes. "I allowed her to get hurt. I could not get here in time to stop the boar from hurting her." I closed my eyes and all I could see was the boar taking her to the ground and the blood blossoming at her side.

"Kyri, listen to me." She turned my head toward where the queen was slowly getting to her feet. I could see a bandage wrapped around her midsection. "She's alive, Kyri, and she might not be if you hadn't put yourself between her and that boar."

"But..."

"No buts! I saw it, but I was too far away to help. She was right on top of the boar when it charged and even you aren't that fast. But without you here watching over us from the trees, my friend would likely be dead. Our queen would be dead. For that I thank you with all my heart." I could see the tears in her eyes as her worry for her queen and friend broke through. I let her hug me and felt a little better myself.

Then, as if I was struck by lightning, a memory dawned on me. I pulled out of the hug. "Do you remember when I told you the story of how my da got the steading?"

Shana looked confused. "Yes, why?" Then she remembered the story as well. "Oh. Didn't he do something similar by saving his king from a wild boar?"

"Yes he did. And now I have continued his legacy…" I trailed off, remembering the best of who my da was and wishing I could have known him longer.

Before I could travel any further down memory lane, we were interrupted by a commotion among the hunters. The queen was heading back to the village and many were going with her now that a boar had been brought down. I was debating whether I wanted to go with them or stay and run the trees a while longer. Shana decided to walk back with the rest while I stayed to watch a few other women processing the beast. They already had it strung up from a tree branch and gutted when I turned to them.

Coryn walked up while I was watching and her friends were noticeably absent. "Not a cloud after all, Kyri Fletcher. Nice work in the trees today."

I looked at her for a heartbeat or two, wondering if there was some hidden meaning. "Thank you."

She gave me an appraising look and I felt heat flood my face. "I look forward to working with you in the coming moons."

I nodded and she walked off. One of the hunters near the boar called out to me. "Kyri, would you like your arrow back? There is no damage."

I took it from her hand, checking the fletching and inspecting down the length. "Thank you…" I looked at her, not sure of her name.

She smiled. "It's Certig. And that was a great shot. I'm very jealous. You know, since you brought the beast down, you are entitled to the tusks as well. If you like, I can give them to you once we get them removed."

"Sure, Certig. That would be very nice of you. If you cannot find me just give them to Shana. She will make sure they find their way to me."

"Are you heading back now?"

I shook my head and searched for the nearest tree up. "No, I think I will hunt some more. I am sure Gata would appreciate a fresh rabbit. See you later, Certig, and it was nice meeting you." With those words I ran up the tree I had picked out and continued across the foliage.

Chapter Seven

The Initiate

I SPENT SO many years learning to be a fletcher and proper archer that I forgot how hard it was to learn different things. My first week of lessons as an initiate was exhausting. I suspected that was the point. They wanted to wear you down to a nub so they could build you into something new. When I reported to the weapons master two days later she told me plainly that I would not be touching my bow in her classes.

"You have already mastered the bow. Now you have to learn what else it means to be an Amazon. We will start with a young girl's first weapon, the staff." She threw a length of wood at me and I caught it in one hand. I spent my first two candle marks of the day learning how to hold a stick and stand on the balls of my feet. Afterwards I wanted nothing more than a nap but found myself rushing to Margoli instead. It was there that my head was stuffed with knowledge about Amazon history and the many wars that the Amazon nations had been involved in. I had no idea their history was so rich and vicious, especially when there were some regions that still thought that Amazons were only a myth. Shana was usually busy during the midday meal so I took food back to my hut and spent a little time with Gata. She did not like being cooped up in my hut all day. I found her usual evidence of the form of two chewed forest fletch arrows and a gnawed rabbit fur. After lunch I made myself ready to go with the scouts. I met up with Coryn and the rest of the troop near the scout hut. It was a small structure that kept a few supplies specifically used by the tree walking scouts. It was easier than having the scouts constantly bothering the weapons master to replenish their equipment. Instead, the hut was kept stocked regularly and the items had their own inventory separate from weapons training. She gave a brief introduction then we took to the trees. As we ran I was given a thorough history of the Amazon scouts. Coryn explained why they were formed, what their duties were, and how they trained.

"Most scout training, well most serious Amazon training, starts right after a girl's first menses. Clearly you've begun your training late but you already appear to have a head start."

I raised an eyebrow. "Head start? I have been running trees

since I was ten. Ask Deka how far behind I am." A few of the scouts with us had heard about the first day I arrived. They remembered the story of how I knew there were people the trees before Shana.

Coryn became irritated at the giggling scouts. "I'm not denying you have some skill, Kyri, but you don't know everything yet."

I looked back and nodded. A few lucky moments should not make me cocky. "You are correct, Coryn, and I apologize."

I learned how it was possible to survive in the trees for days without coming down. I was skeptical of that at first until Coryn explained. The trees could hold both water and food though living on bugs, sap, fruits, and nuts was not my ideal way to survive. I started learning some of the Amazon whistles and hand signals used specifically by the scouts. Shana had taught me a few but I had much more to learn. There was not time during my first lesson but I knew that eventually I would have to see the edge of the Telequire lands, and I would also be instructed in what to do if strangers trespassed.

"Once your training progresses, you and I will spend a rotation with the fourth scouts, the ones who patrol the perimeter of Telequire. That is the only real way to get a feel for the entire Telequire nation. You will also need to know our boundaries when it comes to your first trial."

Eventually my two candle marks came to an end and I bid goodbye to run to the healers hut. Before I could take off Coryn stopped me. "Kyri, would you like to meet for dinner tonight in the meal hall? We could discuss your training more..." If I had not been watching her so intently, I would have missed the brief flicker of her eyes as they scanned the length of my body. Clearly her fire was still burning despite the fact that she had become my instructor. I was glad at that moment that Gata prevented me from eating in the meal lodge.

"Actually, I usually eat outside with Shana because I cannot take Gata into the meal hall yet. I want to make sure she is better trained before I attempt such a thing." I gave her a friendly, if slightly unapproachable, smile. "I just do not trust her with all the people and food."

Coryn laughed but I could tell she was disappointed. "Okay then, I guess I'll see you tomorrow."

"See you, Coryn."

My healing, society and duties, and economics instruction all progressed much the same as war and history. I did get permission from all my instructors to bring Gata, as long as she did not interfere. I decided that it would be best to leave her in my hut for weapons training and scouting, at least until she could listen regularly to basic instruction. After all, wild creatures had a tendency to do whatever they wanted. But overall she was pretty well behaved and I was happy to have her in my life.

MY FIRST MOON of training went by as fast as a diving hawk. I was able to finish the arrows I started back before I became an initiate. Two dozen of those I gifted to Shana. She still helped me with knife lessons every couple of nights. She cautioned me to not push myself and relax at night since I was undertaking so much other instruction. But I told her that I got bored in my off times and that I had the training master's permission. As for my training overall, I knew that I was progressing well, at least with certain things. I could keep up with the scouts easily and I had nearly all the Amazon signs and signals memorized. I could readily recite recent Amazon history and list the various major wars. I knew basic field healing for dealing with immediate life- threatening injuries and the minor ones. Society and duties were a little harder. There was so much to learn about being an Amazon and Basha would frequently quiz me on what I would do in this situation or that situation. Economics I was miserable at, but I was told not everyone had a head for it.

And finally there was weapons training. I think because of the nature of weapons training, I viewed my instructor in much the same way I saw my da. He was a very thorough teacher and I always tried my best not to disappoint him. I felt the same way about Kylani, but there was so much to learn. She had me start with the most basic Amazon weapons, chobos. They consisted of a pair of wood lengths, slightly narrower than a staff and only as long as my arm from elbow to fingertip. Chobos were the first weapon Amazon children are taught and the easiest to create should you find yourself unarmed. Besides chobos, other weapons included in my instruction were bow, staff, sword, and knife. While I was excellent with the bow and proficient with a knife, the rest had me struggling. I seriously bruised two fingers on my left hand within a fortnight trying to master the staff. I was constantly covered with blackened bumps and lumps from chobo practice. And the sword...something held me back with the sword. I grasped all the basic drills, and I could recite sword strategy. I had been thoroughly trained on how to take care of my blade but I had no instinct. Every time I tried to go on the offensive, I would pause. Kylani was at a loss as to how she could help me. We both knew it would cost me my life in the event of a serious skirmish.

On the nights I was not working on knife technique with Shana, I spent time in my hut fletching and adding to my store of arrows. A lot of my free days I went out cutting shaft wood for arrows and straightening them. I traded rabbit furs to the nation's fletcher, Achima, and in turn she gave me a large assortment of arrowheads since I was running low. Even though I did not need any more arrows I was still amassing a stockpile, making the best arrows my da taught me to make. They would be my gift to the nation and I hoped to have a few hundred by the time I was ready to go through my trial.

I WOKE THE morning of my birthday feeling alive and surprisingly refreshed. There would be no instruction for two days because the entire nation considered the times of equinox and solstice as sacred. They celebrated on the eve and the day of each new season because they were revered as a time of change and enlightenment. The queen had sent Shana off to the centaurs and she had been gone for a handful of days. My Amazon sister confided in me that Queen Orianna was sending her away to train with diplomats of different nations. I missed her whenever she would leave but she was rarely gone longer than a few days at a time. Her most recent was the longest trip since I came to Telequire but I understood the need for her training. Besides, I was plenty busy myself. She assured me that she would return in time for equinox eve, but she never checked in the previous night so I resigned myself to not seeing her smiling face on my birthday. That was why I was so startled to hear a knock on my door first thing in the morning.

Gata ran over and lightly scratched at it, looking as if she were trying to answer. She was so funny sometimes, and smart. She had gotten big enough that she could stand on her hind legs to work the latch on my door, so even when I wanted to keep her locked up she did not always stay. At least twice after weapons practice I had tracked her to the council chamber and found her sitting in the lap of Queen Orianna. The queen did not seem to mind, but I was annoyed that I had run all over looking for the cub. I opened the door and was surprised to see Shana. I was glad to see her, not only because it was my birthday but also because I had a promise to keep with the training master. The three of us went to breakfast and I decided to take Gata into the meal hall for the first time. Surprisingly, she was very well behaved. She stayed close to my feet while I got some food from the table near the far wall. Shana ran into the kitchen area to get a few scraps.

She did not think they would want the cub back there, and there was no way Gata would leave my side in the busy lodge.

While she was gone, I was pleasantly surprised to see Queen Orianna walk up to my table. "Do you mind if I sit here?" She pointed to the bench seat across from me, next to where Shana usually sat.

I shook my head and slipped a bit of venison to Gata under the table. "I thought you were supposed to be sitting...you know..." I waved my eating knife in the general direction of the large table in the back. She laughed and all I could do was stare. Her eyes, they just...there was so much happiness and humor there. I blinked to break the spell she seemed to have over me.

Shana returned and having caught my question laughed along with Ori. "That's the first thing she did away with when she became queen. The only time the primary feathers have to eat at the main table is for official functions. Other than that, she's just like the rest of us little birds."

"Wow, that is a lot..."

"Better," she said matter-of-factly. "It's a lot better. I would much rather be out eating with my fellow Amazons, my friends, and family."

We ate a leisurely first meal while Shana told us about her visit with the Centaurs. "Ori, your sister Risiki says hello. And I believe you have a new niece or nephew on the way."

It took a moment before I remembered Ori had a sister that was married to a centaur. The stories of centaurs were fantastical and too far-fetched to believe, with them supposedly being half man and half horse. But pregnant? I wondered how that worked and thought maybe I would ask Shana later...or maybe I would not. I had a feeling she would never let me hear the end of it. My thoughts were interrupted as a hand touched mine. "Heyla, Kyri, are you still with us?"

I blushed scarlet, unable to speak while the queen held my hand. I wanted her to let it go so the bumps racing up my arms would go away. But at the same time I did not want her to let go because it felt really nice. What was wrong with me? I dumbly stared at my plate until Shana whispered something about turning me loose and the hand disappeared. I mourned the loss and did not fully understand the reason for it. Why would my new friend, my queen, affect me so? I gulped. "I—I am still here."

"Good. I was just saying that I'm looking forward to seeing you shoot later."

I shot a quick glance at Shana, then back to the queen. "But how...who told you I was shooting?"

Shana held up her hands. "It wasn't me. I know how you are.

I assumed you wouldn't want a big crowd for that shot. It was probably Kylani."

The queen scratched idly at her temple. "Actually...it wasn't Kylani. It seems your words were overheard by another and quickly spread around." She gave me an apologetic look. "I'm sorry, Kyri, I should have put a stop to it. I didn't realize you wanted it to be private." She went to touch the back of my hand but stopped just before our skin met.

I sat there for a few heartbeats thinking about the situation. An audience did not really matter, the target would be the same either way. Either I would make the shot or not. Though I preferred to make it if I was going to have witnesses, especially if Ori was going to be one of them. "It is okay. I just get nervous with big groups. But a smart friend once told me to focus on the target and the rest would just be trees in the forest."

Shana raised an eyebrow. "Oh, so now you think I'm smart, hmm?"

I laughed. "Only once in a while."

She threw the chunk of bread she was holding and it bounced off my head to the floor where Gata promptly pounced on it. It was devoured in a matter of heartbeats. The queen burst into laughter and I held my breath. When she turned her green eyes to me, I released it in a sigh. All at once I was ready to begin my day. I stood and gazed down at my two meal companions. "I suppose the target will not hit itself so I should probably head over there." I looked to Shana. "Are you coming with me to watch humiliation at its best?"

She grinned and gathered her plate as well. "I wouldn't miss it."

I leaned across and punched her in the shoulder. "Thanks a lot, sister."

The queen stood with us. "Well I'm certainly not going to miss a demonstration of your archery skills." She leaned forward and gently grasped my shoulder. "But I fully expect to see that pendulum stop today."

"You know it is an impossible shot, right?"

She gave me a squeeze. "I have complete faith in you." She released me and picked up her plate. "Actually, if you give me a quarter candle mark I'll grab my own bow. I haven't been to the range in a while. It might be nice to loosen up my string a little." She smirked at the startled look on my face. "I *did* used to be First Scout Leader before becoming queen. It would prick my pride to lose some of that skill while sitting on my royal backside."

We all laughed as we walked out of the large food lodge. The coming day was going to be...interesting. All that was left for me was to do the impossible in front of hundreds of the very people I wished to join as a sister. And in front of their queen who was...bow and branch, but I did not know who she was. I only knew that she was something that affected me deeply in a way I could not understand at all.

The queen was already at the practice range when I arrived. Before I approached the staging area I gave a trilling whistle to Gata and she stopped walking with me. We had been working on that signal and others for more than a moon, and her training was really coming along. I wanted to start taking her hunting with me because she was of an age where she should probably begin learning such things. The cub had already grown to my knees, too big to be sitting in laps anymore. Yet she still did. Spoiled thing.

Shana and I both walked to where the queen stood. We all had our bows strung. "Kylani should be here in a few candle drops. She had some things to take care of first. Why don't we get some practice in, hmm?"

We lined up at separate targets and Shana called out with a wry grin on her face. "I don't even know why I'm doing this. I feel like a duckling amongst two swans here."

I called back to her. "But did you not say you were a scout before you started wandering around flapping your diplomatic yap?"

Shana's mouth dropped open. "Diplomatic yap? You just wait until this 'diplomat' gives you the next knife lesson. I said I was a scout but I don't recall saying I was a great archer. I'm average with a bow on my best day."

The queen added with a laugh, "Well your arrows may not always be on target, but your sweet tongue certainly hits the mark often enough. And that, my friend, is why I send you around to flap your diplomatic yap."

Shana made a rude gesture to the queen, which probably would have carried severe punishment in any other nation. Instead, the queen laughed harder.

Kylani quickly approached. "Ahh, I can see we're all just seriousness and stone here today, hmm?"

Queen Orianna wiped away tears while Shana slowly lost the flush in her face. "Actually, we decided we were going to do a little shooting with Kyri to help her warm up."

Shana called out, "Are you going to join us, Training Master?"

Kylani gave a firm nod. "Sure." She quickly strung her bow and went farther down the line past Shana.

It did not take very long for us to all empty our quivers into the standard practice targets. When we went downfield to retrieve them, I saw the training master speak to another Amazon. The Amazon took off at a jog and pulled out two of the advanced targets, setting the pendulums in motion. And suddenly it was time. I swallowed, a hard lump stuck in my throat.

Shana spoke up, interrupting my growing panic. "I'm definitely not shooting at that. I'll keep my pride somewhat intact, thank you."

Kylani turned to the queen. "What about you, are you interested in a challenge?"

She grinned. "Sure, why not?"

I gaped. "But you..." I trailed off, at a loss for words. Queens did not shoot at impossible targets.

Slowly she turned intense green eyes my way and I sensed my mistake. "But I what?"

In my defense, I had a tendency to babble when nervous. "But you are the queen. Queens are supposed to rule and watch over the nation. Queens make treaties and laws, and they..." I watched her eyebrows disappear into her bangs.. "...they make sure stupid dumb Amazon initiates shut their yap." And with that, I shut my yap.

A chorus of laughter sounded behind me. When I saw the gathered faces, the blood froze in my veins. I did the only thing I could think of and dropped to a knee. "Forgive me, my queen. I did not mean to offend."

When I heard her chuckle, I looked up. "Get up initiate. You didn't offend me. And I would call you neither stupid nor dumb. Although now I find it necessary to prove that I'm no novice at the bow and fletch."

I mentally scrambled backwards. "But..."

She grinned mischievously. "Hush, you. How about we make a wager on this?"

"A wager? What kind of wager?"

She pointed down field. "I hit the pendulum and you have to do a favor for me, for a moon. If you hit the circle and stop the pendulum I have to do a favor for you, for a moon. So what do you say?"

"But you are the queen. Your time is much too important to spend a moon doing me favors."

"That's why your challenge is harder; you have to work harder to earn my time."

I thought about it and chewed my lip. Finally I nodded. "That sounds fair but what favors are we to exchange?" Shana snickered and I shot her a dark look. This was no time for her jokes. The moment was much too serious.

Kylani spoke up. "Sword lessons, my queen. You could give Kyri sword lessons. She is at an impasse with me. Maybe you can help her breach that barrier." I heard another snicker from Shana and she whispered something about 'breaching her barrier.' I would have to get even for her inappropriate comment later.

The queen nodded her head, seeming to get more from the training master's words than I did. "That is acceptable."

Broken string and bent arrows. Winning the wager meant having the queen witness how inept I was with a sword. I tried to get out of it as delicately as possible. "I am sorry my queen, but I do not think I have anything I can give you that is worth your instruction time."

Shana chimed in once again. "How about your rabbit stew, Kyri? You could make it once a rest period, for a moon. That's about four pots."

"But why would she want that?"

Queen Orianna stepped toward me. "Did she say rabbit stew? You make rabbit stew?"

Shana smirked. "It melts in your mouth, it's so good."

A broad smile graced the queen's face. "Done!"

Shana leaned over and whispered to me. "Rabbit stew is her favorite food, and Ori seriously loves to eat." I blushed, ignoring yet another innuendo.

Kylani clapped her hands together. "All right, now that the details have been decided, let's get to it."

"Are you going to shoot with us, Training Master?"

"Oh, no, I'm going to let this little challenge play out just as it is."

I chanced a look behind me and realized even more Amazons had arrived to watch. There were quite a few in trees, trying to get a better view. I wondered how the wager would work. Kylani gestured down field. "All right, there are already two targets set up with pendulums in motion." She turned to one of her other instructors, a stocky woman with sandy blond hair and a friendly smile. "What do you think Culda, two or three?"

Culda quickly replied. "One. I think if they are going to meet their goals, they will only need one shot."

Murmuring worked its way through the crowd behind us. I cast a worried glance at the queen but her face held no emotion. It was then that I realized how out of focus I had become. I thought about my da and all the things he had taught me over the years. I took a deep breath and let it out as I heard Kylani call out to us. "One it is. Archers, are you ready?"

"But who is to go first?"

The queen looked at me and I saw her eyes soften just a bit.

"I'll go first." The crowd seemed to hold its collective breath as she smoothly pulled an arrow from her quiver and nocked it. Her breathing steadied as she focused down field and I watched her study the moving pendulum. When the queen had the motion of it memorized she released. Her aim was true, and when the arrow buried itself firmly in the moving pendulum, the crowd gave out a great cheer. I had not realized until that very moment that Ori...my queen, was a very talented archer. Hitting the pendulum was truly a master shot.

The crowd slowly died down and she raised her hand in acknowledgement before fixing her gaze on me. The expectation in her eyes left butterflies looping and diving in my stomach. After a few cleansing breaths I stepped up to the mark. Her target was adjacent to mine, pendulum starting to slow with the weight of her arrow. Mine was still moving regularly back and forth and the hole looked impossibly small from our distance. As I drew back my arrow the world fell away around me. I ignored the sound of murmuring from behind, the smell of wood smoke, and the knowledge that I was attempting the impossible. I felt the rhythm downfield and estimated the distance and speed of my arrow. And when I knew I was at my limit for a controlled draw, I released my forest fletch. The arrow, made with the skill of my own two hands, flew straight and true. And just when I was sure I would miss completely, I watched the pendulum stop. I heard the words 'by Artemis' said aloud behind me and everyone went crazy. Shana ran up and slapped me on the back, joined by the training master and Queen Orianna. By bow and leaf, I really had done it! The thoughts I cast out into the world came straight from my heart. 'Da, if you are dead and can actually hear me, thank you for all that you have given to me.'

The queen suddenly turned and addressed the gathered Amazons. "Now that you've all seen the impossible, let's get this nation ready for a celebration." The queen turned back to me. "You seem to have the luck of the gods, my friend."

I gazed at her seriously. "Am I your friend?"

She responded with a smile. "I'd like to think so."

With just a few words something great and warm exploded inside me. I grinned back at her, knowing happiness shone in my blue eyes. Then remembering our wager, I sighed. "I suppose the training master told you I was a lost cause with the sword."

She motioned to me and we started walking down the field to retrieve our arrows. "She actually said that you are technically proficient but you lack initiative. Can you think of a reason why?"

"I have not really thought about the why of it."

She nodded as we arrived at her target and turned to tug her arrow out of the wood pendulum. "Well then, perhaps that is what I can help you with."

We walked together to my target and just stared at the arrow. I started to reach for it and she stilled my hand. I could see goose bumps race up both our arms and I felt her fingers tremble on mine. "Leave it, we can always make more pendulum targets, but only one arrow has ever made the impossible shot. I'm going to have Kylani place this next to the training master's office for display. It will give some of our more cocky scouts something to think about, and perhaps a goal to strive for."

I grinned. "But were you not a scout, my queen?"

She winked. "I was the First Scout Leader, so what does that tell you?"

"It tells me that I was perhaps played the fool by my queen in order to get some rabbit stew."

The queen burned my shoulder with a touch. "It's Ori." I looked at her puzzled and she elaborated. "It's Ori that wanted your rabbit stew and Ori that wants your friendship. And when we're alone, you can just call me Ori."

I swallowed back the emotion rising in my throat. "Thank you, Ori. It will be my pleasure to share my mam's famous rabbit stew with you." I decide then that I had to do something for the queen, to honor her for her bravery and sacrifice to the nation. In just a few words Ori had shown me how much she had given up in order to keep her sister, the centaurs, and fellow Amazons safe. I knew how much of herself she had to lose and change in order to take up the queen's mask and I admired her immensely for it. I spent another few heartbeats staring into those beautiful eyes before I turned and began walking down field again. "Come on, Ori. You said yourself that we had a celebration to prepare for." She only laughed and joined me in the walk.

Shana accompanied me to my hut afterward and sat on my bed stroking a sleepy Gata while I replaced the missing arrow in my quiver. I liked to keep an even dozen so I always knew how many shots I had. When I was finished I sat on the bed with her, relaxing after such a stress-filled morning. Shana seemed a million leagues away but she looked up when I spoke. "You know, I'm thinking of taking Gata hunting. She is getting big and I need to teach her to feed herself or all my time will be spent providing small game for her. What do you think?"

She nodded. "That sounds like a good idea."

The tone of her voice caused me to really look at her. "Sister, is everything all right?"

She lifted her gaze and stared straight into my eyes. "Is

everything all right with you?"

"What do you mean? I am fine."

Shana wrapped an arm around my shoulder and pulled me toward her. "I hope you realize that you can talk to me and I'll always keep it in confidence. But I can see you've been keeping something to yourself this past moon and it weighs heavily on you. What is it?"

I stiffened in Shana's embrace and looked away. "I...it is nothing."

She pulled away and gently turned my face her way again. "You are a terrible liar. Is it Ori?"

Ori. Orianna. Queen Orianna. At the mere mention of her name, my heartbeat sped up and I flushed. "No, there is nothing wrong there. She said she wants to be friends and she asked me to call her Ori when we are alone."

She gave me a piercing look. "I see. And do you want to be alone with her?"

"Gods, yes." The words slipped out before I could even think. As soon as they did I scrambled off the bed and felt my face go hot. "I mean no. We are just friends, she is my queen and...I mean..." I could not help the emotion that overcame me. Everything that had been pulsing inside, every single touch and look, it overwhelmed me in an instant and I broke down in tears. Before I could draw a breath Shana was at my side leading me back to the bed. She held me while I sobbed and just rubbed my back.

Once I calmed down and dried my tears she brought me a cloth soaked in water. "So what are you going to do about this?"

I blanched. "Do about this? Nothing. This is nothing." I drew my knees to my chest. "You know as well as I do that I am just some kid who knows nothing of the world, and I have no experience here. I am sure it is just a passing infatuation for me."

She gazed back at me seriously. "I don't think it is."

"What do you mean? Of course it is. It has to be a passing infatuation because I certainly cannot go on like this forever. I dream of her, Shana!"

Shana grasped my shoulder firmly. "No, I don't think it's a passing infatuation for *just* you."

"Wh...what?"

My heart froze with her next words. "Kyri, I've known Ori since we were younglings. When she and Risiki were brought to the nation by a returning raiding party, my mothers took them in. They actually lived with us for a few years. At least until Ori decided she could take care of her sister on her own, halfway through her secondary education."

I had known that she and her sister were orphans but I never thought about what happened to them when they came to Telequire. "Why did she want to live on her own?"

"I'm not sure if you've noticed, but Ori is incredibly stubborn. And she's always had it in her head that she has to do everything, be everything, and her sole focus in life was on protecting her sister. Around the time we were both sixteen summers, she decided she didn't want to be beholden to my mothers and petitioned the queen and council for her own hut and custody of her sister."

"And they allowed that? How did your mothers feel after raising them for...eight cycles?"

"They did and it was...difficult. On one hand I was sad to see Ori pull away. But after Combe and Sikara spoke with the priestess, they seemed to understand. Also, Risiki continued to stay with us on the nights that Ori was away from the village so it worked out. But what I'm trying to say is that I lived with Ori, I know her better than anyone else in this village. And I see her when she's with you. Kyri...I can see that you affect each other in the same way. She's always been good at hiding her emotions but I can see through both of you. She is as drawn to you as you are to her."

I closed my eyes and tried to make sense of what she was saying, fighting back tears that threatened to break free of my eyelashes. "But none of it matters, does it? She is my queen. No, she is not my queen yet because I am not even an Amazon."

I felt Shana touch on my face, wiping away an escaped droplet. "It always matters Kyri, and you will both see that soon enough." She suddenly shoved my shoulder, startling me and waking Gata, thus changing the mood. "Besides, I know for a fact that the quickest way to Ori's heart is through her stomach. You'll have her following you around all the time once she gets a taste of your rabbit stew."

I shoved her back. "Oh, shut your diplomatic yap, you poor excuse for an Amazon archer!" She gaped at me and when she came close to retaliate, Gata stood between us and gave a raspy growl at her. I just laughed. "Good girl, Gata!"

Once the laughter died down I stood and walked over to my old cloak, the original my mam had made me. I took it down and brought it back to Shana. Holding it up to her I asked, "Is there someone in the Telequire tribe who can help me make something like this? I know my mam's techniques but I do not know where I can get the cloth and materials. My da sent some patterns with me and some of my mam's needles and other tools, but I need new fabric."

Shana thought for a heartbeat. "There's a weaver in the nearby village of Gelta. The nation trades with her for bolts of fabric. We can talk to the supply master and see what we can do for you. Why do you want it? Are you going to make yourself another new cloak?"

"No, I..." Sudden shyness tied my tongue. "I wanted to make one for Ori. It is probably a fool's idea, right?"

She smiled. "Not at all. I think she'll love it." Curiously, she said, "So you're mam taught you how to do all that? Wow."

"Well, she taught me but I was never as good as her. I thought I would give it a try again. I am not sure if I should make a short cloak or a longer one for her."

Shana snickered. "Well, she is short."

"Ha-ha, you are very funny and no help."

She stopped laughing and actually gave my question some thought. "Well, she doesn't run the trees like she did when she was a scout. I think you'd be safe giving her a standard cloak."

"Okay, that makes sense. I was also thinking about my trial and what I would need to prove my worth."

She cocked her head. "Go on."

I went to the opposite end of my hut where I had my fletching equipment stored. I moved a bit of scrap leather and showed her the forest fletch arrows I had amassed in the corner. Her jaw dropped. "By Artemis, there must be hundreds there!"

"It's about two hundred and thirty actually. Do you think a few hundred arrows and my four horses from the raider attack would be a sufficient proof of worth?"

My friend shut her mouth with an audible click then after a heartbeat she broke out in laughter. "This from the woman who shot the impossible today. Oh sister, I think a million arrows and horses would still undervalue your worth. But yes, I believe your gifts will be acceptable." She stood from the bed and slung her sword over her shoulder. "Now, all this talk of stew earlier is making me hungry. Why don't you have lunch with me before you take Gata out hunting, then later we can meet up at the bathing hut? What do you say?"

I slung my bow and quiver across my shoulders and whistled for the cub. "Well come on then, what are we waiting for?" Our walk was quiet and I spent time thinking about all that Shana had said. What if Ori *did* feel the same way? I knew she could never act on it because within the tribe, I was no one. Even once I got my mask and feather I would still be an outsider, a junior member of the Telequire nation. I was saddened by the thought but I still had the hope of her friendship. Plus, I also had the pleasure of spending time with her over the coming moon. Not that I wanted to humiliate myself in front of her during sword practice, but I was looking forward to having a few meals together.

HUNTING WITH GATA was interesting. I had been working with her for more than a fortnight to climb trees with me and I had even taught her some simple whistling signals. I was actually using the Amazon whistles because I thought they would be easiest. However, I had yet to take her out with the intention of hunting prey. Once I got far enough outside the village I took to the trees. With a running leap, she followed easily by digging in her sharp claws. Her balance was exceptional when walking the branches. I led for quite a ways before I signaled a stop and wait. We hunched down and I kept my bow ready. She actually heard the slight rustling in the underbrush before I did. Two rabbits came into view below our tree, exactly what I was hoping for. I gave a low whistle for 'go' and pointed down. She hesitated for only a heartbeat before leaping from the tree. One rabbit hopped away as fast as it could while the other was pinned beneath her. Then she clamped her jaws on its neck, suffocating the hare in her grasp. I had been training her with food in my hut but it was time for the real test. When I could see the animal was dead I reached down slowly to take it from her. I whistled to her 'stop' and 'wait.' Then in a calm voice I told her, "Gata, leave it. Gata, release!"

She opened her jaws and let go of the rabbit. I motioned her back. "Back, Gata." As she backed away I breathed a sigh of relief and I picked up the dead animal. I made short work gutting and cleaning it while she watched impatiently with a twitching tail. Once I was done I cut off a leg and threw it to her. Then I wrapped the body in a scrap of leather and stuffed it in the pouch at my side. Once the meat was taken care of, I dug a shallow hole with a stick and deposited the mangled skin and entrails. We repeated this with two more rabbits, but I only let her have a leg from one. I wanted to see how she acted without a reward. By then my pouch was overly full and Gata seemed well sated. I was satisfied in two things. First, that she would listen to me, even in a dangerous or wild moment. And second, that she would be able to hunt and fend for herself out in the wild. Overall it was a pretty good day and the celebration had not even begun.

Chapter Eight

Judgment of Six

EQUINOX EVE WITH the Amazons was like nothing I had experienced before. They truly revered seasonal cycles as sacred and took every opportunity to commune with their goddess Artemis. I respected the idea of Artemis and all she stood for. After all, she is supposed to be the goddess of hunting, wilderness, wild animals, transition, and childbirth. She is said to even be the protector of girls until the age of marriage. The bards sing of the virgin goddess, and how she walks the forests with a stag and a she-bear. I had always enjoyed the stories but none of them ever touched me within. They were just stories to me. Knowing how much the nation revered the Goddess of the Hunt, I spoke with the priestess, Glyphera, shortly after my arrival. She assured me that as long as I revered the same things as the Amazons, it did not matter if I had Artemis in my heart. I could live with that.

The Telequire Temple of Artemis was one of the most grand that I had ever seen. The area on the west side of the nation was rocky with quite a few caves. I had often wondered if that was why the countryside was dotted with hot springs because some of the caves were quite warm. The temple itself was inside the largest cave of the area, with its opening near the base of what was either a large hill or a small mountain.

The outside had been carved into a bas-relief of stone columns surrounding a cave entrance. Inside there was a great statue of the goddess Artemis, which was surrounded by two smaller statues of a stag and bear. Every time I saw the level of artistry that went into their sacred place I was in awe. The inside had a high ceiling and was easily large enough for the entire nation. The call to temple was signaled by horn blasts that were repeated throughout the nation. Two times the horns would blow with a quarter candle mark between. By the time we congregated for the ceremony, torches were lit along the walls and I could hear the bleat of a goat tied to a pole near the altar in the very back of the large cave. When I asked Shana about the goat she said it was Artemis's favorite sacrifice. The goat was to be sacrificed to the goddess, then the meat would be roasted for the festival so nothing would go to waste. Having gotten there before the first horns, Shana and I were lucky enough to be standing toward the front where I could see best.

Even the forest scouts gathered for the short temple and fire lighting ceremonies. When I asked why there were no concerns about invaders, I was told that Artemis would protect the nation while they honored her. Shana later admitted that the Centaurs and volunteers from the men's village helped watch our borders during festivals. I felt safer after that. Once the ceremonies were done, the interior and perimeter scouts would grab some food and return to the trees to run short shifts for the next two days. The short rotations would give everyone a chance to participate in the festivities and games.

A hush fell over the crowd when everyone was assembled. The priestess stood at the altar and called forth Artemis's chosen. At that point the crowd parted and Queen Orianna walked forward. She was resplendent in a leather outfit dyed the deepest of reds. Her short hair gleamed golden in the torchlight and her feathers swayed with each step. She wore a beaded necklace made from bone, porcupine quills, silver, and turquoise. To my eyes, the queen was no longer simply beautiful, she had become magical. I noticed that while she still wore a sword across her back, it was not her usual weapon. The new one had a decorative cross guard and a moonstone set in the pommel. When I asked why the sword was different, Shana put two fingers over her lips warning me to be quiet. The queen walked up the stone steps and over to the great statue of Artemis where she went down on one knee. Drawing the sword, Ori held it up with both hands, perpendicular to the floor. When she spoke, her voice was low and melodic.

"Hail to our goddess Artemis! You are both the hunter and the hunted with your thundering pulse and sure steps. You wield the bow that brings prey down to forest loam. You are the roe deer fleeing certain death through the surrounding wood."

The crowd around me chanted. "Silvered moon, mighty huntress of the dark, hear us, Artemis!"

The queen stood and walked to the altar. Turning, she offered the priestess her moonstone sword. The priestess received the sword and held it up in the same manner before continuing the invocation.

"Goddess Artemis, hear our prayers and bless this season of hunts! We are your children, seeking darkness and the forest ways. We are also hunters and hunted, following the laws you decree. Goddess of the Crescent Moon, you are the virgin huntress with your silvered gaze."

Once again, the gathered Amazons answered. "Silvered

moon, mighty huntress of the dark, hear us, Artemis!"

"You who are fearless, you who could track reflected moonlight back to a forest pond, hear us. You, the shy deer who runs from the fumbling steps of your sisters and kin, feel our hearts. Let the beams of moonlight shine down and show all your secrets. Let the winds blow through the forest and uncover that which you hid beneath the leaves and loam. Show us what you hold in your heart, all those things that are seen only once, then never again as long as we breathe."

I began chanting with the crowd, sensing something greater in the air. "Silvered moon, mighty huntress of the dark, hear us, Artemis!"

The priestess's voice swelled in response. "Huntress with hounds who chase us in our weakness, who will not let us sleep the sleep of compromise. If compromise would cause us to stray from our hearts, let it be buried deep in the woods like offal of a hunted stag. Goddess, remind us of our duty to land and nation, and cast the moonlit shadow so we may always know your path."

She and the queen joined the amassed Telequire nation. "Silvered moon, mighty huntress of the dark, hear us, Artemis!"

All the torches went out. No one made a sound. I held my breath, unsure what I was waiting for. After a candle drop, I heard a scraping sound and a torch flared near the altar. I could see the queen carrying the flame to the others on the raised dais while the priestess brought the goat to the altar. Once the queen returned, she stood at one end of the altar and took the rope holding the goat. The priestess held the sword in front of her, beneath the neck of the sacrifice.

"Lady of silver moonlight, dark goddess rising over the trees of the forest. Lady of the deep forest pools that sustain the hidden life of the darkness. You who knows the hidden ways and who sees the things that are often left unseen. Our light in the darkness, our shining Goddess of the Silver Bow. On this day of change when the seasons are in a balance of transition, let there be clarity. On this day when the sky and the land below seek each other like lovers, let there be peace. We ask you, Goddess of the Forest Waters where all wild things slake their thirst, to show us our own secret pools of wisdom. Give us your blessing that we may send our wildest parts to drink in safety from all that would harm them. And let us accept those parts of us, and find comfort in their continued freedom." When the last words were spoken the queen pulled the rope tight, and the priestess quickly slit the goat's throat. The blood, looking nearly black in the few torches that were lit, was allowed to empty into a wide wooden bowl. Once the goat was drained the queen came around and gently carried it off to the side of the altar. After that, she returned and cleaned the sword with a cloth and re-sheathed it. The priestess then lifted the full bowl high above her without spilling a single drop. "In this nation of followers of the Goddess of the Hunt, we revere women and wild things and we honor the life giving forest. But there are those among us whose hearts walk directly in the goddess's footsteps for a short while. With this beast, with this blessing, let me call forth all those that honor the virgin goddess. Come forward and receive your mark." She once again lowered the bowl of blood and waited.

I watched as many young girls past puberty, a few women my age, and even some older started walking toward the altar. I felt a poke in my side and gave Shana a questioning look. She nodded toward the dais. I understood that portion of the ceremony and Shana's intent but I shook my head and whispered, "I am not an Amazon yet."

She whispered back. "The priestess is calling all who are within range of her voice. Go!"

I was unsure if I wanted to stand in front of the gathered nation and admit to walking in the footsteps of their goddess when I myself did not carry Artemis within my heart. With one more poke to my ribs I relented. As I stepped into the aisle and walked forward, I swore that I could hear whispers following me. I ignored them and joined the line of other women heading up the steps to the dais. Unfortunately, because of my hesitation I was last in line. I watched as Glyphera dipped her finger into the goat's blood and marked the forehead of each supplicant before me. The priestess would recite the same words with every symbol. "I mark you in the name of Artemis, who knows the hidden ways. If and when this mark should fade, remember that it is not necessary to walk in the goddess's steps to continue following her path."

Finally it was my turn and the priestess recited the words. When she made the mark on my forehead I let my gaze wander to the queen. I could see surprise in her eyes before she quickly masked it. She then gave me a smile and the barest hint of a nod. Once I had my mark, I found my way off the dais and back to Shana's side. The entire thing seemed hazy and surreal.

When the bowl was cleared away the priestess turned to the crowd. "The sacrifice has been given and the blessings have been made. Oh Artemis of the silver light, give us a sign that you have received our gifts and are pleased."

The waiting silence was so complete it was almost as if the crowd was holding its breath. I was not sure what we were expecting but I did not really believe anything would happen. I glanced at Shana but she was completely still watching the altar. The queen and the priestess stood staring straight ahead. Heartbeats went by, then candle drops, and still we waited. When I thought the crowd would surely give up, all heads turned to the sound of a scratchy little leopard cry. Shocked, I looked back at the aisle only to see Gata running toward the dais.

Shana spun her head around and whispered, "Is that?" I nodded, suddenly embarrassed that my charge was interrupting the ceremony. I moved to grab her but Shana stopped me. "Do not interfere."

"What?"

She held my arm tighter. "Watch."

The entire Amazon nation watched as Gata ran up the steps and made her way across the dais. She rubbed against the priestess on the way by, but only stopped when she got to Queen Orianna. There she sat back on her haunches and gave another raspy cry. The priestess suddenly raised her hands and called out, "The sign has been received and Artemis's messenger has been sent. Goddess of the Hunt, Goddess of the Wild Animals, we thank you for your blessing today."

The entire crowd chanted the end of the ceremony. "Silvered moon, mighty huntress of the dark, hear us, Artemis!" And then it was done.

Women started to disperse, many to finish preparing for the celebration. A few were scouts heading out to grab food early, before the ceremony of light. I stopped Shana before she could leave. "I do not understand. Gata is not a sign from the goddess, she escapes all the time. Why would they believe that?"

Shana looked at me patiently. "Gata does escape all the time but she is also a wild creature. Today she escaped at exactly *this* time. And she came to the temple at exactly this time. She didn't come to you as she often does. Instead she called out and ran to the altar. She touched the priestess and only stopped at the queen. She sat at the feet of Artemis's chosen and called out again. All of this happened while we were waiting to see if we had Artemis's favor. Now you may see all this as coincidence and maybe it is, but it seems like an awful lot to me. And it was enough for me to believe. She is my goddess, Kyri, and I believe."

With those parting words she left me there. I was confused and somewhat in a daze. The dried blood on my forehead was starting to itch and I had to go find Gata. When I looked at the dais, I could see the queen and priestess still there. Gata herself was sitting on the altar allowing the priestess to stroke her soft fur. I approached the steps. "May I come up?"

The priestess gazed at me silently, as if she searched for

something unseen in the depths of my eyes. "The ceremony is over, you may go where you please. Come up and get your charge, Kyri."

I jogged up the steps and across the dais. Gata gave me one of her little mewling roars. I scooped her into my arms, though she was getting much too big to do so. She easily weighed as much as child of six summers. The queen laughed and commented, "She was determined to join us today, perhaps you should have just brought her."

Without looking at either of them, I responded. "But then where would you have gotten your sign of Artemis's favor?"

The priestess once again stroked the soft cub in my arms. She spoke cryptically, as the pure followers of gods were known to do. "Perhaps we have had our sign all along..." She turned and walked away. I glanced to the queen, but she did not say anything about the priestess's comment. Instead she smiled.

"So how did you like your first equinox ceremony?"

I thought for a heartbeat or two. "It was beautiful, and different. Having so many women together talking of honoring all those things I hold most dear, it fills my soul with light. But I confess that I am no follower of Artemis nor am I such for any of the gods. I just do not hold beliefs like that in my heart."

She lightly ran her finger along the mark on my forehead. "And yet, you walk in Artemis's footsteps..."

I shivered at her touch and closed my eyes. "Perhaps I have simply led a sheltered life and now I am merely waiting."

She withdrew the finger. "And what are you waiting for, Kyri?"

Before I could guard my answer I started to speak. "I think maybe I have been waiting for..." I never got to finish because Basha suddenly entered the cave and called out.

"My queen, you are needed to prepare for the ceremony of light."

Ori sighed. "I'll be there in a few candle drops, Basha. Please make sure the witnesses are ready."

"Yes, my queen."

She once again left the temple and Ori turned back to me. "Now, you were saying?"

When the regent left, my bravery went with her. I could not finish what I had previously started to say. "I...it was nothing, my queen." I cast my eyes downward and felt as though I disappointed her.

The woman who so dominated my thoughts reached across and lifted my chin until I could once again see into those hypnotizing green eyes. "It's Ori, please."

I smiled back at her, shyly. I liked Ori much better than the queen. "Okay, Ori. Well, maybe we can discuss philosophy and reasons some other time?"

She gave me a warm smile. "I think I would like that, perhaps over a nice bowl of rabbit stew." Shana was right, Ori's eyes actually twinkled at the mention of food.

"That would be great."

"Okay then. Now, I really have to go or my regent will have some sort of fit." I laughed which made her pause for a heartbeat. She then turned and with a forward flip off the dais, she jogged out of the temple. I set Gata down — my back threatened to give way from her weight — and replayed the queen's flip from the dais a few times in my head. In that moment I had found my goddess, and it was not Artemis. I waited to see if I would be struck down for my thoughts and when I was not I made my own way out of the temple.

When I returned to the village center it looked like a bee's hive of activity. The great bonfire was ready to be lit and cook fires were spread around the festival area. The dais was set up and I could see different competition areas being organized. I knew that the celebration featured numerous events and games, which let the Amazons show off various skills. All the events would be held the next day, on equinox. There were weapons competitions, which included sword, chobo, staff, knife, archery, and unarmed combat. There were feats of strength, balance, speed, and agility. I was especially happy to hear there would be storytelling and song contests. I was only slightly surprised to hear that the queen had entered the ones for sword and archery. When I found Shana again and asked her about it she just laughed. "Why wouldn't she? She is a master swordswoman and archer and I hope she wins both." Shana entered knife and storytelling, and made her own suggestions for me. "You should also enter the archery competition."

I shook my head. "Why would I do that? It would not be fair to everyone else. Besides, we already know what kind of shot I am."

She thought for a heartbeat. "Well then what about the skill event, and the tree race?"

I cocked my head. "What exactly do those entail?"

"Well, the tree race is exactly what it sounds like. Everyone starts in a tree and you have to race around the perimeter of the village and training grounds, and return before everyone else. You can't leave the trees, and you can't touch any of the other contestants."

"Oh, I can do that!"

"You know Coryn always enters that one and she has won the last two seasons. Before her, Ori used to win regularly."

"I would not be ashamed to lose, and I also would not be ashamed to win. We will just have to see who the trees favor tomorrow. Okay, so what is the skill event?"

"Well, it's not so much a contest as it is a chance to show off your greatest skill. Usually the crowd and conference of elders determine who has the most impressive demonstration. It can be anything from balancing on a tightened length of rope, or something that demonstrates who can skin a rabbit the fastest. It's a very open event."

I looked at her in consternation. "I already told you it is not fair of me to shoot my bow — "

"No, no, I wasn't referring to that. I was thinking that you could...maybe..."

I raised an eyebrow, daring her to continue. "Just what other skills do you think I have, Shana? I am not going to make my mam's rabbit stew for everyone."

She laughed and shook her head. "I bet you'd get everyone's vote though. No, I was thinking that maybe you could do a demonstration, similar to what you did with Deata and the crossbow bolts..."

I gave her a piercing look, hoping my blue eyes were making her as uncomfortable as I suddenly felt. "Shana..."

She put a hand on my arm. "No, it will be perfect. Listen to my idea, hear me out please?" I nodded and she continued. "What if we do this? We'll make it a showman's event, to really draw the crowd. I can wear wood blocks, like Deata did. And when you come up to demonstrate your skill, you can pick me as the target. That way no one will be endangered and the crowd is none the wiser."

"Okay, but who will be the shooter?"

She thought for a heartbeat. "Maybe we can get Kylani to help out, or perhaps ask for a volunteer from the crowd."

"Sister, I don't think anyone will want to shoot an arrow at you not knowing that you are protected and safe."

With my words she thought for an entire candle drop. Suddenly she cried out, making me jump. "Ori!" I gave her a strange look. "Ori can help. I'll explain it to her, and she will make sure the shot is true."

I mulled the plan over in my head. "We would have to make sure we had a safe enough distance for me to shoot my bow."

"Well...actually..."

"What now? Spit it out, Shana."

"I was thinking that you could catch them in your hands.

Then we only have to make sure no one is behind me."

I rubbed my chin while considering her new suggestion. "You know, that actually might work. And you trust me to catch the arrow?"

Her voice was serious and solemn. "With my life."

I grinned. "Well, it will not come to that with you wearing the wood blocks."

"See, it's perfect!"

I just shook my head. "All right, I am in for both."

She pumped her fist into the victory sign. "Okay, I'll have a word with Ori later this evening to make sure she is in on the plan. Then we'll be all set for tomorrow."

SHORTLY AFTER MY conversation with Shana, the next horn rang out indicating the final ceremony was to begin and Gata came with me to the ceremony of light. The crowd no longer bothered her as it did when she was much smaller and she was very well behaved. Once again, I found myself watching from the crowd as the queen and regent climbed the steps onto the dais. They were followed by the council. The queen walked forward to the edge of the raised platform and the crowd fell into a hush. The only sounds heard were the crackle of cook fires with their spits of roasting meat and the rustling of wind through the trees. Unnecessarily, she raised her hands for attention. "Before we begin the lighting ceremony on this equinox eve, we have a few announcements." She called eleven young women to the dais, reciting their names and their parentage. They seemed to be past puberty, but not yet into adulthood. When all the girls were present next to her, she continued. "You were all chosen to be our first fosterlings to our sister Amazon nations. You will spend six moons training and learning with the foster tribe and parents. In return, those tribes are sending fosterling to us for the same six moons. The fosterlings will be exchanged with our wagons of trade goods."

The crowd murmured and she held her hand up for quiet. The queen then called out each fosterling's assigned nation. I smiled as a young woman named Rochelle was assigned to the Tanta tribe. Once all assignments had been given, the fosterlings filed back off the dais and the queen continued. "As you may have just guessed, our extended offers of trade agreements have been accepted and will be honored by all twelve Amazon tribes." With that, there was a great roar of approval. Everyone knew how valuable trade agreements were, especially between other Amazon tribes. Each had their own unique skills and growing climates. It was a major accomplishment for such a young queen. Queen Orianna let the cheering and clapping die down then started her next announcement. "Will Shana, daughter of Combe and Sikara, please come to me?"

Shana had not mentioned anything about being in the ceremony. She gave me a slight wink as she went by in the crowd. Once she was up on the dais she took a knee before the queen. Ori touched her shoulder lightly. "Sister, please rise and face the Telequire nation."

The regent came forward and held out a feather that had been dyed jade green. The queen took the feather and addressed the crowd of women before her. "For the first time in many suncycles, the Telequire nation finds itself in a place of favor with not just other Amazon tribes, but with our neighbors and a variety of allies. Because of the increased demands of communication and diplomacy, the council and I have created a new position in the Telequire nation. Shana has displayed true Amazon perseverance through trial and adversity in order to honor our nation's wishes for such diplomacy. She was given the task of creating ties between two nations with a history of hatred and anger and she returned to us with success. Shana has also taken training with the Centaurs, the Shimax Amazon ambassador, and the city council leaders of Gelta, Distrato, and Perivoli." She turned toward Shana and lifted the feather. "Because of your bravery, diligence, and silver tongue, Shana of the Telequire Amazon Nation, you will become our first Ambassador of Nations." She tied the feather into Shana's hair next to her Amazon rite of caste feather. "May all your diplomatic endeavors bear us sweet fruit!"

I thought my heart would burst as I gazed up at my sister and first Amazon friend. She had earned honor for her actions and I was really glad that Ori and the council saw her worth properly. She would make an amazing ambassador. The new ambassador's eyes appeared slightly watery as she made her way off the dais to a crowd of well-wishers, but she did not shed a tear. The crowd settled down again, sensing that the queen was not finished. Shana made her way to me and I gave her a quick hug. "I knew you were destined for great things, sister!" We quickly composed ourselves and waited for the queen to speak. I was curious when I heard her call a number of familiar names to the dais.

"At this time, I would like the following witnesses to come to me. Margoli, Basha, Kylani, Steffi, Coryn and Thera."

I could feel butterflies flutter upward in my belly and my voice came out as a whisper. "No, it is much too soon." Perhaps the queen was just acknowledging my progress. There was no way the names called could have a connection to my trial. Shana reached down and gave my hand a squeeze and that was the moment when I knew different. My breath came faster and sweat formed under my arms.

The queen looked to the assembled women on the dais. "You six Amazons have been called as witnesses to the passage of an initiate to her trials. Do you understand the duties that were set before you and swear to give accurate testimony before the gathered nation?" They all gave their assent and Queen Orianna called out loudly. "Kyri, daughter or Mira and Galen Fletcher, please come to me."

I paled and clenched my fists. Shana leaned toward me and whispered, "Go. It will be okay, I promise." She gave me a pat on my back and I had no choice but to make my way to the dais. While all my instructors were lined up to the queen's right, I was made to stand on the queen's left. Gata had followed me up and sat on the dais between us but no one paid her any mind.

Next, the queen called out. "Margoli, please step forward and give your judgment."

The military advisor took one step forward. "In the case of Amazon wars and history, I find the initiate Kyri well versed in the past of the Amazons and in our outcomes and tactics of recent wars. She is ready to move on. I recommend Amazon trial." She stepped back when she finished speaking.

"Basha, please step forward and give judgment."

The queen's regent stepped forward next. "In the case of Amazon society and her duties to the nation, I find the initiate an apt and appreciative pupil. She has satisfied my requirements and I recommend Amazon trial."

Despite two affirmatives, my stomach remained tense. My fists were still clenched at my sides and my gaze was rooted far in the distance. "Kylani, please step forward and give judgment.

The training master stepped forward confidently. "In the case of Amazon weapons and training, I find the initiate a master of archery, well-versed in knife, and proficient at sword, staff, chobos, and unarmed combat. She has satisfied my requirements and with the stipulation that she continue her training until she attains mastery of all items mentioned, I recommend Amazon trial."

My eyebrows rose at her conditions. Mastery? There was just no way I would ever master the sword. She stepped back and the queen called for the next person in line. "Steffi, please step forward and give judgment.

"In the case of Telequire economics, I find the initiate hopelessly acceptable, just as I find the majority of Amazons I've trained..." She was interrupted slightly by laughter rolling through the crowd, then continued. "...with this judgment, I recommend Amazon trial." She once again stepped back.

"Coryn, please step forward and give judgment."

I was curious what the head of the scouts would say about my training. She stepped forward. "In the case of scouting, I find the initiate a master level tree walker and hunter, and I find her proficient at hand signals, whistles, signs, and encounters. She will make a fine scout for the Telequire nation and I recommend Amazon trial." I was pleased and slightly surprised by her words. I had not realized that she held my skill with such high regard. She always kept any praise very minimal.

Finally, my last instructor was called. "Thera, please step forward and give judgment."

Thera stepped forward and glanced at Ori. "Oh, she's all right, my queen. Kyri's been very good at all the healing stuff. Let her have her trial already!" I glanced to my right as the crowd broke out in laughter and saw a smile grace the queen's face.

Ori looked toward the healer and spoke. "So your recommendation is for Amazon trial?"

Thera nodded. "Yes, my queen."

Ori turned back to the gather crowd. "So it has been agreed and judgment given. Kyri will begin her Amazon trial the day after equinox. That dawn, she will report to the scout hut and it is then that she will be given the challenge of running the trees around the entire Telequire nation. Should she pass all three challenges of her trial, she will receive her Amazon mask and rite of caste feather, and she will be known in our histories as a Telequire Amazon. Let Artemis smile on her at that time." Understanding the dismissal, we filed off the dais while the queen continued with the lighting ceremony. All she had to do was recite an invocation to Artemis and call for the bonfire to be lit. The sun was sliding down the late afternoon sky and I was starting to feel the pangs of hunger. Of course it was not helped by the smell of roasting meat wafting all around us.

The bonfire was lit and I found Shana again and punched her lightly in the arm. "Did you know about this?"

She rubbed her arm and grinned. "Well, a little bird may have mentioned that you might be ready for initiation..."

I growled under my breath. "Come on, I am starving. Let us go find some food."

Ori and Basha found us while we were eating. Basha gave Shana a big hug and congratulated her again on being made ambassador. While they were busy talking about the promotion, Ori leaned over and whispered to me. "Were you surprised?"

I turned and was frozen by the nearness of those green eyes.

When I moved my gaze downward, all I could see was her lips. They looked so soft and warm. I watched them moving and it took me a heartbeat to realize she was talking to me. "Heyla, Kyri, I think you disappeared again."

"I am sorry, what?"

"I asked if you were surprised."

I blushed. "Oh, yes. I had no idea that my instructors thought I was ready to go through my trial."

She smiled and winked. "You are more than ready, and I look forward to putting a feather in your hair."

At that point in our conversation, Shana and Basha were both listening and Shana burst into laughter. I blushed nearly purple, knowing that Shana was laughing about the tradition of lovers. Apparently when two Amazons became lovers and promised themselves only to each other, they exchanged their rite of caste feathers. It was certainly not the feather Queen Orianna was referring to though my heart fluttered at that thought. It was always innuendo with Shana. Basha got it instantly and joined her in laughter. I sighed, wanting to crawl under the bench while Ori only smirked in Shana's direction. I cleared my throat and answered with as much dignity as I could muster. "Thank you, my queen. I look forward to that day as well." I stood and decided I needed some time with the trees. "Now if you will excuse me, I am going to take Gata out to hunt for her dinner."

Shana looked at me in confusion. "But, Kyri, there's plenty of food here. I'm sure Gata would get her share of scraps…"

Ori seemed to understand. "Go ahead, Kyri, I hope you both have good hunting. We'll see you later?"

I nodded. "Yes, I will be back in a few candle marks." And with those words I took off into the trees. Little Gata Anatoli, who was not so little any more, easily followed.

We rose into the canopy together and made our way around until we were somewhere near the temple. My mind was a mass of confusion and I was not sure why I felt I had to leave. Yes, I was embarrassed by Shana's teasing but it was more than that. I was also very aware of the great chasm between me and Ori. I had desperately craved her friendship for over a moon. And in just a few short candle marks of time, I realized that I desperately craved more. I was not even sure what it was I wanted, but I knew that the urge to touch her when she was near was getting harder and harder to deny. And I did not want to ruin our new and delicate friendship with my strange emotions. Nor did I want to lose sight of my goal to become a Telequire Amazon. I had to do it for myself and for my da. I needed to live and be happy. In my head and heart I knew that I had to be free and be nothing but myself, or he will have died alone in vain. I would not throw away his gift to me. Twice he helped give me the gift of life and I will forever honor his memory.

The woods were fairly quiet on the temple side of the village. The dark was slowly working its way up from the forest floor, as darkness always spreads. We had to be careful in the trees though I had to watch a little closer than Gata. She had much better eyesight at night than I. We waited, hearing a rustle in the leaves below us, and I saw a roe deer walk under our branches, unaware of the danger above. He had small antlers rising a hand span above his head that ended in three little points. Despite his small size, I knew he was too big for Gata to take down on her own so I had an arrow nocked. I whistled the signal to 'wait' while I drew back. I released my arrow into a beautiful heart shot. The deer took off, as they do, and I whistled for Gata to 'go'. She leaped from the tree before it had gone three steps and took the small deer to the ground. With an arrow in its heart, the struggle was very short and it soon bled out. When I was sure the deer was dead, I signaled for release and Gata backed away. Twice in one day she had hunted with me, and twice she shown that she could be trusted with fresh kill. I quickly processed the deer, saving the torso, heart, skin and antlers for myself. I gave the rest of the organs to Gata then buried the entrails under the loam. I waited while Gata made short work of her portion. The other forest creatures would finish whatever she left. When she was sated, I bundled the meat and skin as best I could and went back to the temple. I made my way inside and up to the altar, which was once again set to receive offerings. I was not sure why, but I felt it necessary to leave something for the goddess. I retrieved the saved heart from my bundle. It was still oozing and there was a large hole in it from the head of my arrow. After I placed it onto the offering plate I rinsed my hands with the provided water pitcher. The heart was a delicacy and I assumed it would be a worthy offering for a goddess. I said the only words I could think of. "I am unsure if you are real, Artemis, and I do not know if you are not real. But I do know that my feet already follow your path and my soul will always walk your trees. I am placing this offering here because my mind and heart are not closed to the idea of you."

I rose and Gata and I made our way back to the festival. The cooks were grateful for the meat I brought with me and I was happy to help out. I decided to head to the bathing pools for a quick cleanup before rejoining the celebration. Gata started to follow me into the cave with the smallest hot spring, then quickly made her way back out. It was obviously too warm for her and I had a feeling she would be fine on her own. I lit the torches around the small chamber, quickly undressed, and then sank to my neck in the warm water. It was a welcome feeling of bliss and I was grateful each day to be living in such a place with the Amazons. My friends, and all the people I had met since coming to the Telequire nation, were all starting to feel like family to me. I smiled at the thought until I sensed a presence in the cave with me. I quickly opened my eyes, surprised to see Coryn. A strange look passed over her face, then quickly disappeared.

"I'm sorry, I didn't mean to intrude. I just got back from assigning patrol duty and wanted to clean up a bit before I go eat. I can go find another pool..."

She made the offer but I noticed that she made no move to leave. I sighed quietly, knowing I should do the customary thing and let her join me. "You do not have to leave Coryn. I was just doing the same myself. You are welcome to join me in this one."

She grinned, perhaps a little too triumphantly and I simply untied the leather thong and began to unravel my braid. She got in as I ducked under the water to wet my hair. When I came up again, Coryn was a little closer than I expected, which startled me. She laughed. "Sorry, Kyri, I didn't mean to scare you. I was just noticing your scar." Coryn reached out to my shoulder. "Do you mind if I touch it?"

I shook my head. "No, go ahead." Once again, being so close to the First Scout Leader, I was reminded of just how attractive she was. Her dark blond hair was loose, falling just below her shoulders, and her hazel eyes looked dark and brooding in the torchlight.

She reached out, tracing my blackened scar with her fingertips and I could not stop the goose bumps that marched across my upper body. "Was this from the leopard attack? Gata's mother, right?" She continued to trace each line.

I swallowed at the sensation. "Yes."

She looked at me but did not still the motion of her fingers. "Does it still hurt?"

My pulse sped up with her nearness and touch. "Yes, I mean, no. It no longer hurts. Neither does my leg and that injury was the worse of the two."

She removed her fingers and I was finally able to breathe again. "Oh? Did you blacken the leg as well?"

"No, that one was a little deeper and Shana had concerns about it healing clean. So she left it alone."

She moved a little closer and my heart pounded in my chest. "How big is the scar on your leg? I don't recall ever seeing it. The leather strips of your skirt cover pretty well."

I held my hand out of the water, spreading the fingers to show its size. If Coryn noticed the slight tremble she did not comment. "She was a full grown leopardess. Her weight took me to the ground. Even though I put an arrow through her, she was still able to claw me before I could slit her throat."

"Wow. That is some feat. Do you mind if I feel the scars on your leg?"

I swallowed and decided to let her satisfy her curiosity. I had heard that Coryn was a great huntress herself, so I supposed it was only natural that she would be interested in my attack. I took her offered hand and laid it on my scar under the water. As she ran her fingers across it, a strange feeling came over me. My stomach had butterflies and my belly felt heavy. I barely heard her words as my hands uncontrollably clenched under the water. "Goddess! That must have been a great cat to leave a mark this large." I nodded, unable to speak. She was my height, so sitting on the rock ledge in the pool she could easily look me in the eyes. She must have saw them grow wide when her hand wandered beyond the boundaries of my scar. My lips were slightly parted as I began to breathe a little faster. I could feel a hot flush race through my body and I started to tingle. She leaned a little closer and whispered in my ear. "You're very beautiful, Kyri...and very brave."

I gasped at the nearness of her lips. "I...I am, um..." I cleared my throat. "I am not brave at all, just lucky."

I felt the barest touch of her tongue on my ear then just as quickly it withdrew. I turned my face to her with no small amount of shock showing. That was when she leaned forward again and kissed me. It was...overwhelming, the feel of her lips and tongue caressing my own. It was beyond the tentative and shy kiss I had shared with Baeza. The feel one of Coryn's hands on my thigh, and the other making its way across my ribs. I could not handle it. I moaned, and hearing my own voice, suddenly pulled away. I tried to catch my breath and when she started to follow me back I put my hands on her shoulders to hold her in place. I surprised myself when I managed to speak. "No."

She stopped and looked at me in surprise. "*No?*"

I tried again a little more firmly. "No."

She smiled and licked her lips. "I can feel your desire, Kyri. What's the matter? I know you find me attractive, just as I feel the same way about you." I was unsure how to answer her. She pressed me a little more. "Why are you stopping me? Doesn't this feel good? Doesn't it feel right?"

Despite me holding her shoulders back, her hand started to move again toward my inner thigh. Shock and arousal hit me like a lightning bolt and I stood abruptly. Water cascaded down my body and I noticed that her eyes did not follow mine upward. With one deep cleansing breath I found my words at last. "It does feel good, Coryn, and you are very beautiful yourself. But I am not ready to leave Artemis's footsteps just yet. Please respect my decision."

She instantly pulled back and I could see her face pale even in the torchlight. "Kyri, I'm sorry. I had no idea." She stood as well and her eyes never left mine. "Please accept my apology and respect for the goddess." She held out her hand.

I watched her eyes for a heartbeat, trying to gauge her sincerity. Satisfied with what I found I clasped her forearm like a warrior. "I accept your apology, but I am afraid only Artemis can accept your respect. No harm done, Coryn. Would you like to finish our bath?"

The scout leader smiled, her demeanor completely changed. "Sure, I'm ready to join the festivities. Have you entered any of the competitions tomorrow?" We both resumed our seats and bathing activity.

I smiled back. "Yes. Shana talked me into two of them, the skill show and the tree race."

She laughed. "Oh ho, so I'm going to have some competition this season? Well may the best competitor win, hmm?"

"We shall just have to see." For the next half a candle mark, we actually had good conversation. In that short time we found that we had quite a few things in common. By the time we finished bathing I felt as if Coryn and I could actually be friends. It was a nice feeling and much better than that of being pursued. I was surprised by her reaction when I told her I was not ready to step out of the goddess's footsteps. Whether I believed that I actually followed in Artemis's footsteps was not what mattered. I knew I was simply not ready for what Coryn had to offer. And I was okay with that.

Chapter Nine

Trial of the Initiate

BY THE TIME we returned to the celebration, the dancing had already started. The first person I saw when Coryn and I walked through the crowd was Shana. She raised her eyebrow when she saw the two of us approaching from the bathing area. I said my goodbyes to the scout leader and made my way to the person who came closest to being a sister to me.

She scowled at the departing scout. "And just where have you been? And with Coryn?"

I raised my palm. "Peace, sister, I am not sure why you have issues with Coryn. We both bathed and had some good conversation."

She snorted. "Oh? And what else did Coryn have with you? She's not one to pass up an opportunity..."

"Oh, she definitely is not. But we worked it out and I think now we can actually be friends. And stop worrying about that all right? I know my path and no one is going to make me stray."

Her eyes glanced behind me and she smirked. "No one, Kyri?" I turned to follow her gaze and felt my breath catch.

Ori walked up with Gata pacing along next to her. She graced me with a beautiful smile and my heart felt as if it stopped. "I think I found someone that belongs to you."

I forced myself to breathe and knelt down to the cub. "Oh, she does not belong to me, my queen. She belongs to no one but herself. I am simply lucky enough to be her friend."

I watched Ori's smile warm. Her response was naught but a whisper but I still heard the words. "I think she's the lucky one." She seemed to give herself a mental shake and her face changed to one of curiosity. "So, Shana gave me a strange request earlier. Can you really catch arrows with your hands?"

I stood and felt a little embarrassed smile take hold, thinking about my strange talent. "I have done it before back at Tanta nation. I caught an arrow that would have taken their training master's life, and she set up a test for me later to prove the skill."

"And you think you can just do this whenever you choose to?"

"No, Queen Orianna, I know I can do it whenever I need to."

My queen raised her hand and grasped my shoulder. "I look

forward to your demonstration tomorrow."

I nodded with a smile and she wandered off into the crowd. Shana snickered and murmured, "I bet she is..." I punched her shoulder yet again. She could never leave things be.

We spent a few candle marks walking around the celebration until Shana met up with one of her owl friends and they wandered off together. Shana explained that when two friends sought to spend the occasional evening of pleasure together without wanting to exchange feathers, they were called owl friends, meaning they were friends mostly at night. I went over to the great bonfire to watch the dancers. As I watched, I thought about the Amazons and their owl friends. After getting close with both Baeza and Coryn, I definitely understood the allure of owl friends. But I was not willing to risk the distraction when I was so close to my goal. But someday...yes, eventually. My attention was caught by the laughing form of a short blonde dancing around the fire. Ori seemed so free amid the other dancers and her inner light challenged the fire in brilliance. Chosen of Artemis, my queen, and my friend. Yes, maybe someday I would be ready to let someone all the way in.

EQUINOX DAY CARRIED even more excitement than its eve. I was up early like the rest of the nation seemed to be. I assumed Shana would be with her owl friend so I did not wait for her to go to the meal lodge. When I walked in I could see that most of the food was comprised of leftovers from the day before; however, they added some of my favorite boiled eggs, porridge, and morning bread. Gata was well sated from her large meal the previous evening and seemed content to lie at my feet. I noticed the queen arrive and grab her own plate of food shortly after I sat down. I smiled as she walked my way and sat on the bench across from me.

She chattered cheerfully, clearly not feeling the wine that many others seemed to feel after a great feast. "So, are you ready for your skill demonstration? That is the first contest to start today after the distance runners are released. Then the weapons contests will begin. Those should last until midday. The afternoon will hold the tree race and archery competition. I hear you entered the tree race too."

I cut half a boiled egg off and mashed in onto a piece of bread before answering. "Yes, I saw the preparations when I walked by this morning. Shana was the one who talked me into the tree race."

Ori laughed. "I bet she talked you into both didn't she?"

I blushed. "Yes, she did. What about you? I hear you entered the archery and sword contests."

She smirked, her green eyes twinkling. "Of course I did. I have a reputation to uphold after all. Once a scout, always a scout. This queen's not too proud to compete." She winked at me and started on her own breakfast.

I shook my head at her cockiness. I had enjoyed getting to know Ori, and not just the queen. I ate a few bites before my curiosity got the better of me. "I'm surprised you have not said anything about me not entering the archery contest."

She looked up and set down her eating knife. "For one, I'm glad you aren't entering because it actually gives me a chance." I laughed at that and started on my bowl of porridge and dates as she continued. "And for another, I understand why you didn't."

I cocked my head. "You do?"

She smiled. "Sure. Archery contests, competitions, wagers, they're all about proving yourself. Whether it is to prove yourself to others or simply to your own heart, it's about constantly striving to be better. It's about putting yourself out there in challenge, not knowing you will be the one to come out on top." She laid her hand on mine. "But you, Kyri...you've already made the impossible shot. You've done what no other archer in the Telequire nation could and there is nothing left to prove. In your mind it wouldn't be fair to enter knowing the outcome in the end." She rubbed the back of my hand then moved to pick up her knife again. "That is a very noble thing to do and I admire you tremendously for it."

I was left speechless, amazed that she could so easily read what was in my heart and mind. "Th...that is exactly it. How did you know?"

"Because if I had your skill that's exactly what I would do." She smirked. "But I'm still glad you didn't enter, if only to improve my own chances."

I reached across and gave her shoulder a little shove. "You are bad, Ori. And just so you know, I plan on watching both you and Shana compete at weapons today. So I expect to see some wins from you two."

"Well, I'm sure we will both do our best."

There was not much of our meal left after that and before I knew it we were making our way to the skill area. I could see a dozen Amazons wandering around with red strips of material tied around their thigh. Red was said to be one of the sacred colors of Artemis and it was also bright enough to distinguish the contestants. Others were talking with friends while waiting to watch the event. The conference of elders agreed to judge the skills contest each season. They would listen to the crowd feedback as well as give their own assessment for each competitor. It was a good arrangement because while they were all too old to compete themselves, they still wanted to be part of the action. I was scheduled to go sixth so I had a little time to watch and prepare myself. Shana wandered up after the second person finished. She gave me a wink so I would know she already had the wood blocks strapped under her loose buckskin shirt. I was reassured because I really did not want there to be any risk. While the second contestant's skill was walking on a rope that was strung between two trees, the third contestant was juggling sharpened swords while walking on an empty wine barrel. She would walk the barrel forward and backward while maintaining all the sharp blades in the air. The three of us were talking next to the juggler and Shana was telling Ori the story of when I shot the crossbow bolt out of the air when facing the brigand. I heard the juggler cry out just as she lost her balance on the barrel and her swords flew through the air. I did not think, I simply pulled Ori to my chest and spun us away from a wayward sword. I looked down into startled green eyes. "Are you okay?" Then realizing that she was still crushed to my chest, I released her and stepped back. I felt lightheaded after having her so near.

She took a deep breath and took stock of herself. "I'm fine, and thank you. You always seem to be putting yourself between me and danger."

I smiled back and answered honestly. "I will always put myself between you and danger, my queen."

The scattered swords were collected, luckily no one was hurt. After that the judges ordered the crowd to step back ten paces to prevent any more near accidents. It hardly seemed like any time passed before it was my turn. My name was called and I walked into the demonstration area, then called out loudly to the crowd. "For my demonstration of skill I will need two brave volunteers." Shana and Ori were right at the edge waiting for my signal and stepped forward immediately. I motioned them toward me and quickly removed the bow from my back and strung it. I then removed my quiver of arrows and held both into the air. "As you can see, I have my bow and quiver here. One of my volunteers will be the archer and one will be the target." I paused for a few heartbeats while a few people gasped and anxious murmuring rolled through the crowd. I continued, "No harm will come to the target because my hands will be her shield." My words prompted an even greater furor and I stepped toward my friends. I held the bow out to Ori and she gave me an inscrutable look then shook her head. I briefly wondered if she had changed her mind. "Ori?"

She smiled and took the bow and quiver, then promptly handed them to Shana. The ambassador lowered her voice so the crowd would not hear. "Ori, no. I have to be the target because I'm protected under my shirt!"

The queen would not be dissuaded. "No, I will be the target." Then she looked me right in the eye. "I trust her."

She had issued me a challenge that I could no longer back down from. I pushed the bow and quiver firmly into Shana's hand. "Go on, Shana. I will not let anything harm her. I promise." She nodded once and started counting out paces away from us. When she got to forty she stopped and turned. Ori was supposed to shoot from fifty but I knew Shana was not as confident with her archery.

That was the moment that the crowd finally caught on to the fact that someone would be shooting an arrow at their queen. Many were not happy. One of the judges called out, "My queen, are you sure about this?"

She waved at the gathered crowd, which seemed to be growing by the heartbeat. "Yes, I'm sure. Let Kyri demonstrate her skill." We moved into place, and I stood to the queen's immediate left. There was not a hand span between my body and hers. If she was afraid, she never showed it. I took a deep breath and then another. She spoke quietly next to me. "I trust you, Kyri."

I gave Shana a nod and before anyone else could protest she drew and released. I heard the rustle in the air and suddenly found my hand wrapped around one of my forest fletch. Then I immediately heard another rustle and instinct took over as I found my other hand full. The crowd gasped in shock, and I whipped my head toward Shana. Two arrows were never discussed. What if I had not caught it? I lowered the two arrows and moved my gaze to the queen, expecting her to be angry at the added amount of danger. But I saw nothing but a twinkle in her eye. The assembled spectators started cheering and hooting at what I had done just as Shana arrived with my bow and quiver. In a low voice tinged with anger I turned to her, shaking. "What did you think you were doing? You could have killed her. What if I had not caught that second arrow, Shana?"

Ori put her hand on my trembling arm. "Peace, Kyri, I signaled for two."

I looked at her incredulously. "You what?"

She smiled and held up two fingers. "I signaled for her to shoot two. I told you that I trusted you, Kyri. You should trust more in yourself." With my mouth hanging open, the queen gave me a wink and walked away.

I was flabbergasted and quickly apologized to my friend. "I am sorry, Shana. I did not mean to yell at you. I was just scared and had no idea she would do that."

She slapped me on the back. "It's all right, sister, I know you were just worried. But you have to admit, she certainly guaranteed you the win." She laughed then and I joined her. A short while later, after the rest of the contestants had competed, she was proved right. I did win the contest and received a little fired clay statue of Artemis with the simple word 'skill' written across the bottom. I slowly turned it over in my hand. I had won. Suddenly, I could not wait for my trial.

THE DAY SEEMED full of equal parts exaltation and heartbreak for the many women competing. I was finally able to see the queen with a sword in hand. Afterwards I was convinced that no one else could glide like her. She moved like a panther, all speed and precision. Her sword was a blur and many women found that she simply was not where they tried to strike. I had never seen anyone with such skill, and after Ori's first match I completely understood why Shana bragged of her queen's fighting prowess when speaking with the Tanta nation. After systematically defeating all other competitors in the event, she was eventually handed the clay statue. The simple word 'sword' was engraved on the bottom. When she held it up to me, in triumph, I gave her the victory sign. Once the queen was able to pull away from her well-wishers, she walked to where Shana and I were standing. Shana pulled her into a quick hug and joked, "Just how many of those do you have now from playing with that big blade of yours?"

Ori smirked. "A few. What about you, are you going to show us what you can do with those tiny little blades of yours?"

I laughed at their easy banter and added my own teasing. "Yes, Shana, we have both won statues now. I think it is your turn."

She just gave us a pained look. "Gee, no pressure though, right?"

The knife competition started right after sword, so the queen stayed by me to watch. Shana won her first match and another match had started when I turned to the woman at my side. "Shana is really quite good. I guess I never realized how talented she is. I have only seen her with a knife when she trains me."

"Shana tells me you're getting pretty good at the knife, yourself."

I blushed. "I have long arms, I think that is my only

advantage. But I do enjoy our lessons. I got firsthand experience at how important knife skill can be when we were on our way here from Tanta nation."

She shot me a glance. "You did?"

"Yes, when we were attacked by a group of men two thirds of the way here. It was the day we picked up those eight horses we arrived with. I am surprised she did not tell you."

"Oh, that fight. Yes, she did report on the attack, but she didn't give any details. She just said that you were attacked by eight warriors on the road and that you had put an arrow in all but the leader."

I smiled ruefully. "Well, technically that is true. But the last man came at me with a sword after I had tossed my bow away. I managed to block his downward stroke with my knife and stabbed him in the chest with one of my forest fletch arrows. So yes, I put an arrow in him as well."

She shook her head. "You never cease to amaze me, Kyri."

We continued to watch the event until the final match arrived. Shana made it to the final round and she was scheduled to fight Deka, the Second Scout Leader, for the clay statue. Right from the beginning I could see they were well matched. They fought with a knife in each hand, making it seem even more dangerous to me. There was a lot of circling and staying low on the balls of their feet. One would parry and the other would block, then the dance would reverse. Within a quarter candle mark both women were sporting a dozen small cuts, though none serious. Then Shana was forced to block and Deka got a solid kick in to her midsection. She doubled over in pain and the scout took advantage, scoring a slice along her left arm. Shana lost one of the blades. Clearly in pain, Shana scrambled back a few paces to get her bearings. I heard Ori gasp and I shivered as she grabbed my hand. I held it tight knowing that she was as worried as me. Blood ran freely down Shana's arm and Deka came at her from a position of strength. Just before Deka could strike, Shana grabbed one of her wrists to stop the forward motion and blocked the other blade with her own. They seemed at a momentary impasse, both straining to win out. Deka knew Shana's strength would quickly flag with the arm slice so she continued to press. Then in a movement almost too fast to follow, Shana swept the scout's feet from under her, dumping the other woman hard in the dirt. She kicked one of Deka's knives free and quickly pinned the woman to the ground. One hand held Deka's remaining knife hand safely away, while the other pressed a blade to her throat. Knowing she had been beat, the scout called out loud enough to the judge to hear. "Yield!" Just like that, the match was done.

Shana rolled off and a healer rushed to clean and bandage her arm. I turned and hugged Ori. "She won!" Just as quickly I realized what I was doing and stepped back. My face was red. The queen neither acknowledged my hug nor my mortification. She just clasped my shoulder and smiled. "Yes, she did. Now, let's go tease her for taking so long to do it." I laughed and followed her to where our friend sat with the healer. Ori tapped my sister on the shoulder of the arm that was not being tended to. "Heyla, Shana...it took you long enough. Why, I think that elder Kevara would have won in less time. Ask Kyri, I think I grew gray just watching you two."

Shana chuckled tiredly and held up the clay statue. The word 'knife' was clearly scribed along the bottom. "I still won, Ori." Then she stuck her tongue out at the queen.

I pointed at her waggling tongue. "Should you not be saving that for one of your owl friends?"

Shana's tongue slipped back into her mouth and she gaped at me. The queen roared with laughter. "Bu...wha...what do you know about it?"

My face reddened but it was worth shocking her. I smirked. "Oh, I pick up stories here and there. I am not completely innocent you know."

Ori was now doubled over in hysterics. She could barely get any words out. "Y...your face Sh...Shana! Right now it's worth more than gold!"

Shana finally gave in and joined us laughing.

THE REST OF the games went well and were a lot of fun. I came in second to Coryn in the tree race, but I knew that I would be doubly determined to win at the spring equinox competition. Amazons did not hold games during winter solstice because the cold weather made too many of the events dangerous and difficult. Instead they celebrated winter by exchanging favors and gifts with a series of special meals leading up to the solstice eve. I looked forward to learning all the different traditions with my new family in the moons to come. When the clay statue for the archery competition was handed out I clapped and hooted with the rest of the Amazons, thrilled that Ori had won. I continued to be impressed at the skill of our queen, seemingly in all things. But it was disconcerting to feel equal parts proud and inadequate.

A fleeting thought blew through my mind after Ori had won her second statue of the day. Why would she ever consider me? I put a stop to the words before they could continue to their end. It did no good to think about impossible things. As the day wound down to evening the feast began. A large group of us took up one of the great tables. Seated on the benches were Shana, Basha, Ori, myself, and even Kylani, Steffi, Coryn, and her friends. It was an amazing time and I was once again reminded of how grateful I was for my new life with the Amazons. There were a lot of congratulations for the various winners, as well as a strong dose of revelry and bragging. Coryn ribbed me good-naturedly about her win in the tree race. Others asked how I was able to catch arrows with my bare hands. Some at the table had not seen the skill demonstration so Shana told them that tale, as well as some of our stories from the road. When it became late enough for the drums to start I said my goodbyes. A few asked me to stay but I told them I wanted to be ready to start my trial the next day and they understood. Shana and Ori each gave me a brief hug and said they would see me at dawn.

When I got back to my hut I found Gata curled up on the bed. She had grown so fast that I knew there would eventually be no room for me. I built up the fire to ward off the chill then placed my statue on the shelf with all my other mementos. It held a place of honor, right next to the bronze arrow. Once my bow, quiver, and knives were put away I had nothing left to do but think. I changed into a light shift and decided to fletch some arrows to help find a bit of calm. I had about twenty straightened shafts with nocks already carved, so I sat down to the delicate task of gluing on my blue and green dyed feathers. I had always preferred the shield cut feathers with their more angular nock end, over the parabolic that had a rounded nock end. It was personal preference I suppose, but my da used it before me and his da before him. I guess it was just our way and I never saw any reason to change. However, unlike my da, I did not care if they were right wing or left wing feathers. I was always careful to keep them separate though, as they could not be mixed on an arrow without compromising its flight. But I had always found that my arrows flew true with either wing. I marked a finger's clearance on all twenty arrows as a starting point for the fletching. As I was gluing the feathers onto my third arrow there came a knock at the door. Gata looked up and yawned but just resumed her nap. When I answered, Ori poked her head in. She looked at me, taking in my shift. "I'm not intruding, am I?"

I waved her in. "No, not at all. What brings you by?"

She looked at my fletching tools and half-finished arrows. "Are you sure you're not too busy? I don't want to take up your time. I know tomorrow is a big day for you."

My stomach clenched—I did not want her to leave, not yet anyway. "No, please, come in and sit down. I was just passing the time until I got sleepy." I looked at the cub on my bed. "Clearly Gata has no problems with that."

The leopard only gave an ear twitch at my words. Ori cocked her head and peered closer at my bed. "Did she track wood onto your coverlets?"

I smiled. "No, those are chips of cedrus wood. My mam always used it on our bedding to keep pests away. I sprinkle some all around my hut and on my bedding. It seems to be working so far. Although, to Gata's credit, she seems to be fairly pest free." I cleared some of my tools out of the way and we both took a seat at my little table. Once we were across from each other, I got nervous. I had one of my fletched shafts in my hand and spun it back and forth between my first draw finger and my thumb. Ori seemed content to watch me fidget for a candle drop then reached over and stilled my hand. Gently taking the shaft from me, she peered at the nock and the blue and green feathers.

"This is really good work, Kyri. Didn't you say you were supposed to get your Master's Mark before your father sent you away?"

I nodded and swallowed down the knowledge that I would not be carrying on my family's legacy. "Yes. Da had called for another master to come test me but Shana and I had to leave before he arrived."

I got a solemn look in return. "The Master's Mark means a lot to you, doesn't it?"

"Yes. Da, and his da before him, were fletchers. It was my family legacy but I fear that will end with me."

Ori cocked her head. "You know you can always find a master and go through your test if it means so much to you. There is nothing stopping you, Kyri."

I sighed. The truth was, I had thought about it many times over the moons since I had been with the Amazons. While the events of my life had caused me to change my priorities, they had not stopped me from wanting that old dream of being a master fletcher. "There *is* something stopping me. My da made me promise that I would seek a new life and family, to be free and follow my heart. And right now my heart is telling me that I need to be an Amazon. Becoming an Amazon and learning about the nation and its people has to take precedence over any childhood dreams I may have had." I gave her a serious look, because I did not want her to worry about my childhood dream. "I am all right with not getting my mark, Ori. I have come to terms with it and now I really want to focus on settling into my life here."

She pursed her lips, silent for a few heartbeats. "Well I'm not all right with it but we can discuss this again after your trial." She stood suddenly. "I should probably be going so you can get back to what you were doing."

I rose with her, confused by her abrupt departure. I still had no idea why she had visited me. I was also confused as to why it would matter to her whether or not I had my mark as an Amazon. I followed and stopped her at the door. "But why?"

She met my eyes steadily but I couldn't read her expression. "Because as the queen I want to make sure our members have the best skill set, and that all my Amazons are happy."

"But...but the Telequire nation already has a fletcher with her own apprentices, and a Master's Mark has no meaning within the Amazon tribes. So what is the real reason?"

Her gaze grew melancholy and she tried again. "Because as your friend, I don't want you to have any regrets."

As I listened to her answer I became aware of our proximity to each other. We stood close, perhaps too close. I felt hot yet I shivered and goose bumps marched up and down my arms. I could feel my body react under the light shift I wore and I abruptly felt self-conscious in the face of her probing gaze. Looking into her eyes, I had to ask. "Do you have any regrets, my queen?"

In a quiet moment of stark honesty, she answered, "I find lately that I do." She let those words settle between us for a heartbeat. "Good luck tomorrow, Kyri." With that she stood on her tiptoes and gently kissed my cheek, then slipped out the door.

With her exit I had a sudden attack come over me. I thought perhaps I was getting the condition my da had. My heart raced and I could not breathe. My knees grew so weak I sat down. I leaned over trying not to panic as my chest constricted. Why? Why did she do that? I shut my eyes and focused on breathing. Deep breaths in with slow exhales. I repeated the motions of conscious breathing until I felt in control again. Then I continued to sit and let my thoughts tumble around in my head. In the end I decided to simply push it all away. I blew out my candles and banked the fire, then wrapped myself around Gata. My trial would start in the morning and I needed the sleep.

Daylight dawned while my eyes were busy peering into the darkness. Halfway through my night of restless dreams I decided I could get more solitude in quiet contemplation. After dressing I grabbed my weapons, scouting kit, and cloak. I already had light provisions packed for a day, so I just needed to fill my water skins from the well to be fully equipped for the trial. I arrived at the scouting hut a little early but saw Kylani and a few council members already there. Coryn walked up with yet more council members, then finally Shana, Basha, and the queen arrived. I peered closer at Ori and took in the dark circles under her eyes. I suspected that we slept much the same the previous night. Queen Orianna looked back at me without emotion. "On this day following fall equinox we are gathered here to witness the Amazon trial of Kyri Fletcher. The first challenge will be to run the trees from this point to the first outpost, and then continue through the trees around the entire perimeter of the Telequire nation until you once again reach the first outpost. After that you will return to this spot in whatever manner you choose, no later than dawn tomorrow. If you leave the trees for any reason, or if you receive help of any kind, you will be disqualified and unable to go through the trial again for one full season. There will be scouts taking turns pacing you throughout your run. You are not allowed to interact with them in any way. The penalty is also disqualification. Do you understand the instructions and rules you have been given?"

I nodded. "Yes, my queen."

"Do you have any questions at this time?"

I swallowed at her disconcerting lack of emotion. "My queen, I have two."

"Go ahead."

I glanced around at the ten gathered Amazons. "Do I have to take a full day between challenges?"

The queen looked to the council members, and then glanced at Kylani and Basha. One of the oldest members answered. "It isn't against the rules. It's merely customary courtesy to offer a period of rest after such difficult challenges."

I nodded at this. "Then may I request to complete the second challenge on my way back from the first outpost?"

The queen's face still showed no emotion, but I could see Shana looking at me with worry. I heard her whisper. "Kyri...don't push yourself."

Queen Orianna glanced at the council members and one by one they nodded. She turned back to me. "We see no reason why you cannot combine the challenges, if you find yourself with the opportunity. The second challenge is as follows: You have one day to provide game enough to feed twenty Amazon warriors. You can bring many small game animals or one large game animal, as long as it feeds twenty. If you choose to complete your second challenge on the way back to the village, you must still return by dawn or lose the first challenge." She stopped and added. "What is your second question?"

I looked at the cub sitting near my feet. "Would you please keep Gata for me until I return from my challenges?"

It only lasted a heartbeat, but I saw a warming in her eyes.

"Yes, I can do that. Now, do you have any other questions?"

"No, my queen."

In a loud voice the queen recited the final invocation. "Initiate, by the will of Artemis, great huntress of the dark, you have one full day to complete your challenge. If you choose to complete two challenges at once, you still have to return to this spot no later than one candle mark past dawn tomorrow. Do you subscribe to the judgement of the goddess?"

I signaled for Gata to stay with Ori. "Yes, my queen."

She pointed in the direction of the first outpost. "Then your challenge has begun. Go!"

Her words still hung in the air when I took off for the trees. Easily running up the nearest one, I found my rhythm among the branches. I knew keeping to an average pace would have me out to the first outpost in less than one and a half candle marks. Then it would be another eight or so candle marks around the Telequire perimeter. The real challenge was the fact that if I rested for too long I risked being caught in the trees after dark. As it was, my return to the scouting hut from the first outpost would be on the ground after sunset. That was when I had planned to hunt for my second challenge. Again, the darkness would provide the most problems.

Mentally gathering myself, I pushed on even faster. I took a short break for water and a scout bar once I reached the outpost. The small bars made from nuts, compressed grains, and honey were a valuable source of energy when on duty. It was at the outpost that I picked up my first watcher. Unfortunately for the scout she was only able to keep up with my fast pace for about a candle mark before she fell behind. The second scout watcher was able to match my pace, and that was how it continued throughout the day. I tried to take short breaks every few candle marks. My only judge of time was the passage of the sun above the trees and the changing scouts that paced me.

I discovered eliminating from the canopy was difficult but not impossible. I estimated that I was about halfway around when I finally allowed myself a longer break. Fatigue had started to set in but nothing too bad. Spending a lifetime running the branches had been the perfect preparation for my Amazon challenge. It was as if my da had known what I was to become and spent his last seasons and energy to help me ready myself for the Amazon initiation. After another scout bar, some cured meat, a bit of goat cheese, and an apple, I continued on my way. By late afternoon my slower speed was obvious. My muscles were tiring more rapidly, but I estimated that I still had a couple candle marks before I once again reached first outpost since I had just picked up my fourth scout. They had been pacing me about one every two candle marks. After another water and food break I set out to complete the rest of the tree portion of journey.

When I completed the full circumference around the Telequire lands and arrived back at the first outpost I saw Coryn and Kylani. Both nodded in acknowledgement that I had completed the circuit and could now drop from the canopy. I had made very good time, leaving me with about a candle mark until sunset. That was not a lot of time to kill and gut something that would feed twenty warriors. I knew a roe deer was out of the question because it would be too small, but a red deer might be too large for me to carry. After resting for about ten candle drops I took off in the basic direction of the village.

Once I started seeing rub marks on the trees I quickly took to the branches again and strung my bow. Then it was a matter of waiting. I knew how plentiful the game was in the Amazon forest. I had hunted the trees many times and knew the deer often liked to travel at dawn and dusk. I said a brief prayer to the Goddess of the Hunt, thinking it could not hurt. And by divine happenstance, or simple coincidence, I heard something approach. The sky was turning orange in the distance as the darkness quickly rose from the ground and I knew I was running out of time. I had my arrow nocked and I was taking slow steady breaths when he approached my tree. It was the greatest stag I had ever seen and he would more than fulfill my challenge. His chest and neck were thick, well-muscled to hold up the two hand's worth of points on his antlers. With the season turning colder, the meat would be a welcome addition to the tribe. The problem was that there was no way I could carry the beast back to the village. It was at least three of me in weight. Watching him slowly approach, I had to make a decision. I could leave him and continue on my way empty-handed, then attempt my second challenge after a day's rest. I could let the buck go and stay in the tree hoping to shoot another in the short time I had until full dark. Or I could take the buck and risk not returning in time to complete my first challenge, thus being disqualified and forced to try again in the dead of winter.

Then, as if the goddess herself placed him in front of me, the great stag turned broadside not twenty paces away. My decision made, I put an arrow through his heart and then knowing I would not be able to track him in the darkness, sighted the leaping form and dropped him with second arrow. After retrieving my arrows I looked around for something I could use to aid in the gutting and cleaning process. Finally, I spotted a large tree that had fallen and was resting against the trunk of a great oak. I pulled the coil

of rope from my scout pack and tied one end to the center of the
dead tree, then looped it up and over another large sturdy branch
that was coming off the oak. Finally, I attached the other end of
the rope to the hind legs of the stag. I was out of breath from
dragging the great beast just ten paces to the base of the oak tree,
there was no way I could get it back to the village without at least
gutting and cleaning it. Once the rope was tight I went to the
leaning dead tree and starting shoving it off the trunk onto the
ground. Finally, with a great heave and a yell I got it to tip over.
Just as planned, the weight of it pulled tight and heaved the great
stag right into the air. I cheered aloud despite no one around to
hear me. The sky had turned a deep red and the woods around
appeared gloomy and ominous. I quickly skinned and cleaned the
deer and wrapped the prized organs in the skin before burying
the offal. Next I used the small hand axe from my pack to cut both
long and short branches and some vines and began lashing
together a simple travois that I could drag behind me. Once
complete I cut the rope and dropped the carcass to the ground. I
lashed it and the skin and organs to the travois then wiped my
hands on a rag in my scouting kit. The poles would normally be
difficult to maneuver through the underbrush but I was near a
regular trail. The hardest part would be to lift and push nearly
my body weight the rest of the way back to the village. I took a
few swallows of my second water skin. I had depleted the other
while still in the canopy. It was full dark with the moon just
barely rising by the time the travois was ready. By leaf and bow,
at least I had a full moon to guide me. Then with one great breath
I lifted the crossbar and started moving forward at a very slow
pace. Half a candle mark in I removed my old cloak and used it to
pad the crossbar. I was grateful for the cool night air because it
helped keep me from overheating. Given my slow progress I had
serious doubts my strength would last until I made it back to the
village. Time went by and my internal clock told me that I was
two candle marks in, but the trail markers showed that I was not
even half way. Fear of failure was rapidly rising within me but I
kept walking. One step, two steps, they all seem to blur together.
My legs tremored with each pace forward and my shoulders
burned with agony. With each break I took, I was afraid I would
not be able to start again. I feared that I would give in to
exhaustion and weakness and lie down on the soft loam,
slumbering until well past dawn. Or perhaps I would never wake
again. Candle marks passed, or maybe just drops. At one point I
collapsed into the leaves and tried to control my breathing. I
looked up to the moon. It was high in the sky and I no longer
knew the time. I was exhausted when I started the final part of

my journey and I had no words for what I had become as the stars whirled the sky above. Twice I had to rub cramps out of my legs and I developed blisters on both my hands. Yet I still found the strength to rise again and go on. Despite my ability to push forward through my exhaustion, I knew I neared the end of my strength. I began stopping more frequently and I had completely run out of water in my skin. Long after the blisters broke, my steps slowed as if I was wading through water. My arms and legs turned to stone as my back became a blaze of fire. My body was telling me that I needed to lay down and let the forest take me but my head and heart pleaded for perseverance. Every breath became a battle as my eyes grew heavy. Eventually the forest around me began to lighten with each inhale and exhale of sobbing breath. Every hundred paces I stopped simply because I could not continue more than that without a break. The moon started its decent and I knew the sun would soon break the horizon. I started taking my rests crouched on a low tree branch around the same time the morning birds began calling. I figured that if I slipped into sleep I would lose my balance and fall from the branch. It was the only thing I could think of to keep me awake. I fell off during two stops.

The sky started to turn pink as I emerged from the trees about fifty paces from the scout hut. I could see the same people gathered that had sent me off the morning before. Turning off my mind and ignoring my body, I slowly trudged forward. The only thing that mattered was taking one more step. I had to become an Amazon and fulfill my da's wishes for freedom. I would be free.

"Kyri..."

I did not consciously hear the voice, but something did. I tried to take another step, but my load became immeasurably heavy and my breath poured out of me in great heaving sobs. "I have to make it. I have to keep going..." My throat hurt and the words were raspy from fatigue and thirst.

Finally, the voices began to break through. "Kyri, little one, stop."

I looked up, hands still clenched around the crossbar of the travois. I could not tell dream from reality. "Sh...Shana?"

Another voice broke in to my scattered thoughts. "Kyri, let go. You did it."

I looked toward the other voice and saw those green eyes. "Ori?"

"Let go, Kyri." And I did. As soon as I dropped the sled, my body gave up its fight and I collapsed. Many hands grabbed me but I was beyond caring at that point. I did it, she said so. I smiled, then was claimed by the darkness.

I woke in a strange place and tried to move but could only wince in pain. Every muscle hurt and my hands were bandaged. After looking around I realized that I was in the healer's lodge. I could see late afternoon sun casting long shadows through the room. I tried to call for Thera but barely made a croaking sound. The noise must have been enough though because she bustled in from the back and smiled at me.

"Oh! You're awake. How are you feeling?" She gave me some water.

I groaned. "Like a tree rolled over me, then someone scraped all the skin off my hands and ran spikes through both my shoulders." I looked at her anxiously. The end of my trial was hazy. "I do not remember. Did I make it?"

She grinned broadly. "You made it, little one. I'll brew you some tea. You just rest here a bit longer. You didn't wake enough yesterday to be aware but your friends have been stopping by to check on you since you returned. Shana promised to stop by again before evening meal. She said she'd walk you to your hut if you were awake and didn't want to stay here any longer." I nodded and waited for my tea, amazed I had slept so long.

Shana arrived about a half candle mark later. "Heyla, you're awake. Nice to see that smiling face of yours."

I grimaced. "Broken string and bent arrow, it is either smile at you or cry." I gave her a serious look. "Thera said I finished on time, did they determine if the deer satisfied the second challenge?"

"Are you serious, Kyri? That was the biggest buck the nation has ever seen. No one knows how you got it back in one night and no one understands how you were able to drag it so far, for so long. Especially not after running the trees for ten candle marks straight. People are starting to think you are touched by the goddess."

I snorted and quickly realized that hurt too. I wished the tea would work a little faster. "More like touched in the head by crazed spirits."

She laughed, and took my bandaged hand. "I was really worried about you, sister. So was Ori. I'm so glad you are back to us safe."

I squeezed her hand in return. "I am sorry I worried you. I just had to do this my way."

A few heartbeats later, she let me go. "Feeling better yet? Are you up for a walk to your hut?"

I took stock of my basic aches and pains then gave a nod. "Sure." I got a lot of strange looks during our walk. When I asked Shana about it she just laughed and said I was becoming a legend.

I hung my head with her words. I did not want to become a legend, I just wanted to be an Amazon. She left my hut with the promise of returning with some food. I decided to lay down again to wait for her and promptly dozed off. I missed Gata. I was pulled from my slumber by knocking. Startled, I took in the dark cabin around me and shivered with the chilly air. Besides answering my door, a fire would have to be first priority. I tried to sit up and grimaced so I just called out to whoever was knocking. "Come in."

On my second attempt to stand Ori walked in, trailed by my Gata Anatoli. The golden haired queen smiled, and I found that my butterflies were mostly too tired to flutter. "You're up and around I see. I wasn't sure if you would be so soon after your trials."

"I am neither up nor am I around, I am merely vertical." I could see she had brought food with her so I made the effort to walk to my little table. It was slow and much too embarrassing. Hunched over and hobbling, I walked like a gran of four generations. Once I was seated, Gata came over and rested a paw on my leg. She gave her scratchy little roar, and I smiled. "Did you miss me, little Gata? I missed you."

The queen bustled around my hut, starting my fire and lighting a few oil lamps. I had used my last candle the night before the trial and I had no opportunity to get more from the supply hut. Candles were valuable so we were only allowed a few each seven-day. Olive oil lamps were plentiful but I did not like the smell and they were not as bright when I stayed up late fletching. The queen's actions in my hut took me by surprise and I was more grateful than I could say. Ori chuckled quietly while she worked. "She certainly did miss you. She paced around my hut for candle marks after you left." She reached out and gently touched her fingers to my bandaged hands after taking the seat across from me. "Yesterday you were so...out of yourself. How are you feeling today?"

I could only look at her and give a pained shrug. "I feel like someone strung me up like a skinned buck and used me for chobo practice."

She pulled her hand away and smiled at me. "I suppose that's to be expected after one spends a day and night doing the impossible."

I looked up, confused. "What do you mean?"

Ori sighed and ran a hand through her hair, careful not to dislodge her feathers. "Oh, Kyri, where do I even begin?" When she looked back at me something had changed.

"Ori, what is wrong?"

My queen laughed but there was no humor and no smile. "You broke my heart out there, Kyri. I was your last tree watcher."

My eyebrows shot up. "Before the first outpost? No, I saw someone else out there. I would have remembered you."

This time she grabbed both my hands in hers. "No. I was the watcher for your return to the village. I saw your hunt and every painful step of your journey back. I could neither speak to you nor could I interfere." She swallowed and looked down at our hands. "Why did you have to hunt? Why didn't you just wait another day to complete the second challenge? No one would have thought less of you." Suddenly she looked up with those intense green eyes. "Why did you go through so much pain and risk yourself like that?"

I could only stare at her, unable to look away and very aware of my aching hands being cradled in hers. I thought about my motives and all my reasons why. I wanted to give her an answer that made sense. One that she would understand. But I was unsure if I had any of those kinds of answers. I could not tell her of my fears of inadequacy. I did not want to admit that I was pulled to greatness simply out of the necessity of worth. "I...I have had a lot of confusing things in my head lately. There are things weighing me down, and things lifting me up. There is a constant pressure to do and be more as an Amazon. And those reasons why...I cannot tell them to you at this time, I...I am not ready. But what I can say is that this is who I am. Sometimes I have to do things my way even if it is the hardest choice. I have to prove to myself that I have earned something or no amount of praise and honor in the forest will convince me that I have done right."

I was not sure if it was the result of the trial and its toll on my body or something more, but I could feel the walls crumble. My eyes burned and I removed my hands from her grasp to cover my face. I did not want her to see me cry. I was an adult and I had completed the hardest two phases of the Amazon trial, I should not cry. Crying was for that girl on the homestead, the one who thought she was losing everything. I did not know how long I sat there silently gasping into my hands but I could feel my bandages wet through. After a few candle drops, or maybe a hundred, I heard Ori stand from the table. I assumed she would leave rather than watch me break down. While I did not want her to see me so weak, I also did not want her to go. Before I could expend another breath thinking about it, she embraced me from behind. "Shh, Kyri. It's going to be okay."

I lowered my hands, surprised at her compassion. When I

turned my head she was right there, inches from me. Her eyes looked so sad I could feel my own heart breaking. "I am so sorry, Ori, I did not mean to scare you. You are right, what I did was stupid." She could not have been very comfortable, bent over slightly and holding me in such a way. Yet she did not let go. But the look between us crossed that safe border, it was simply too close for too long. I could feel the flush start and the urge to lick my suddenly dry lips took me. She watched the movement of my tongue, sighed, and pulled back. Keeping that distance between us, she massaged my shoulders and I could not help the moan that escaped. "Oh bow and leaf, that feels amazing." I dropped my chin to my chest and enjoyed the relief to my screaming shoulder muscles.

She chuckled lightly. "I can imagine it does after hauling that loaded travois around like some sort of deranged heard beast. Perhaps we should assign you to till the fields in the southern end of Telequire instead of the plow horses, hmm?"

I turned my head and grinned. "Is that what my official job will be with the nation, my queen?"

"It's Ori, and we don't know what your job will be yet. What do you want to do?"

"I...um, I guess I do not know. I just assumed that I would end up as a scout. I have had the most training as a fletcher. I have also been trained in working with dyes and sewing, as my mam was a master cloak maker before she died. I am not nearly as good with cloth and the nation already has a fletcher and seamstress. However, you always need scouts and hunters..." I trailed off at the look on her face.

"But what do you want to do?"

I thought about it. The further I looked inside myself, the more confused I got. What could I possibly want to do, other than what I had always done? I had no other skills. But did I want to continue my set path or did I want to strike out in another direction and learn something completely new? I closed my eyes and searched as deep as I dared go...and found nothing. Hesitantly, as though saying the words aloud would cast me adrift, I whispered my answer. "I do not know anymore."

Ori just nodded and moved away from me again. She returned to her seat at the table and began unpacking food from the basket she brought. "Tomorrow at midday you will be called to prove your worth to the nation, then you will be given your rite of caste feather and your mask. Finally, there will be a feast tomorrow evening to welcome our newest member." She winked at me. "I heard a rumor we're having venison."

She had clearly planned on taking her meal with me since she brought enough for two. We ate in comfortable silence but after a handful of candle drops I thought of a question. "How do you and the council measure proof of worth?"

She swallowed and gave me another one of those smiles, the kind that crinkled the corners of her eyes and made the green seem especially bright. "Well, if it were up to me, I'd say you have proven your worth many times over. Honestly, it's a hard thing to measure but the proof itself doesn't have to be too much. We've had women display a skill or ability that would bring considerable worth to the tribe, such as wine making or horticulture. Having a master level ability could be considered proof. A very few come to us with wealth of one type or another, or we've had women donate something they have made that will benefit the nation as a whole." She looked at me curiously. "Why do you ask, haven't you decided on your proof of worth yet?"

Hesitantly, I admitted to my idea. "I actually have been working on a gift since I became an initiate." I stood and walked slowly to the corner where I kept my arrow store. I moved the cover and showed her. "So far I have about two hundred and fifty completed to donate to the tribe. I also plan on donating those four raider horses. Do you think that will be sufficient proof?"

She burst out laughing and I realized that perhaps I had been worrying too much. Nibbling on some of the roasted tree fowl, she spoke with a little more merriment than I thought necessary. "Goddess, are you really asking me if more than two hundred master quality arrows are sufficient as your gift? And you seem to think that you need to add four valuable horses too?" She shook her head and continued to eat, chuckling some more.

I covered the arrows and resumed my seat across from her. Picking up a piece of flatbread, I continued my own dinner. "Perhaps it has been on my mind a lot but I had to be sure."

She shook her head again. "Well, have your gift bundled and your horses ready if you're insistent on donating it all. We certainly won't turn it down."

I nodded. "Thank you, for everything." Then without warning, I found myself in the middle of a great jaw-cracking yawn. "Ugh! I am sorry, Ori. I still feel so drained."

"It's okay, completely understandable actually. You need to build up your internal stores after running yourself empty yesterday. Get some sleep, tomorrow will come soon enough." She quickly stood and cleaned up our meal and then I walked her to the door. In a move that surprised me, I was pulled into a strong hug. While I loved every heartbeat of it, I found it difficult to let her go at the end. We pulled apart again and both of us paused. Looking into those green eyes, I finally knew. Everything

Shana had been trying to tell me, all the worry Ori expressed over my trial, it suddenly became clear. There was something drawing us together and it scared me. I suspected it scared Ori as well. My gaze was so focused on the softness of her lips that I was startled to feel her calloused palm on my cheek. I swallowed nervously and she spoke. "Should you decide to talk about all the reasons you cannot say to me right now, I'm here for you and I will always listen." She paused and gave me another searching look. "Have a nice night, Kyri." Then, much as she had before my trial, she kissed me on the cheek right at the edge of my mouth. My heart hammered in my chest long after she had gone.

Chapter Ten

The Secrets We Keep

I WOKE THE next morning feeling nearly new again. I was also ravenous so rather than waiting to see if Shana would come find me, I took Gata to the meal lodge. Many women greeted me on the way and I felt bad for not knowing their names, but I knew that names and familiarity would come in time. I made my way to the tables after I put a plate of food together and grabbed some scraps for the cub. I scanned the lodge for Ori but disappointment rolled across me in waves when I did not see her. However, I *did* see Coryn as she smiled and waved me over. "It's the big game hunter! Are you looking for me, gorgeous?"

I blushed faintly but did not let her rattle me. "I was actually looking for a cute scout to have good conversation with. But I suppose I will have to be content with very simple conversation and you. Fear not, I will refrain from using large words." I smirked and began eating. The next thing I knew, a roll bounced off my head.

"Why you little woods weasel!" Our attention was diverted as Gata pounce on the roll and both of us laughed uproariously. We laughed so hard that it took a few candle drops for us to calm down again. "Seriously though, that was the largest buck I've ever seen. I still have no idea how you got it back here within the time limit. You had nothing left to give by the time you collapsed."

I shrugged. "Actually, when it comes to getting what I want I have everything to give. My biggest priority right now is receiving my Amazon rite of caste. You all feel like family to me now and I just want it to be official. The people in my life have a habit of slipping away and I will not let that happen with the Amazons. This is who I am, who I was always meant to be."

She held up her hands. "Whoa, sister, peace. We all feel the same about you. There isn't an Amazon in the Telequire nation who would turn you away. As far as I'm concerned, you've always been an Amazon. You just didn't have your feather yet. And where feathers are concerned, should you ever decide to hand yours out...hmm." She gave me a sly smirk and a wink.

I burst out laughing again and swatted her arm. I knew she was not serious for I could feel a real friendship developing between us since our talk in the bathing hut. "Oh please. I know your story Coryn, leader of all the scouts. Rumor has it that some of the rutting stags in the woods spend their days racing through trees."

She gave a mock affronted look, which did not at all fit on her smugly attractive face. "I have no idea what you're talking about. Who would spread such rumors about me?"

I snorted at her antics. "I would wager you have been offered so many feathers you could stuff a bed by now."

Shana chose that moment to sit down next to Coryn, bumping shoulders with the attractive woman. "She's completely right you know. You are nothing but a feather ruffler."

Coryn held up a hand. "Stop already. Goddess but you two are good for bringing my head down out of the trees."

I took a deep breath and attempted a serious smile. "You are right, Coryn. We should not pick on you so much. Perhaps we should pick on Shana, with her barn full of owl friends..."

Coryn roared. "Oh ho, she got you there!"

Shana grinned unabashedly and kept eating. When we were all finished, my sister-friend asked, "Are you ready to receive your rite of caste?"

I threw my shoulders back and sat a little straighter on my seat. I had finally passed the tests and that in turn gave me confidence I had not felt before. "Definitely. Are you ready to help me bundle a few hundred arrows and round up my four raider horses?"

The scout leader raised her eyebrows. "You're giving the nation all that?"

I nodded.

"Wow, you're a generous one, and now I'm really glad we're friends. You know, winter solstice is coming up and I'm very good at receiving gifts..." She waggled her eyebrows. This time Shana and I each swatted an arm.

Shana remarked, "I swear, you are nothing but a rutting hare."

The tall blonde looked back at her, eyes twinkling in merriment. "And just what is wrong with that? A lot of people like a good rabbit stew."

Assuming she heard about my wager with the queen, I whined. "Now why are you dragging me back into this? Hush both of you." I stood and took care of my meal dishes, calling over my shoulder. "Hurry up, Shana, you have work to do."

I stopped a little ways from the meal lodge and waited for her to catch up. She and Coryn exited at the same time then Coryn pulled her to a stop just outside the door. They looked like they were having a serious conversation, not at all the light-hearted banter that was being exchanged a few candle drops before. I was intrigued when I saw Coryn reach up and caress Shana's cheek. That was the moment that Shana noticed me waiting and quickly stepped back from the head scout. She said a few more words to Coryn then started walking toward me.

Shana did not stop when she reached me though. She just kept walking. I stood agape for a heartbeat before rushing to catch up. "What was that all about?"

She sighed. "It was nothing."

"Funny, it did not look like nothing. What was she saying to you?"

The ambassador stopped abruptly and turned to me. "I said it was nothing now let it be, Kyri."

She started walking again and I hustled behind her, my head whirling. Was that Shana? Was that the person as close to me as a sister? No. When we entered my hut I shut the door and grabbed her arm. "Stop."

She spun around and shot me a look that was both upset and angry. "Why can't you leave it be?"

I stepped forward and looked straight into her eyes. "Because you are my sister and I love you. Now tell me what she said that made you so upset. I thought we were all friends here." I cocked my head. "It almost looked as if...well, I do not know what it looked like. Were you two close once?"

Shana turned away and ran a hand through her hair. "Goddess, were we close once?" She laughed mirthlessly and started pacing. "Well she certainly wasn't close."

"Shana?"

My friend stopped mid pace. "Why don't you keep any wine here?"

"Maybe because I do not drink it?"

"Well it would be nice for when you have guests."

"It is only *halfway* to midday."

When she growled at me I grabbed her hand and lead her over to my bed. Pushing her down, I sat next to her and gently rubbed her back. "Talk to me."

She sighed, a distant look in her eyes. "So I told you that Ori, Basha and I have been good friends for many sun-cycles right? We all grew up together." I nodded. "Well, Coryn is also our age. She was always the golden child growing up. She was the best hunter, so tall, and goddess was she attractive." I stood to pour us both some water and she continued. "She practically cut a swath through half the eligible girls not long after we went through Ilio Choroú. Ori, Basha and I joked about it all the time. Basha even admitted that she'd spent the night with her once. Ori though...Ori always kept her distance. Some of it was probably due to the fact that she had beat out Coryn as First Scout Leader, which caused a little rivalry between them. But me..." She laughed again, a thoroughly unhappy sound. "Me...I was just a little nobody, not even in her field of view. And I was hopelessly in love with her."

Oh, broken string and bent arrow! Suddenly I understood a lot more about my best friend. "What happened, did you say something to her?"

She shook her head. "No. One night we were all drinking wine and sitting in the large bathing pool. We had stocked it with plenty of food and skins and it turned into an impromptu party of sorts. The next thing I knew, Coryn was on my side of the pool sitting very close. She started talking about how beautiful I was and how nice it would be to spend the night together. She said my eyes looked like the purest amber. Then she started kissing and touching me and I nearly melted into the water."

I nodded, understanding the feeling well but decided it best not to mention how familiar I was with Coryn's touch or kisses. "Like me with Baeza?"

She looked me right in the eye. "Yes. *Just* like you with Baeza, *exactly* like that." She was trying to tell me something and she waited a heartbeat for me to get it. Then I figured it out.

"You still walked in the goddess's footsteps?"

She nodded and I watched her swallow down the rising emotion. "I believed her that night and I let her lead me to a pile of furs in the back of the cave. It was wonderful and more beautiful than all my imagination had previously provided. The next morning I woke in her arms and I swear it was bliss. But when we were dressing it got awkward. She didn't really say anything and refused to meet my eyes. When she left, she just said that she'd see me around."

"Did you say anything to her or try to talk to her about it?"

Shana shook her head. "No, I just assumed that I was another one of her conquests. I thought that I was only good looking enough to share pleasure with after she'd had plenty of wine. So I let it go and I got over it."

"Are you kidding me?" I looked at her cascading dark curls, then at her eyes. She had the longest eyelashes of anyone I had ever met and her eyes were the most interesting shade of honey brown. There was a reason that my sister was a very popular owl friend. "Shana, you are gorgeous. I mean, I did not know you back then but I doubt that you have changed much. I also doubt that was the reason she left the way she did."

She just shrugged. "Well it hardly matters now, does it? Its ancient history and I've moved on."

I thought about all her owl friends, and the fact that other than me, and a select few good friends, Shana never let anyone close to her. I did not think my sister had moved on at all. Instead, I suspected that she let what happened to her affect all other relationships since that morning. "What did she say to you after I left?"

"She said that she had never seen me laugh so much before today and that she was really glad we were becoming friends. I told her that I wasn't interested in any more friends, that my life was busy enough. She just told me that everyone can use more friends."

Sensing more to the story, I prodded. "And?"

She took another sip of water and continued. "Then when we got outside and I looked up at her and she made a remark about how the sunlight made my eyes look just like the warmest amber."

"Let me guess, that is when you caught me staring and you walked away from her?" Shana nodded and I pulled her into a hug. "Come here. You are gorgeous, funny, kind, smart, and fierce with a knife. You're the best friend I have ever had. And you have a quiver's worth of regular owl friends. Do not for a heartbeat think that you are not wanted."

"Why didn't she want me?"

I sighed and held her tight. "I do not know, Shana, perhaps you were misunderstanding the situation. Everyone carries their own story and you will never know hers until you ask. Did you ever talk to Ori or Basha about it?" She shook her head. "Why not? They were your best friends, Shana. They could have helped you at the time and it sounds like you really needed someone to lean on."

"I just couldn't. I didn't want to think about it anymore. I didn't want to admit to them that I fell for all that charisma and charm like a hundred other women." We sat in silence, both of us lost in thought. I could feel her slowly regain control of herself and gradually pull away. She gave me a tremulous smile. "When did you get so wise, oh great huntress?"

Smiling back, I winked. "Well, I have had a few good friends to help me along the way."

She finally gave me a real smile and seemed to shake off her depressed mood. "So did you hear the news?" I shook my head, unsure what she was talking about after such an abrupt subject and mood change. "Rumor has it, we're having venison tonight. Apparently one of the hunters brought in a deer big enough to feed an army."

I punched her in the arm and she snorted at me. "Are you not here to work? Because I am pretty sure you came over to help me." We bundled the arrows into groups of twenty and left them by the door. "Let us go get the horses then we can probably tie these bundles together and drape them over their saddles."

She nodded. "Good thinking."

I managed to snag an apple for Soara on my way out the door. I felt guilty that I was only able to ride the mare a few times a seven day due to all my training, but she seemed happy enough and the stable master had already spoken to me about breeding her in the spring. We had to detour to Shana's hut on the way so she could pick up her ceremonial outfit and Amazon mask. While scouts were expected to wear it whenever they were on duty, most others kept them put away until special events. Once the horses were back at my hut and hobbled outside, we were able to get all the arrows tied to their saddles and packs. They were not bad looking animals considering who their previous owners were. Shana said she was not sure what she was going to do with her four and mentioned selling them on the next trade trip. Once they were loaded we went inside to change. I combed and re-braided my hair then grabbed my fall cloak.

Shana looked at me critically. "Take out your braid." I raised an eyebrow. I always wore my hair braided to keep it out of my face. "It will make it easier to receive your feather." I nodded, loosened my hair, and once again stood for her approval. "I think you'll do." She wrapped her arm around mine before I could fuss any longer. "Come on, let's go make an Amazon out of you!"

I could only mumble "Oh, gods…" before I was pulled through the door into the bright sunlight.

When we arrived at the center of the village, I looked for Ori but did not see her. My hands were sweating and Shana leaned near to whisper in my ear. "Calm down, you'll be fine." Suddenly there was a ripple in the crowd and I watched the queen and council walk through and up the steps of the dais. The regent and conference of elders followed close behind. Once all were in place, the queen stepped forward to address the nation. Everyone on the dais wore their masks and I did not like the fact that I was unable to see Ori's face. The crowd hushed immediately and she began to speak.

"For generations the Amazons have been tasked with certain duties by our goddess, Artemis. We have been given the duty to build a nation of strong women, to protect them, and nurture them. We have been tasked to watch over the forests and creatures of the land. And over those many generations, the tribes have grown to number twelve, strong and plentiful. Girl children are born and grow up to be Amazons if they choose the way of the goddess. But there have been some occasions where women come to the tribes and prove that they too have the soul and heart of an Amazon." She took a breath and looked around before letting her masked gaze fall on me. "The Amazon rite of caste is both a privilege and a duty. The trial you face to earn your privilege is only the beginning. The real test of being an Amazon happens over a lifetime. It is in spending the rest of your days putting your sisters and the good of the nation first in your mind. The real test of an Amazon is in devoting your life to protecting women and innocents, and giving up that life if necessary."

She paused while Basha stepped forward carrying a beautifully carved mask. "We are here today to bear witness to an initiate receiving her Amazon rite of caste. Kyri Fletcher, please come forward." The crowd parted and I brought my four loaded horses through. I stopped in the area just below the dais and went down to one knee. She continued. "Though unconventional, you have successfully completed both the first and second trial at the same time. The only thing remaining is for the nation to accept your proof of worth. Stand and state what you bring to the Telequire tribe, as an Amazon."

I rose and spoke loud enough to be heard by the assembled people. "If it pleases the nation, I bring with me four horses with full saddles and tack. I am also donating two hundred and fifty of my forest fletch arrows. I was set to test for my Master's Mark before traveling to the Amazons, so while they are not official master level, I have all confidence that they are master quality." I let the reins of the horses drop to the ground and took one more step toward the dais and the masked queen. "I also give myself. I am a tool for the nation to use and take value. Let me be a hunter or a scout for you. Let me be a fletcher or your seamstress. It matters not what you need me to do, because my spirit is yours to command." I tried to see the green eyes hiding within her mask. "If the nation is threatened let me be your shield, and if the nation seeks retribution for a wrong done, you will find no other arrows as true as mine. My heart and soul have always been of an Amazon. I have only been waiting for my feather to truly fly."

The queen waited a few heartbeats to make sure I was done, then turned to the council members. "Council, what is your judgment concerning the initiate's third challenge?"

As one they intoned. "The initiate has been found worthy."

The queen then turned to the conference of elders and the Regent. "What is your judgment concerning the initiate's third challenge. They answered in much the same manner. "The initiate has been found worthy."

Finally, she looked out at the gathered nation and posed the question to the amassed women. "Telequire Amazons! What is your judgment concerning the initiate's third challenge?"

As one, the crowd roared around me, a great and echoing word cried to the heavens. "Worthy!" When the gathered women fell quiet again, the queen looked straight into my eyes.

"Kyri, daughter of Mira and Galen Fletcher, please come to me." On wobbly legs, I walked up the steps of the dais and took my place next to her. "With kindness and compassion, you have shown us your heart. With skill and perseverance, you have shown us your soul." She reached into her hair and untied a feather that she did not have before the ceremony. She reached over and tied it into my hair, a few fingers behind my temple. "With the blessing of Artemis and this feather, may you soar above the Amazon nation to watch over all of your sisters." She then received the mask from Basha and placed it over my head. "With the blessing of Artemis and this mask, may you strike fear into all those who would trespass against us and let its wood surface remind you of the forests that Amazons have sworn to protect." Once the mask was in place she grabbed my hand and raised both of ours high above our heads. "Please welcome Kyri, our sister and newest Telequire Amazon!"

In that moment I learned another important use for the Amazon mask. They were good for more than just instilling fear into the hearts of our enemies. They were also good at hiding my tears of joy. I sent out a prayer to the heavens on the winds of my exaltation. 'Thank you, Da, for forcing me to do the right thing even though it hurt. This is my family now, these are my people. I finally feel like I have come home.'

The queen turned to me and I finally saw the green of her eyes. They looked as though they were swimming, but it could not be. What reason would she have to cry? She spoke in a voice just loud enough for me to hear. "Congratulations, Kyri."

THE CELEBRATION THAT evening was the happiest night of my life. Even though I was the uncomfortable center of attention, the laughter, friendship, and love that poured from my new Amazon family put me at ease. I got the privilege of eating with the queen and council on the dais. Maybe privilege was not exactly the right word. Everyone had stared at us through the meal like we were fish in a pond and I figured out why Ori hated official dinners so much. But afterwards was wonderful. I joined in the games and activities with a lot of giggling and silliness. I

also joined in the dancing and singing even though I was no
master at either. Shana talked me into a bit of watered wine,
insisting that it was not bad. And she was right, I actually
enjoyed that as well. I figured out that, as with many other things,
moderation was the key. The only thing that marred my perfect
evening was the fact that Ori had not come to say hello once the
ceremony was complete. We did not get much opportunity to talk
during dinner and afterwards she kept to herself. At one point
after losing a round of wrestling, I looked up to the dais. Ori was
sitting on her throne talking to Basha but her eyes were not in the
conversation and her hands were gripping the chair tightly. That
was when I decided to find Shana and ask why Ori was not
joining us.

I pulled Shana from a circle of her friends after promising I
would bring her back, then took her somewhere relatively quiet a
few dozen paces away. She looked alarmed. "What's wrong?"

"Uh...sorry. Nothing is wrong I guess, I just wanted to ask
you why Ori has not come down to celebrate with everyone." A
thought popped into my head that perhaps I simply was not
aware of all the rules and practices for their ceremonies. "Or is it
a rule that she has to stay up there the entire time when new
Amazons receive their rite of caste?"

Shana sighed, scratched her ear, and sighed again. "There's
no rule, Kyri."

"But why then? This is the happiest day of my life, why
would she not want to come celebrate with me?"

Shana looked at the ground for a few heartbeats then back to
me. I did not recognize the look in her eyes. "This is really hard
for me. You know I'm good friends with you both, right?"

I was confused, she made no sense. "Why is it hard? I am
friends with her too."

She shook her head. "No, Kyri. What I mean is that just as
you tell me things in confidence, not wanting other people to
know, she also holds my confidence." She gave me a piercing
look. "If you want to know why she won't come down and
celebrate with you, you'll just have to ask her. It's not my
knowledge to tell."

I swallowed thickly, worried at what Shana could not tell me.
"D...does she not want to be friends with me anymore, Shana?"

Her eyes softened as she reassured me. "No, little one, it's
not that. But you'll have to ask Ori for her reasons."

She watched me, waiting for me to understand. I found that I
only had a small voice left inside. "Okay. Thank you, sister."

She waited to make sure I was okay then walked back to the
circle of her friends. I went the opposite direction, into the edge

of the woods. Gata stayed with me and when I went up into the canopy, she followed. Sitting on the branch of a large oak, I slowly stroked my wild friend. I had not been there long when a voice startled me from a neighboring maple. "The trees around here grow some strange fruit."

I looked up and saw her crouched on a branch of the next tree, about two body lengths from me. "Ori! You scared me, I never even heard you approach."

She grinned. "Didn't I tell you I was a very good scout?" I smiled back, still feeling sad. "What's the matter, Kyri? Why are you out here and not back there celebrating with all your friends?"

I gave her the most honest answer I had. "Because not all my friends were celebrating with me." I peered at her closely and saw her swallow. "Are you still my friend, Ori?"

She shut her eyes, frozen in place. My words must have hurt her because when she opened them again they were swimming with regret. "Of course I'm still your friend. As a matter of fact, I consider you a very good friend."

I turned away from that gaze, it was too much. "Then why? Why have you been avoiding me?" I heard a faint rustling and the next thing I knew she was on my branch. Gata chose that moment to leap down and leave us alone in the tree. Ori sat in the space next to me, so close that our bodies pressed together from shoulder to thigh. She took my hand in hers and sat there for a few candle drops. I did not know what was going on, but her nearness had snared me as sure as any spider's web. I could not prevent the shiver when she turned my hand over and started tracing the lines of my palm with her fingertip. I whispered, "What is wrong, Ori?"

She stopped tracing and sighed. "How do I explain it to you? I don't really know…" I waited, understanding that she would continue when ready. Finally she began again. "Tell me, why don't you leave the nation and go get your Master's Mark when I know that has always been in your heart?"

I looked at her strangely, unsure why the subject was coming up when we had spoken about it so recently. "I already told you. It is because I have things I need to do here. I have priorities and goals and I do not want anything to interfere with that. I told you this before, why do you ask again?"

She continued. "And how would you feel if someone kept tempting you into leaving, trying to convince you to forget about those goals and responsibilities and let your heart take over? What if you knew there was a master fletcher in a town nearby and all you had to do was leave Telequire for a few days to find him. Would the temptation be greater?"

I still did not understand. "It would be hard for someone to keep tempting me with what was in my heart, and even harder if I knew that which I most desired was so near. Why are you asking me these things?"

Pressed together as we were, her face was very close when she finally looked up. Peering into her eyes I found that everything was written there for me to see. All the words and the glances, all the things I had not previously understood, everything had become bare on the planes of her face. I swallowed back the fear and elation and continued to look at her, to search for her meanings. My voice was a mere whisper when I finally spoke. "Is that what I am to you, a temptation?" She finally broke our gaze and I asked again. "Am I the Master's Mark that would keep you from your goals?"

Her hand clenched around mine but she refused to look at me. Her voice, when it finally came, was quiet like fog. "Yes."

All the breath left me at once and my heart soared. Then, taking in the actions and demeanor of my queen, it quickly plummeted to the ground. My queen....Ori was my queen. I realized the dilemma, I understood exactly why she felt pain in my presence. I was beneath her, and no temptation in the world would rise me up. I was just another lowly Amazon, barely into my feather and mask and with no real profession to speak of. I had nothing to offer. She could not love me and be queen. Every single thing before that moment, every heartbreak I had suffered until then, seemed small and incomparable. But I knew that if I still wanted a friendship with her I could never let her see my pain. Pulling myself back mentally, I let out the breath I had been holding and separated our hands. "I understand, my queen."

She immediately looked up in alarm and even though my heart was breaking, I smiled to reassure her. "I will always be here for you, Ori. No amount of heartache or disappointment can break the bonds of true friendship." I sat up straighter and looked down at the forest floor. "Now, are you ready to join the celebration with us? I hear the guest of honor is tall as a tree and no small hand at shooting a straight arrow. Shall we go see?"

She laughed and I politely ignored the pain of it. "Thank you, Kyri." She put a hand on my arm and gave me another one of her looks, ones that were previously unreadable to me. "I want you to know that I feel the same way. Now, I think it's time we should be getting back." After a heartbeat's hesitation in order to take in the full meaning of her words, I stood. Then with a grin I did a flip down to the soft loam beneath our tree and she did exactly the same. "I hear the guest of honor is pretty fast in the trees too."

I laughed. "Hey, want to hear a joke?"

"Sure."

I grinned. "How many men does it take to sew a dress?"

"I don't know, how many?

"None, sewing is a woman's work!" She growled and punched me and I laughed even harder. I had heard the joke in a village near my homestead and thought it stupid then. But I knew it would make even less sense in a nation of women. The rest of the evening went much the same way. We found Shana and Basha, and all of us joined a group dancing around the fire. At one point Shana asked if the queen and I had spoken. I simply nodded but did not say any more. She was right, sometimes there were things we held in confidence for others. And I was learning that sometimes those things were merely our own secrets we kept to ourselves. It was late when I finally got to bed, the moon had long since risen, but not so late that I could not take the time to hang my new mask reverently from a peg on the wall, next to the shelf with my other memories.

DESPITE HOW DIFFERENT having my mask and feather made me feel, my schedule remained just as busy after my trial was complete. The only real change was that I was temporarily assigned to the moon shift scouts. It was different for me, having to adjust my sleep schedule to accommodate the late shift, but I enjoyed working with the scout leader, Dina, and all my sisters in the trees. Coryn warned me ahead of time that Dina was a bit of a practical joker. She also gave me a heads up that the moon shift scout leader was as much of a feather ruffler as she was. I thought it unlikely that anyone could rival the First Scout Leader in that regard but thanked her for the warning nonetheless.

Things were so busy with settling into my new scout troop, and continuing my training with the weapons master, that it took a fortnight before I could start to make good on my wager with Ori. I went searching for Gata one morning not long after first meal. Acting on a hunch, I went to the queen's hut and knocked on the door. Ori opened it and I saw my wild friend lying on a large cushion near the queen's chair. Though the leopard was growing at an alarming rate, clearly someone still spoiled her like a little cub. I laughed aloud at the cat lying in luxury. "Oh ho, look at you. Clearly the queen's chamber holds a lot more comfort than mine." She just opened an eye and flicked her ear at me.

Ori laughed. "She likes to keep me company while I review scrolls and write treaties. I didn't want her on my bed but I felt bad so I had a cushion made for her."

I shook my head and knelt to stroke her soft spotted fur. "You spoil her, Ori. She will never want to return to the wild when she is grown."

Ori looked at me then down at the hand I had running through Gata's fur. "Did you really expect her to?"

I realized what she meant immediately and blushed. "Ah, I see what you mean. Perhaps she is a bit too tame to really survive and thrive out there with the other predators." I sighed, sad that I had partially failed at trying to foster the cub. "Anyway, I actually came here to take her hunting with me and see if you are interested in dinner tonight?"

"Dinner? Don't you usually eat in the meal lodge?"

I smiled, glad I could surprise her for once. "Well, I do when I am not planning on making a large pot of rabbit stew."

Ori's eyes widened and her voice dropped a little lower. "Rabbit stew? You're making rabbit stew?"

I grinned, seeing the reaction I had hoped for. "Well, yes. After all, we did have a wager."

Another surprised look washed across her face, then one of apology. "Oh. I'm so sorry, Kyri, I completely forgot. I've been so caught up with the Thessaly Agreement..." She waved her hand toward the table next to the door. It was covered in scrolls, short lists, and half a dozen mangled quills. Ink stains dotted the wood surface and her fingers.

I held up a hand. "No problem, I completely understand. I have been busy adjusting to the moon shift anyway."

She smiled in relief and waved at hand toward a chair so I took a seat. "And how are you liking the moon shift scouts? Were you warned about Dina yet? That one's got a golden tongue on her. She'll talk you into your gran's cloak if you let her...or out of your own skirt." She chuckled, clearly remembering the scout well.

"Yes, I was warned by Coryn of all people. I think she was legitimately worried about me."

"Coryn?" The queen roared with laughter. "Like she's one to talk. Why, I think the only one that rivals that woman for owl friends is Shana." She stopped and a thoughtful look came over her. "I wonder if they've ever spent the night together."

I wisely said nothing since it was not my story to tell. However I was glad Ori did not see my face just then because I had never been good at hiding my emotions. I was a terrible liar and I knew it. But her words gave me pause. Shana, who had a barn full of owl friends, adapted her behavior in response to being hurt when she was younger. It made me wonder if there was a similar reason behind Coryn's promiscuity. I shoved those thoughts away until I had more time to consider them. "Anyway, my time with them has been good, if busy. Kylani is also running me around, trying to instill some staff and chobo proficiency into me. Shana has moved me up to using two knives during our practices together so I must not be a total failure there. But the sword..." I was at a loss when it came to describing my hesitancy with the large blade. I just shrugged at her instead.

"You want to talk about it? We could go over your schedule and see which days would work best for sword instruction." Her eyes darted to my bow and quiver and she suddenly remembered that I was in her hut for a reason. "Oh, sorry! I forgot you were here to pick up Gata. We can talk about it another time if you like."

"Actually, I stopped by to take Gata hunting with me. But if you are not too busy, you could come with us so you can see the training I have been doing with her."

I could see her consider the idea, glance at her scrolls on the table, then grimace. Finally, just as I was about to tell her not to worry about it if she had too much to do, she gleefully responded. "Sure. I need a break from all this anyway. Let me grab my cloak and my gear."

No sooner had we walked out the door when Basha approached. "Or..." She shot a quick glance at me and suddenly realized she was in public.

"Queen Orianna, have you finished with the newest trade agreement? Head councilor Gerta is asking to review it."

The queen grinned at her, unabashedly. "No I haven't, and you can tell her I won't have it for two more days."

Basha sighed. "Maybe you should tell her. You know how testy she gets when it starts turning colder."

Another unapologetic grin. "Nope, I'm busy."

The regent raised an eyebrow. "And what is more important than the Thessaly agreement?"

Finally Ori gave her a serious look. "Rabbit stew."

Now Basha's eyes twinkled. "Of course it is." She looked at me and laughed. "I should have known the cause. Now you've done it, I'm afraid rabbit stew is Ori's greatest weakness."

Basha did not catch it but I clearly heard Ori's murmured words. "Not any more..."

I smiled at Basha's comment and ignored the queen's. "Perhaps I could make enough for everyone, if you are interested. You two, Shana and myself. We just need to find a place big enough to fit all of us and someone has to bring bread."

My suggestion immediately caught Basha's interest. "Oh, that would be great. I'll bring a couple loaves of bread. And Ori's hut is big enough for twice as many people."

I nodded, and Ori spoke up. "Can you let Shana know to save her meal time for us later? We're heading out to hunt rabbits right now. That way Kyri has the afternoon to let the stew simmer."

"Yeah, I can do that for you." She turned and called back over her shoulder, "Have fun you two. And bring back lots of rabbits."

HUNTING WITH ORI was fun, but hunting with Ori and Gata was an entirely different experience. I showed her all the signs that Gata had learned and she was considerably impressed. The first two rabbits followed our normal process, but I only gave Gata a single leg from each. Ori was shocked that the big leopard cub would bring the animal down then let me take it from her. She seemed convinced that I was touched by the goddess. All my exasperated explanations were not sufficient to change her mind so I made a suggestion when we hunted the third rabbit. "Since you refuse to believe that I am not touched by the goddess, I will let you give the signals to Gata for the next rabbit."

The queen scoffed at my idea. "She won't listen to me."

I smirked. "There is only one way to find out. Now hush." Just as predicted, the cat followed every signal Ori gave her. In the end we had five rabbits, but I let Gata have the very first one we killed as a reward.

Ori looked thoughtful on our way back. "Do you think she'd listen when hunting larger prey?"

I considered the idea. "I do not see why she would not. We hunted a dear on equinox eve." I watched my friend as we walked back to the village and her face turned dark.

"What about against men?"

I stopped walking, completely taken aback. I had not thought of anything beyond hunting. But it made sense for her to help with more if she was able, and the queen would be the person concerned most with the safety of our nation. The entire Amazon culture was centered on protecting our land and way of life, and protecting women in need. The idea had interesting symmetry. Instead of the Amazons protecting a wild creature, a wild creature would be protecting us. Ori stopped with me and waited for my thoughts to catch up. Looking into her questioning eyes, I shrugged. "I never really considered that before. Perhaps I should try taking her out scouting the next time I rotate out to fourth scouts and see how she interacts with the others. And see how she interacts with any strangers we come across."

The queen nodded. "I think taking her out on perimeter

scouts is a great idea. I'd like you to keep me informed on her progress when you try it. Just ask Coryn to set up a trial rotation."

I smirked and bowed. "Oh yes, my queen, anything for you."

She pointed at me and laughed. "Impertinent pup! You clearly spend too much time with Shana."

Even I had to admit that the stew turned out wonderful. My mam would have been proud. But the meal was far surpassed by the camaraderie of friends. Ori said she could make time every other day for sword practice, and I told her I would make stew every seven day. That would coincide with my off days from scouting. Life was very good, and that helped soothe the pain I had buried deep within my heart.

Chapter Eleven

The Gifts We Bring

THE WEEKS OF Fall ran together. Before I knew it, the leaves had abandoned the trees and all the Amazons had switched to their winter wear. While it was known to get cold in Telequire nation, we rarely had to deal with the water freezing over. And it was practically unheard of to get snow, unlike the Tanta nation. They had stories about great blizzards and snow piled up to your waist. Thankfully there was nothing like that in our forest. But scouting in the trees with your fingers stiff from cold and your breath coming out in great white clouds was no fun.

Winter solstice was rapidly approaching and besides all the other things I had been doing to stay busy, I had also been working on gifts for my friends. I spent the most time and energy on the cloak I made for the queen, having decided to slightly alter my mam's original design, adding a removable inner lining. It was long, just as Shana had suggested. The cloak itself was made of tightly woven wool and dyed in a patchwork of greens. It had small leaf-shaped pieces of material sewn across the shoulders, which were layered down the back. The removable inner lining was made from all the rabbit furs I had saved from my stew hunts, pieced together into one large fur. The fur was a mottled variety of browns and was very soft and supple to provide the most comfort against the skin. I sewed leather laces to the inside of the cloak, to make it easy to attach the rabbit liner. Once it was all put together, I tried it on. It was a few inches short for me but it was the most comfortable thing I had ever worn.

For Shana, I traded a few pots of my rabbit stew and some custom fletched arrows to the blacksmith for help creating a set of matching daggers that had handles made from my wild boar tusks. I got a great trade because she already had the blades created, we merely had to carve the handles and join them together. One dagger had the Amazon symbol meaning 'Brave' inscribed along the length of the handle, and the other had the symbol for 'Beautiful.' The blacksmith did a masterful job and I considered ordering my own set from her. Or maybe I would order my first sword instead. I had not chosen one at the time I received my rite of caste because I did not feel that I was good enough to carry a sword. But after a few moons of instruction from the queen, I was finally confident enough to pick out a blade. I used more rabbit fur to create a scroll satchel for Basha, and I learned Coryn's favorite colors and created two dozen arrows with custom fletching for her.

The day before solstice eve, Shana stopped by in the morning to take first meal with me. We missed eating together when I was scouting on the moon shift. But since I had returned to the morning shift troop, I was able to meet with my friends more regularly. Before we could leave, I stopped her to show off the cloak and get her opinion. I had it rolled up and stored with some cedrus wood until the time came to give it to Ori. "Hold on, Shana, look at this before we go." I unrolled the cloak and held it up so she could look at it. "I finally finished the cloak for Ori, what do you think?"

She took it from my hands and her mouth gaped open. "Kyri..." she breathed out.

I prompted anxiously, "Well, what do you think?"

She spun it behind her and put it on. "Goddess. This is beautiful, Kyri." She sighed and rubbed her face into the fur liner. "I am so jealous right now, you have no idea how magical this feels."

I laughed and held out my hand. "Okay, I understand. Now give it back."

She pouted but did not remove the cloak. "Can't I just wear it to first meal? It's so warm."

"No, she might see it. Now hand it over, you woods weasel."

She laughed and begrudgingly gave it back. "So what did you get me for solstice, hmm?"

I once again stored the cloak and pushed my Amazon sister toward the door. "The guts of fifty rabbits. Now get out of here, I am starving."

She continued to pester me all the way to the meal lodge. "What about my birthday, would you make me one of your cloaks for my birthday? Next solstice?"

Once we had plates full, we turned and Coryn waved us to her table. I could sense Shana tense behind me but she nodded when I glanced at her. When we sat down, Coryn gave us both a big grin. "Heyla, ladies, are you both ready for solstice eve tomorrow?"

I grinned at her, excited because I had finished all my gifts. "Yes, I am." I then addressed both her and Shana. "Are the solstice and equinox eve ceremonies different for each season, or are they all the same?"

"Different."

"Mostly the same."

I snorted. "Oh, you two are a real help."

Just then, Basha sat down with a full plate and joined in. "You wanted help with something and asked these two hoot owls? Sister, you sure are getting your information from the wrong sources."

"Oh? Who would be the right source?"

She spoke around a bite of food. "Well, the priestess is the best one, or even Ori. The queen plays a role in the ceremony, just as with all other ceremonies. Ask Ori."

"Ask Ori what?"

I looked up into a pair of smiling green eyes. Her blonde hair looked tousled like she had just woke up and I briefly wondered if she had rushed to meet us for morning meal. I moved over to make room, wanting yet not wanting her to sit next to me. "I was just asking whether the solstice festival would be the same as equinox, or if it is different for each season." She crowded in next to me, causing a little shiver down my spine. Did I purposely leave her a small amount of room? I was pretty sure I would not do that. I briefly considered moving over so our legs did not touch under the table...then changed my mind. I liked the feeling too much.

She interrupted my internal debate. "Oh, that's easy enough. It's mostly the same, and yet completely different."

The hoot owls across the table started flapping in response. "I told you so. No, I was right." The bickering continued for another candle drop or two. Basha laughed again, setting her eating knife down to avoid hurting herself.

I turned to the queen. "As you can see, the entertainment is lively this morning."

She snorted and shook her head. "If you want, stop by this evening when you're finished with scout shift. I'll try to explain it a little better than our friends across the table."

My heart stuttered for a beat, as it always did when faced with the prospect of spending time alone together. "Thank you. I will." Coryn and I had to rush since we had to start scout shift. When I got ready to leave, I saw Gata settled in by the queen's feet. I gave a little whistle, signaling it was time to go. She flicked an ear in my direction and ignored me. With a muttered "spoiled..." I whistled again a little louder. She finally stood, if reluctantly, then stretched and padded after us.

Coryn, who had watched the entire exchange, chuckled. "She's getting spoiled."

"Thanks for pointing out the obvious. You can blame the royal one back there. She has a giant cushion for Gata in her hut." She nodded solemnly in what I thought was agreement. "Oh yeah, that's much worse than letting her take up half your bed." She smirked and I made a rude gesture, one of several I had learned. No one could say my time with the Amazons had not been educational. She laughed even more. "It's a good thing you walk the path of the goddess, otherwise you'd have no room for your owl friends."

I blushed. "Oh ha-ha, you are very funny this morning, Coryn."

"I try." She smiled. "Now, let's move a little faster. It doesn't look good for the scout leader to be late for duty. Race you to the trees!" She took off with a good two- stride lead and sadly I had only made up a stride by the time we caught up with the rest of the group. We had a rivalry but it was all in good fun. I think it helped that I had no plans on being a scout leader. I liked having a lot of free time to work on my other crafts. Scouting was a duty for me, but not my passion. The shift was uneventful, which was a good thing since the scouts were all more boisterous than normal. When we were finished with our circuit I started to head to my hut when Coryn called out. "Kyri, can you wait for me? I have to give my report to Deka, and then I'd like to talk to you about something."

I sighed, already hoping to spend some time in one of the bathing pools before heading to see Ori. "Sure."

After a few candle drops she came jogging over. "Ugh, I need a bath."

"I do too. Why not grab your stuff and meet me at the smallest hot pool? We can talk there, it is private."

She grinned. "That is a great idea. Okay, I'll see you there in a quarter candle mark." After a handful of moons with the Amazons, I had finally gotten used to their openness when it came to all things, including nudity. That still did not stop me from blushing when Coryn undressed and stepped into the pool. It was only natural to look. She was my height, athletic, and extremely attractive. I was not surprised she had so many owls after her. Once she settled safely in the water, she started talking. "I don't usually give out many solstice gifts, mostly because I've only got a few close friends."

"I understand that. I am only giving out a few this sun-cycle too. Still, it is a lot more than when it was just me and my da."

I could sense that she seemed a little nervous, which was probably why she started washing her hair while continuing the conversation. For a distraction. "Anyway, my question for you is, do you think it would be odd if I made gifts for Ori, Basha, and Shana? I mean, we were never very close friends before. We just ran in different crowds I guess. But since you and I have become good friends, I find that I'm hanging out with all four of you a lot more."

I thought about her question honestly. "You are right. When I first arrived, you never seemed particularly close to them. You and Shana actually acted a little antagonistic toward each other. But now you *do* spend a lot of meals with us so I think it would be all right." When I mentioned Shana, a strange look crossed her face but she quickly hid it. However, I was not going to let that little worm of information disappear in the soil of our conversation. "What? Is there something wrong between you and Shana? Did you have a falling out in the past?"

The scout leader shut her eyes and blew out a long sigh. "You could say that."

"What in the world could you have had a falling out about? Did you steal one of her owl friends?" I smirked but watched her closely to see how she acted in the face of my questions. I felt a little bad for leading her but I was tired of seeing Shana in pain whenever the attractive scout was near. I really wanted all my friends to get along, though I knew logically that you could not always have your wishes met so easily. The pinched look on Coryn's face spoke of uneasiness and remorse. Sensing her shell was cracking, I tapped a little more. "What happened, Coryn? What is the matter?"

She finally opened her eyes and they were swimming with tears. "Can I talk to you about something private, just between us?"

"Sure, I will not break your confidence." I could keep her secrets just as well as I had been keeping Shana's.

We both continued washing while she spoke. "I made a mistake cycles ago, not long after I got my Amazon mask. You may have guessed by now, but the stories people tell about me are mostly true. I do like to have a lot of owl friends. I enjoy nightly pleasures and I like meeting and getting to know a variety of women. Everyone wants the same thing and it's all good. In the end it's just a game, only playing my way everyone wins." She looked up and I nodded to let her know I was paying attention. "There have been a few people that I've liked as more than owl friends, but I'm so used to playing the game that I didn't want to pursue something and end up losing a friendship over it."

She paused and took a deep breath. "Coryn, I do not see anything wrong with that when no one is getting hurt. It is your life to live as you choose."

She leaned over to grab the water skin she had left near the pool. She took a swallow, then passed it to me. "But someone did get hurt. Do you remember the night in the bathing pool when you told me that you walked in the footsteps of the goddess and weren't ready to leave them? I stopped then and accepted your friendship instead. Do you know why I never pushed you again?"

I blushed, remembering the feeling of her hand on my thigh and mouth on my neck. "Yes, I do remember that. You are not exactly easy to forget, Coryn." We both laughed. "I remember that it bothered you a lot. Why?"

Again, the regret came back and it was completely out of place on the confident scout. She went on and I could tell that it was hard for her. "Because I took someone from that path once, unknowingly, and I've regretted it ever since." Her gaze was far away as she remembered what she had done. "It was after a celebration, a big group of us were drunk on Amazon wine and we decided to relax in the big hot pool. I ended up sitting next to Shana, and I think we both know how beautiful she is." I nodded and gave her a smile. "Well, she had been telling funny stories about when she took a wagon of Amazon trade goods to market and ended up returning with three times their worth. She...Goddess, but she was amazing that night. And no, it wasn't just the wine. Shana was someone I'd been watching for a while." Her voice was a little raspy so I tossed the water skin back to her. After a few more swallows, she finished her tale. "Anyway, we spent the night together and it was incredible. She was so sweet and passionate and sharing pleasure with her touched something deep inside me. But it wasn't until the next morning when the wine was out of my system that I realized I had taken her from the path of the goddess. I felt terrible because that is something that should be special, with someone special. I didn't know how to act after that and I think I made everything worse. I took something from her that should have been saved and I know she will never forgive me."

"Coryn..." She looked up at me in question. "How did she act after?"

The stoic woman thought back again. "She seemed happy, we both were. I remember falling asleep together on the furs and then waking up with a headache. I stood to find some water and noticed a little blood where we had been lying and quickly thought about all her previous behaviors...and I knew. She wasn't just shy, she was inexperienced."

I pushed again gently. "And how did she act when she woke up? Was she sad, or mad at you?"

"No. Again she woke and smiled at me. And even with both of us sleep tousled and the wine shooting arrows into my head, she was just as beautiful as the night before. But I'll admit that I was a coward. She tried talking to me but I just ran. I avoided her for a long time after that because I felt so guilty for what I'd done. To this day, I still feel guilty."

"Oh, Coryn...you big, dumb, beautiful woman." She scowled so I quickly continued. "It does not sound like she was mad at you for taking her virginity."

"But I did take her virginity and she's hated me ever since."

I shook my head. "No, Coryn, you took her pride. She gave you her virginity as a gift and in return you ran away and refused to speak to her. How would you feel if the situation were reversed?"

The notion dawned over her with slowness and wonder. "I...I would be hurt. And I'd be furious. Oh goddess, what did I do?"

"You did nothing, and in turn that did a lot."

She looked truly shaken, anxiety plainly written across her face. "But how do I fix it? It's been too long now, the hurt has had too long to grow."

I cocked my head and gave what I thought was a hopeful smile. "Well, you have to give back what you took from her. Return her pride and go from there. I am not saying you can fix it, but I think that may be a good place to start." I cast my own hope into the ether that Shana would not want to kill me for shoving them together. I could only hope that she would be as willing to let go of her pain as Coryn was to take it from her. Seeing the thoughtful look on Coryn's face, I realized I should get out of the pool. It was going to be really late by the time I got to the queen's hut. "I have to go for now, Coryn. I promised to meet Ori after shift. But I really hope that our talk helped."

Her gaze lifted from the water and she grinned broadly. I was glad to see the return of the cocky scout that I had come to know and love. "No, you've been great, Kyri. You've given me a lot to think about and I want to make this right. Wish me luck."

I winked at her. "You are the luckiest woman I know. You do not need any more luck."

She splashed me and I just laughed at her while I got dressed. On a chance, I went by the meal lodge to grab enough food for two people then made my way to the queen's hut. I barely finished knocking on her door when it was pulled open and a hand dragged me inside. An indignant blonde greeted me, and I saw Gata was already on her special cushion. "Where have you been? I'm starving. I was just getting ready to head over to the meal..." She looked at the basket of food in my hand and stopped mid-rant. "Oh. Heh, thanks." She began unpacking the food while I took off my cloak and scouting gear and hung them by the door. When I turned around her voice rose in shocked pleasure. "Honey cakes!" She looked at me with suspicion. "And just how did you get these? They don't put them out unless it's a special occasion."

I smirked and took a seat at her table. "A little bird told me that they were all made for tomorrow's festival. So I asked the cooks if I could have a couple for the queen since I was taking evening meal to her tonight."

A surprised look crossed her face, and then she started laughing, taking her own seat. "Woods weasel!" She waved a rabbit leg at me for emphasis. "Kyri Fletcher, you are sneaky!"

"Queen Orianna, you benefit from my sneaking, so hush." She just shrugged and kept eating. "So tell me about the ceremony tomorrow. Coryn says it is different and Shana said it is mostly the same."

Ori smiled and wiped her hands on a cloth that was sitting on the table. "So the basic structure of the ceremony is the same. We have a sacrifice and invocation of Artemis, then we call forward those who walk in the steps of the goddess. After that point is when it changes. Because we consider winter solstice the end of the sun-cycle, we have something called confession of stones." I gave her a confused look so she explained. "The confession of stones is the part of the ceremony where any Amazon can stand in front of the nation and speak of a negative action that is weighing on their heart. Once they have spoken of their deed aloud, they will pick up a red pebble and drop it into a bowl of sacred water. The nature of this ceremony is to lighten one's spirit so they can better move forward into next sun-cycle."

"When do people usually exchange solstice eve gifts? My da and I would have a nice dinner and we would each remember things we loved about my mam, and then we would exchange little things that we had created over the sun-cycle."

"Well, we don't have a big feast on solstice eve the way we do for other solstice celebrations. Because it's so cold, most Amazons prefer to have private celebrations and make their own meals. The meal lodge will have solstice treats, like the honey cakes. They'll also have some standard stuff for scouts that go out and others that don't like to cook, but they won't have much. And gift exchange, for those who wish to participate in it, is also done whenever we feel like it."

Her words struck me with inspiration. "What if..." I suddenly felt unsure of myself. Maybe everyone already had their own traditions and my suggestion would be unwelcome.

I was startled when she put her warm hand on mine. "Yes?"

I nervously swallowed. My thoughts, her hands, everything in my head was jangling. "Do you think my friends, all of you, would want to get together for a big pot of stew and stories? And anyone that has gifts can exchange them at that time?"

A broad smile creased her face. "Kyri, that's a wonderful idea, provided you are the one making the stew and only if it's rabbit."

Her enthusiasm was contagious. "Do you have something against venison stew, my queen?"

She gave me a serious look. "Nothing at all, as long as the deer has long ears and hops along the forest trails." We looked at each other for a heartbeat, then we both released peals of laughter. She wiped her eyes. "Oh goddess, what is it about you that has me so often in high humor?" I was acutely aware of her hand on mine. Sensing the change in mood she straightened in her chair, but she did not remove her hand. "Kyri..."

I did not want to look at that dark and aching place in my heart again. I could not bear to hear her give reasons why or why not so I gently slid my hand from hers. When I looked into her eyes they were full of sadness. "It is okay, my queen. Nothing need be said about that which is between us. I cherish your friendship and would not want to do anything to endanger the bond we have." I stood, knowing I had to leave or lose all control in front of her. The last thing I wanted was to embarrass myself in that way. It was better if I left to cry out my pain to the trees. I gave her a smile that I knew did not reach my blue eyes. "So tomorrow, can we all come here?" She nodded, I think afraid to speak. "Okay, I will be sure to get plenty of rabbits for everyone. Who would you like to invite?" I listed all the names I could think of. "Basha, Shana, what about Coryn?"

She nodded again. "Yes, Coryn. How about Deka, Dina, and Kylani? I was close to them when I was First Scout Leader. And maybe Steffi. She is un-partnered right now, and I think she'd like the company."

"How about Thera? She always seems to be patching me up and I would like to share the evening with her too. She reminds me of my gran before she died."

"Yeah, that sounds like an interesting group. Are you sure you're going to be able to feed us all?"

I mentally counted off the people in my head. "Let me see, ten people means I will have to borrow one of the large pots from the meal lodge. I will take Gata hunting in the morning so it can simmer all day. Maybe everyone could bring some food or drink to go with it. Perhaps bread, wine, and maybe something sweet?"

"I think that is a wonderful idea. I don't know why we have never done something like this before. Let's invite everyone tomorrow morning at first meal."

"Okay, that sounds good." I waited a heartbeat then started

putting my cloak and gear back on. Once I had everything together again, I turned back to her. "Thank you for telling me about the ceremony, and thank you for humoring me with a group dinner tomorrow. It..." I swallowed down a lump of emotion. "It will be my first winter solstice without my da."

Ori stepped close and cupped my cheek in her palm. "Well then, I think you should tell some stories about him and your mam to honor their memory. "

I gave a tiny nod, not wanting to dislodge her hand. "Thank you." In that moment, I could no longer ignore that hurt part of my heart. I turned my face farther into her hand and closed my eyes, simply because I could not bear to see the regret she was sure to be showing me. I stood frozen and against my will a sigh escaped. "I have to go Ori, tomorrow will come soon enough."

She quickly pulled me closer and kissed the corner of my mouth. A great fist circled around my chest with a squeeze. With heart hammering and blood rushing through my ears, I barely heard her whisper. "Sweet dreams, Kyri Fletcher."

I nodded once and walked out the door. I did not run to the trees, which were my usual escape. It was too dark and too cold to spend the time outside and my da did not raise a fool. Instead, I went to my hut where I stored my gear and changed into a winter weight shift. I left my boots on so my feet would stay warm and built up the fire in my hearth. It was then that I turned to my other solace in life, fletching. I tried to blank my mind and work with only the memory held within my hands, but I was unable. My head was full of images, words, and small sighs. My world lived and died with every single touch of her hand. And each time I managed to wall the hurt, her kiss or her eyes would tear it asunder. I was on my path and walking with surety, but I was as lost as any lamb in the wood. The words of my own personal prayer echoed through my head. 'Orianna, I may be your temptation and your Master's Mark, but you are surely the huntress. You would be my personal Artemis if I shared your belief in the gods. As true as my finest forest fletch, your arrows pierce me clean through the heart. I bleed for you.'

THE NEXT MORNING dawned gray and I left early to hunt. Gata did not return with me the night before so I assumed that she stayed with the queen. I did not actually need her to hunt, I just liked to keep her skills and training fresh. I estimated that I would need about eight rabbits for ten people. I planned to pick up the vegetables and the pot from the food lodge when I returned from the woods. There were multiple reasons why I was

excited to hunt on such a dreary morning. Obviously I needed the
meat for our solstice meal but I also needed something to keep
my mind busy and away from those losses that I was feeling most
acutely. I also wanted rabbit furs because they were in their
winter white. It took me until just after midday to hunt, start the
stew, clean and cure the rabbit furs, and clean myself. I had made
a few adjustments to my Amazon wear to accommodate for the
cold. I wore buckskin breaches instead of my leather strip skirt,
and I wore a long sleeve buckskin shirt with fur lining the collar
and wrist holes. To decorate the shirt, I sewed bits of bone, wood,
and quills from a pin pig, in circular patterns across my chest and
shoulders. Many of them were dyed using the same materials I
used for my fletchings. I continued to use my fall cloak even
though it no longer blended into the trees. I thought perhaps I
would use my white rabbit furs to make a cloak like I made for
Ori. Maybe I would dye the outer wool layer in black and grays to
blend in with the leafless trees. But for the day of solstice eve, the
buttery brown of my leathers looked good with the fall turned
colors of my cloak. I managed to find Shana in the crowd of
women heading into the temple just as the second and final horn
was sounding. Together we watched the ceremony and spoke the
correct words when expected. I remained a non-believer but
figured it could not hurt to participate with everyone else. Once
again I went to the dais with the others who continued to walk in
the goddess's footsteps. And once again I received my blood
mark. The queen maintained her decorum through the entire
thing but I could see a hint of a smile when I passed. I also
noticed that Gata sat next to her on the dais the entire time.

I paid close attention for when the winter ceremony broke
free from the fall one. The priestess removed the sacrificial bowl
and returned with another. I watched intently while Glyphera
turned with her back to the crowd and looked upward toward the
great statue of our patron goddess. She recited her words
carefully. "Artemis, Goddess of the Hunt. Artemis, Goddess of
Women and Wild Things. Turn your gaze to us, lend us your ear
for our confession of stones." Then she turned back to us. "Come
forth, any who wish to lighten their hearts with words sent to the
goddess's ears. Come forward all those who would remove a
weight from your soul and move into the new sun-cycle with a
free spirit. Confess and drop a stone in the water and I will take
away those weighted thoughts and memories and return them to
the river for cleansing."

A double handful of women came to the dais, each reciting
their sorrow or guilt, and dropped a stone into the water. I sensed
Shana tense beside me and noticed someone unexpected in the

confession of stones line. It was Coryn. I was pretty sure I knew what was to come. Shana urgently whispered to me. "What is she doing up there?"

I shrugged. "I do not know, just watch." Looking around the dim light of the temple, I could see that a lot of people were surprised to see the charismatic and carefree scout participate.

When she got to the altar, she removed one red stone and held it clenched in her hand. In a voice loud enough to be heard she told her story, or at least a very short version.

"Sun-cycles ago I led a beautiful woman away from our goddess's footsteps and feeling unworthy of such an honor, I ran in fear and took with me her pride. I have mourned my actions and regretted them with everything I am for many seasons. And while I know it may be too late, I wish to return her pride if she can bring herself to accept it from me. Guilt and regret are strange emotions and can trap us like insects in amber for a lifetime. With this confession I am seeking to start the new cycle with both of us unweighted by daemons of the past. Thank you." She nodded once, perhaps to reassure herself that all the right words were spoken, then dropped the stone into the bowl and left the dais. I immediately understood why she added the part about insects being trapped in amber. I suspected that the First Scout Leader had been trapped in Shana's amber for a long time. Shana remained silent beside me.

When the second bowl was cleared, I sensed the end of the ceremony was near. The priestess turned to the crowd and recited some familiar words, and some new ones. "The sacrifice has been given, the blessings have been made, and all confessions have been dropped in stone. Oh Artemis of the silver light, give us a sign that you have received our gifts and are pleased. Give us a sign that you will continue to share with us your wisdom and bounty in the coming sun-cycle."

We held our breaths again and I wondered what the newest sign would be. Gata was already on the stage, so she would not be walking up the aisle to interrupt. Suddenly, a strong and frigid wind blew in from the opening to the temple. It continued for a couple candle drops until everyone was well chilled and all the torches were extinguished but the two behind the altar. When the wind had at last calmed, the Queen and Priestess both raised their hands palm up in supplication, and Gata chose that moment to let out another one of her raspy choking roars. It was not very loud but it was just loud enough. The priestess did not look surprised and continued as expected. "The sign has been received and Artemis's messenger continues to walk among us. Goddess of the Hunt, Goddess of the Wild Animals, we thank you for your blessing today."

Then the entire crowd chanted the end of the ceremony. "Silvered moon, mighty huntress of the dark, hear us, Artemis!" And my second seasonal ceremony had come to a close.

With Shana's help we were able to carry the hot pot of stew to the queen's hut without losing any. Basha and Kylani were already there when we arrived. I made sure the stew was placed near the fire then ran back to my hut to retrieve the solstice gifts I had made. When I arrived a second time, the queen's large hut seemed small. But walking in to nine people socializing with laughter and smiles gave me a good feeling inside. An extra table and more chairs had been brought in to accommodate everyone. A few people brought bread and there were multiple skins of wine and a basket of sweet honey cakes. I also noticed a spicy scent in the air and when Shana saw me sniffing she grinned. "You like that? Thera made it earlier and had me carry it over for her."

I looked around and noticed a smaller pot by the fire. "What is it?"

Thera walked over to stand by me with a steaming wood cup in hand. "This, my young friend, is mulled wine. It's heated through and has added spices."

Shana took a mug over, filled it from the pot, and then brought it back to me. "Try it, I swear I wouldn't steer you wrong. You're going to love it."

Hesitantly, I took a sip of the warm liquid. My first thought was indeed of heat and spices. It was sweet and I rolled the flavor around my tongue. There was a slight warmth in my belly that was partly from the heat of the fire and partly from the wine itself. "Wow, this is good. Now if only Tanta had this stuff when we were there." Shana laughed and Thera enjoyed my praise of her wine.

After the meal there was a little chaos as people milled around giving gifts to various friends. I gave Coryn her arrows, Basha her scroll bag, and I even gave Thera a little leather herb pouch. I saw the queen was busy talking to Kylani so I took the opportunity to give Shana her gift. I pulled the two daggers out of the bag I was using to carry everything and handed them to her. Her eyes widened in shock then she looked back to me. I smiled. "Take them, I had them made just for you. The handles were carved from the boar tusks I got back in the fall."

She pulled them from their sheaths and looked at the blades. Then she took in the engraved handles and their meaning and I saw her eyes tear up. "Thank you, sister. I'm so glad you came into my life and found your Amazon path."

I hugged her. "I am too." She gave me my gift then, and I started at it in awe. It was a detailed carving of Artemis in profile shooting her bow. It was a hand span tall and could easily stand upright. I already knew it would hold a place of honor on my shelf. I put it in a pile with the wool lined deerskin boots from Coryn, the scroll of leaf drawings from Basha, and the little hollowed wood bowl of wound salve from Thera. I waited patiently until Ori was free before I approached her with my gift. I kept it rolled into a bundle and held it out.

She looked curious and reached for it. "What's this?"

I felt shy all of the sudden, unsure if it would be good enough. I tried to explain. "I actually started that moons ago. I thought you should have something for all the things you do for the nation. When it took so long to complete, I thought maybe I should just give it to you for solstice. I...I hope you like it."

She slowly unrolled the cloak, and when it got to full length, she just stared. "Oh Kyri..." She put a hand to her mouth.

I showed her the laces that held the liner in place. "You can take the fur out when it gets warmer outside, and just use the outer cloak..." I trailed off because she still had not spoken.

Our silence was interrupted by Basha. "Holy goddess, that is beautiful!" Unfortunately for me, her words drew the attention of everyone else in the room. Voices all crowded what I thought was a private exchange. "Wow!" "Would you look at that, it's amazing." "I still want one!" The last voice I knew belonged to Shana. I blushed under all the attention and continued to wait for the queen to speak.

She looked at the pattern on the outside, the way the bits of fabric looked like leaves dappling the shoulders. She gently ran her hand along the rabbit fur inside, enjoying the softness against her skin. When she put it on and pulled it around her at the front, a strange smile came over her face. "This is the most beautiful gift I've ever received and I will treasure it."

I tried to lighten the moment with humor. "Well after making all those rabbit stews, I had to do something with the furs." The crowd broke out in laughter then and everyone resumed their own conversations.

Ori smiled at me and gently removed the cloak. "Deh, but it's a warm one."

"Well that is the point, my queen."

She hung it on a wood post in the wall near her bed then came over and slapped my arm. "Woods weasel! You've been working on this for moons and hiding it from me the whole time."

My blush returned. "Well, I wanted it to be a surprise." She took that moment to walk over to a chest against the far wall. When she returned, she was carrying a wrapped bundle. She handed it to me and my first thought was of how heavy it was in my hands. When I unwrapped it I could only stare in surprise, much as she had done with my gift. I pulled the blade from its sheath and saw that it was wide at the base and tapered toward the end. The cross guard was in the shape of an eagle with outspread wings. The handle had roughened braided leather and the pommel was shaped like the point of an arrow. I loved it. "Thank you Ori, for everything. If not for you, I still would not feel comfortable carrying this sword. You are an amazing swordswoman and teacher."

She sported her own blush at my praise. "It really was nothing. It's not like I made it myself. But your gift, goddess, it just amazes me that you created something so beautiful for me. I don't deserve it. Maybe you should keep the cloak. It's much too special."

"Ori...it needed to be special. You are the queen of the Telequire nation and you deserve nothing less than the best I could give. You have given me the trees when I thought I would lose them forever. And you gave me the freedom to walk my own path. For that I will always be grateful."

She looked at me then, really looked at me. "Do you mean that? Do your really believe you are walking your own path?"

A dozen heartbeats hammered by. Her questions brought a sudden clarity to my emotions and fears. "I do not have to know my destination in life to be sure that the path I am walking is the right one. I have found my home here, and I have found family again. And..." Was I ready for so much honesty?

She hung on my words, lips slightly parted. "And?"

I pushed my nervousness down. "And I am ready to talk about all those things that have been weighing me down, and the person that lifts me up. I am ready to tell you my reasons, but first you have to answer a question for me."

She cocked her eyebrow, green eyes boring into mine. "What is that?"

I set the sword on the table behind me then turned and took her hand in mine. "Queen Orianna, my queen...do you find this initiate worthy?"

Her eyes twinkled in the combined lamp and candlelight of the hut. "Yes, I do." With three little words, I felt all that weight slip away.

I smiled and the pain in my heart disappeared. I finally understood that she had concerns like Coryn. She was afraid that I would be pulled from my path, that I did not truly know my heart's desires. But all of her concerns were without merit. I was, and would always be, my own person. I was still walking my path, and I continued to search for my ultimate contribution to the tribe. But as I looked into her expressive eyes I knew for certain that my words were true. I was on the right path because there was a surety to my steps that would not be there otherwise. My desire to get my Master's Mark remained and I would do it someday. But in the meantime, I had found plenty of other skills to explore. I looked at Ori for another beat or two then around the room. I had my friends who were family to me, I had Gata, and I had my queen. My queen, Orianna. Another thing I knew for certain, whatever path she found herself on, I would be in the trees above watching out for her. In a way, her path had become mine. We were inexplicably bound together, by Artemis or by circumstance, and I could not possibly be more content.

I let go of her hand and graced her with my biggest grin. "Hey, do you want to hear a joke?" She did not answer me. Instead she immediately slapped my arm.

A nearby Basha overheard me. "I want to hear a joke!" Ori sighed and shook her head. I laughed with her, enjoying the twinkle that had returned to her eyes. And I was comforted by the lack of pain in my own heart. I knew that the fear would still be there when I told her of all those things I held inside, but I also knew that everything would be all right. She had been waiting for me to take flight. It would dishonor us both if I let her down. I shut my eyes for a brief heartbeat and cast my thoughts into the ether. 'Thank you, Da, for letting me go.'

About the Author

Born and raised in Michigan, Kelly is a latecomer to the writing scene. As an introvert with self-taught extroversion, she has traveled to nearly every state in the US and draws from her experience with everything she writes. Over the years she has loved playing a variety of sports including volleyball, bowling, softball, and most recently, roller derby. But when bad knees became worse Kelly returned to the comfort of fan fiction to fill the void. Reading the amazing tales she found prompted her to try her hand at writing again. The ability to turn out an engaging tale was discovered and a bittersweet new love affair began.

Kelly works in the automotive industry coding in Visual basic and Excel. Her avid reading and writing provide a nice balance to the daily order of data, allowing her to juggle passion and responsibility. Her writing style is as varied as her reading taste and it shows as she tackles each new genre with glee. But beneath it all, no matter the subject or setting, Kelly carries a core belief that good should triumph. She's not afraid of pain or adversity, but loves a happy ending. She's been pouring words into novels since 2015 and probably won't run out of things to say any time soon.

OTHER YELLOW ROSE PUBLICATIONS

Anna Furtado	The Heart's Desire	978-1-935053-81-1
Anna Furtado	The Heart's Strength	978-1-935053-82-8
Anna Furtado	The Heart's Longing	978-1-935053-83-5
Anna Furtado	Tremble and Burn	978-1-61929-354-0
Pauline George	Jess	978-1-61929-139-3
Pauline George	199 Steps To Love	978-1-61929-213-0
Pauline George	The Actress and the Scrapyard Girl	978-1-61929-336-6
Melissa Good	Eye of the Storm	1-932300-13-9
Melissa Good	Hurricane Watch	978-1-935053-00-2
Melissa Good	Moving Target	978-1-61929-150-8
Melissa Good	Red Sky At Morning	978-1-932300-80-2
Melissa Good	Storm Surge: Book One	978-1-935053-28-6
Melissa Good	Storm Surge: Book Two	978-1-935053-39-2
Melissa Good	Stormy Waters	978-1-61929-082-2
Melissa Good	Thicker Than Water	1-932300-24-4
Melissa Good	Terrors of the High Seas	1-932300-45-7
Melissa Good	Tropical Storm	978-1-932300-60-4
Melissa Good	Tropical Convergence	978-1-935053-18-7
Melissa Good	Winds of Change Book One	978-1-61929-194-2
Melissa Good	Winds of Change Book Two	978-1-61929-232-1
Melissa Good	Southern Stars	978-1-61929-348-9
Regina A. Hanel	Love Another Day	978-1-61929-033-4
Regina A. Hanel	WhiteDragon	978-1-61929-143-0
Regina A. Hanel	A Deeper Blue	978-1-61929-258-1
Jeanine Hoffman	Lights & Sirens	978-1-61929-115-7
Jeanine Hoffman	Strength in Numbers	978-1-61929-109-6
Jeanine Hoffman	Back Swing	978-1-61929-137-9
Jennifer Jackson	It's Elementary	978-1-61929-085-3
Jennifer Jackson	It's Elementary, Too	978-1-61929-217-8
Jennifer Jackson	Memory Hunters	978-1-61929-294-9
K. E. Lane	And, Playing the Role of Herself	978-1-932300-72-7
Kate McLachlan	Christmas Crush	978-1-61929-195-9
Lynne Norris	One Promise	978-1-932300-92-5
Lynne Norris	Sanctuary	978-1-61929-248-2
Lynne Norris	Second Chances (E)	978-1-61929-172-0
Lynne Norris	The Light of Day	978-1-61929-338-0
Paula Offutt	Butch Girls Can Fix Anything	978-1-932300-74-1
Surtees and Dunne	True Colours	978-1-61929-021-1
Surtees and Dunne	Many Roads to Travel	978-1-61929-022-8
Patty Schramm	Finding Gracie's Glory	978-1-61929-238-3

Be sure to check out our other imprints,
Blue Beacon Books, Mystic Books, Quest Books,
Silver Dragon Books, Troubadour Books, and Young Adult Books.

VISIT US ONLINE AT
www.regalcrest.biz

At the Regal Crest Website You'll Find

- The latest news about forthcoming titles and new releases

- Our complete backlist of romance, mystery, thriller and adventure titles

- Information about your favorite authors

- Media tearsheets to print and take with you when you shop

- Which books are also available as eBooks.

Regal Crest print titles are available from all progressive booksellers including numerous sources online. Our distributors are Bella Distribution and Ingram.

www.ingramcontent.com/pod-product-compliance
Lightning Source LLC
Chambersburg PA
CBHW051658260626
47170CB00004B/1565